"Look, Teal," sug ... om above this room? Then we could look around."

"Sure it's an observatory platform." They climbed the fourth flight of stairs, but when the cover at the top lifted, they found themselves not on the roof, but *standing in the ground level floor where they had entered the house.*

Mr. Bailey turned a sickly gray. "Angels in heaven! We're getting out of here." Grabbing his wife, he threw open the front door and plunged out.

Then there were hoarse shouts from above Teal. He lowered a staircase and hurried up. The Baileys were in the central room. Teal took in the situation and poured three fingers of brandy. "Here, Mrs. Bailey," he soothed, "this will make you feel better."

"I never touch spirits," she protested, and gulped it.

"I thought you two had left," suggested Teal.

"But we did—we walked out the front door and found ourselves up here, in the lounge."

"Homer," Teal said, "do you know what has happened?"

"No, but if I don't find out pretty soon, something *is* going to happen and pretty drastic, too!"

"Homer, this is a vindication of my theories. This house is a real tesseract."

"About this tessy thing," said Mrs. Bailey. "Explain yourself."

"Now as I see it, Mrs. Bailey, this house, while perfectly stable in three dimensions, was not stable in four dimensions. I had built a house in the shape of an unfolded tesseract; something happened to it, some jar or side thrust, and it collapsed into its normal shape—it folded up." He snapped his fingers. "I've got it! The earthquake last night."

"I thought you boasted about how safe this house was."

"It *is* safe—three dimensionally."

—from "And He Built a Crooked House"
by Robert A Heinlein

BAEN BOOKS EDITED
BY HANK DAVIS

The Human Edge by Gordon R. Dickson

We the Underpeople by Cordwainer Smith
When the People Fell by Cordwainer Smith

The Technic Civilization Saga
The Van Rijn Method by Poul Anderson
David Falkayn: Star Trader by Poul Anderson
Rise of the Terran Empire by Poul Anderson
Young Flandry by Poul Anderson
Captain Flandry: Defender of the Terran Empire
by Poul Anderson
Sir Dominic Flandry: The Last Knight of Terra
by Poul Anderson
Flandry's Legacy by Poul Anderson

The Best of the Bolos: Their Finest Hour
by Keith Laumer

A Cosmic Christmas
A Cosmic Christmas 2 You
In Space No One Can Hear You Scream
The Baen Big Book of Monsters
As Time Goes By
Future War . . . and Other Punchlines
Worst Contact
Things from Outer Space
If This Goes Wrong . . .

To purchase these and all Baen Book titles in e-book format,
please go to www.baen.com

IF THIS GOES WRONG...

Edited by

HANK DAVIS

A Baen Books Original

Baen Publishing Enterprises
P.O. Box 1403
Riverdale, NY 10471
www.baen.com

ISBN: 978-1-4767-8202-7

Cover art by Dominic Harman

First Baen printing, January 2017

Distributed by Simon & Schuster
1230 Avenue of the Americas
New York, NY 10020

Printed in the United States of America

10 9 8 7 6 5 4 3 2 1

DEDICATION

This one's for my long-time friend Moshe Feder, fellow SF editor who does agree with me about a *few* things, such as Diana Rigg in general and *The Avengers* in particular (not referring to that mangy Marvel menagerie, of course), classical music, jazz, and I'll stop there. Keep those nifty books coming along, Moshe, even if they're mere Tor books . . .

Copyrights of Stories

Contents

IF THIS GOES WRONG...

WHAT COULD POSSIBLY GO WRONG . . . ?

Introduction by Hank Davis

"IF THIS GOES WRONG . . ." is, of course, a switch on a phrase made famous by the even more famous and greatest of science fiction writers, Robert A. Heinlein (whom I often refer to, more formally, as God to save syllables). It was the title of his ground-breaking and now classic serial, *If This Goes . . . ?* serialized in the February and March, 1940 issues of *Astounding Science-Fiction*. It told of a future America ruled by a religious dictatorship, one of the earlier parts of his celebrated Future History series.

(If you somehow have never, or even hardly ever, encountered the celebrated Future History stories and novels by Heinlein, you should pause in your reading in of this introduction [after paying for this volume before leaving the bookstore, of course], and acquire *The Man Who Sold the Moon*, *The Green Hills of Earth*, *Revolt in 2100* [which includes *If This Goes On*], *Methuselah's*

Children, and *Orphans of the Sky* [the first and fifth of these are currently available in a single volume—bargain!], currently available from Baen Books—plus *Time Enough for Love* and *To Sail Beyond the Sunset*, available from Berkley-Putnam when last seen. Now back to our regularly-scheduled editorial scribblings.)

A story of an America ruled by a religious dictatorship, giving hints of how that future came to pass, is a very undesirable future to contemplate, but Heinlein told of several other possible futures, undesirable, but in these two yarns, far less grim, even humorous circumstances. (Exit laughing?) Accompanying them are a nifty bunch of tales similarly exploring how thing can go wrong in sometimes grim, sometimes humorous stories, to assist you in living by proxy (sometimes, fortunately so) in these variant worlds.

I hope you enjoy the stories and regret that a recent string of bad health episodes (I *am* an old geezer, after all) has kept me from doing my usual garrulous type of intros.

Of course, some may *prefer* this briefer version. Nonetheless, I hope to do a longer version of this curtain-raiser and also longer story intros for the long-suffering Baen website (*www.baen.com*) at no extra cost. Stay tuned.

—**Hank Davis**
October 2016

COMPLAINT

by Robert A. Heinlein

Robert A. Heinlein (1907-1988), master of tales of things that either go on or go wrong, and of course stories that go through the exosphere and beyond, kicks off this set of yarns with a zany tale of a man-machine sorely in need of consumer protection. This was originally part of a letter sent to Thomas N. Scortia and George Zebrowski to thank them for dedicating an anthology of cyborg-centered to him, in which he included this one-of-a-kind riff.

FROM: X-Model 69-606-ZSCCC-Z5-RAH
(formerly "Robert A. Heinlein")
TO: Complex Cyborg Corporation,
an Unequal Opportunity Employer
ATTN: Messrs. G. Zebrowski & T. N. Scortia
SUBJECT: Above model—Field Defects in

1. Help! _____

2 a. Neuroelectronic engineers indeed! That you should have such hutzpah! Before you took me out of the Box, I told you that all my homeostasis was fubar, shaking like jelly. One of you—the uglier one if that be possible—patted me on my dexter gluteus maximus and plonked that it would all steady down once I was on my feet. Drek! I'm no longer shaking like jelly; I'm flapping in a gale. About Richter scale 6.7 at a guess. Worse yet, parts of it in posiive feedback. I'm heading for a door, see? A big frame—and walk right into it. Landlord wants me to pay for the damage. I told the puking obso to have his lawyer send the bill to ComCyCorp and to demand triple damages.

b. That's not half of what my shyster is going to do to you. Your big selling point, your convincer, was your NeverFail Neoflesh Everready Priapus Eternal. Correct, it never fails. I see a babe with jugs like Venus, a prominent pudendum, and a How-about-it? Eyed and at once my mouth waters. No, not that way, you throwbacks, I long for giant malted milks and juicy cheeseburgers. Worse yet, I get up in the morning go to the jakes and am standing at the pot when I whiff frying bacon. *Spung!* Up like a fencepost and I micturate on the ceiling. Followed by a gob of wasted synthosemen. Who crossed those nerves? Can't either of you count up to XII with your shoes on?

c. Worse still, when I try to be philosophical about it, roll with the punch, and be My Own Best Friend, here's what happens: I strip, stretch out on the bed, and think about apple pie a la mode. Old Neverland engorges at once, maybe 20 cm high, and thick to match: I can barely get my fist around it. Complaints? Oh, nothing much, a mere detail. No sensation. None. I told you not to use teflon. Or Elmer's Glue. What happened? Don't ask *me;* you're the "experts." But obviously the thick network of dermal pseudonerves no longer comes to the surface. Permanently detached or broken. Perhaps if you used tiny helices with some give to them— But not you two. I'll take my guarantee to General Motors' Johns Hopkins Division and have it done right. They'll send the tab to you and maybe you can get Medicare and Triple-A to split it. Maybe.

---

3. Don't go away; I'm not through. That "technologist" you sent out to "service" me. The bedpan hustler with one walleye and Parkinson's Disease. I was stretched out on the rack and clamped and he started to remove my skull piece without shutting me off. I reminded him, gently— after all, everone makes an error now and then. "Thorry, Thir," he answered, very politely, and he did shut me down before any real damage was done. Then he flushed out my hippocampus . . . with *Drano!* I saw the can. Then he "cleansed" my amygala cerebelli with his thumbnail, explaining happily that it was so much gentler than a curet. If I could have moved, I would have bitten his thumb off. But I don't hate him; he's just an unfortunate minus. But as for you two—As soon as I'm off the effects of the shotgun antibiotics I've been taking to offset my "servicing," I'm going to call at CrummyCyCorp, loaded past the red line with ATP, switch to SuperSpeed, breeze past your guards like the Invisible Man, so straight to your offices, jerk down your pants, and set fire to the hirsute thickets around your testes. If you have any. What day? Don't worry, you'll notice it when it happens. But I won't take it out on your geek. I did tell him what I thought of him. Didn't faze him. He just shrugged and said, "Thorry, thir, that'h not my department. If you'll examine your guarantee, you'll thee that for one full year you can alwayth go back into the Box at no charge to you. And a ten-year Box privilege with only a nominal charge for labor and parth."

4. *Insult to Injury.* Gentlemen, if you'll pardon the word, you are *not* going to get me back into that Box! If GMC-JH can't repair me, I'll go to Volkswagen-Übermensch, make a deal with a waiver that permits them to photograph and *publish* pix of your work (in the *International Journal of Cyborg Surgery and Prosthetics,* no doubt, with my signed and sworn statement), as they uncover it in rebuilding me. But you'll see me before then. In this morning's mail arrived this week's *Science* magazine . . . and I saw your full page ad inside the front cover: There was that picture of me (taken without my knowledge or consent), bare as a *Penthouse* centerfold, with old NeverFail rampant. I could have shrugged that off. After all, I'm fairly handsome; my mother always said so . . . and old NeverFail is impressive—by appearance, not function. But underneath it said: Our improved and Perfected *Production* model 69-606-ZSCCC (my emphasis added). Call our toll-free number, and some more garbage. That tore it! Oh, I'll sue, of course. But you'll see me so much sooner. Watch Channel Four Wednesday evening for their 11 p.m. adults-only-anything-goes show with Johnny ("Jack the Ripper") as host and X-Model 69-606 et cetera as guest star. With *Science* magazine. With the studio warm enough for skin. With a pot installed to let me demonstrate how I must stand on my hands to pee.

Hope you are the same,
X
X-Model 69-606-ZSCCC-75
(formerly Robert A. Heinlein)

MOXON'S MASTER

by Ambrose Bierce

*While **Ambrose Bierce** (1842-1914), who disappeared in 1913 in Mexico on a trip to interview Pancho Villa, is best known for his The Devil's Dictionary and the short stories, "The Damned Thing" and "An Occurrence at Owl Street Bridge," This early robot story is an equally nifty chiller. I wonder if Bierce had ever heard of Sir Henry Babbage and his failed attempts to build the "analytical engine" of his dreams, limited to steam power by the available technology of the time. Babbage's dream devices had to await electronics, and, or course, are now known as computers, though I think "analytical engine" is such a charming name, that I often think of this gizmo I'm typing on by that antique term.*

"ARE YOU SERIOUS?—Do you really believe that a machine thinks?"

I got no immediate reply; Moxon was apparently intent upon the coals in the grate, touching them deftly here and there with the fire-poker till they signified a sense of his attention by a brighter glow. For several weeks I had been observing in him a growing habit of delay in answering even the most trivial of commonplace questions. His air, however, was that of preoccupation rather than deliberation: one might have said that he had "something on his mind."

Presently he said:

"What is a 'machine'? The word has been variously defined. Here is one definition from a popular dictionary: 'Any instrument or organization by which power is applied and made effective, or a desired effect produced.' Well, then, is not a man a machine? And you will admit that he thinks—or thinks he thinks."

"If you do not wish to answer my question," I said, rather testily, "why not say so?—All that you say is mere evasion. You know well enough that when I say 'machine' I do not mean a man, but something that man has made and controls."

"When it does not control him," he said, rising abruptly and looking out of a window, whence nothing was visible in the blackness of a stormy night. A moment later he turned about and with a smile said: "I beg your pardon; I had no thought of evasion. I considered the dictionary man's unconscious testimony suggestive and worth something in the discussion. I can give your question a direct answer easily enough: I do believe that a machine thinks about the work that it is doing."

That was direct enough, certainly. It was not

altogether pleasing, for it tended to confirm a sad
suspicion that Moxon's devotion to study and work in his
machine-shop had not been good for him. I knew, for one
thing, that he suffered from insomnia, and that is no light
affliction. Had it affected his mind? His reply to my
question seemed to me then evidence that it had; perhaps
I should think differently about it now. I was younger
then, and among the blessings that are not denied to
youth is ignorance. Incited by that great stimulant to
controversy, I said:

"And what, pray, does it think with—in the absence of
a brain?"

The reply, coming with less than his customary delay,
took his favourite form of counter-interrogation:

"With what does a plant think—in the absence of a
brain?"

"Ah, plants also belong to the philosopher class! I
should be pleased to know some of their conclusions; you
may omit the premises."

"Perhaps," he replied, apparently unaffected by my
foolish irony, "you may be able to infer their convictions
from their acts. I will spare you the familiar examples of
the sensitive mimosa, the several insectivorous flowers
and those whose stamens bend down and shake their
pollen upon the entering bee in order that he may fertilize
their distant mates. But observe this. In an open spot in
my garden I planted a climbing vine. When it was barely
above the surface I set a stake into the soil a yard away.
The vine at once made for it, but as it was about to reach
it after several days I removed it a few feet. The vine at
once altered its course, making an acute angle, and again

made for the stake. This manoeuvre was repeated several times, but finally, as if discouraged, the vine abandoned the pursuit and ignoring further attempts to divert it, travelled to a small tree, farther away, which it climbed.

"Roots of the eucalyptus will prolong themselves incredibly in search of moisture. A well-known horticulturist relates that one entered an old drain-pipe and followed it until it came to a break, where a section of the pipe had been removed to make way for a stone wall that had been built across its course. The root left the drain and followed the wall until it found an opening where a stone had fallen out. It crept through and following the other side of the wall back to the drain, entered the unexplored part and resumed its journey."

"And all this?"

"Can you miss the significance of it? It shows the consciousness of plants. It proves that they think."

"Even if it did—what then? We were speaking, not of plants, but of machines. They may be composed partly of wood—wood that has no longer vitality—or wholly of metal. Is thought an attribute also of the mineral kingdom?"

"How else do you explain the phenomena, for example, of crystallization?"

"I do not explain them."

"Because you cannot without affirming what you wish to deny, namely, intelligent co-operation, among the constituent elements of the crystals. When soldiers form lines, or hollow squares, you call it reason. When wild geese in flight take the form of a letter V you say instinct. When the homogeneous atoms of a mineral, moving freely in solution, arrange themselves into shapes mathematically perfect, or particles of frozen moisture into the symmetrical and beautiful forms of snowflakes, you have nothing to say. You have not even invented a name to conceal your heroic unreason."

Moxon was speaking with unusual animation and earnestness. As he paused I heard in an adjoining room known to me as his "machine-shop," which no one but himself was permitted to enter, a singular thumping sound, as of someone pounding upon a table with an open hand. Moxon heard it at the same moment and, visibly agitated, rose and hurriedly passed into the room whence it came. I thought it odd that anyone else should be in there, and my interest in my friend—with doubtless a touch of unwarrantable curiosity—led me to listen intently, though, I am happy to say, not at the keyhole. There were confused sounds, as of a struggle or scuffle; the floor shook. I distinctly heard hard breathing and a hoarse whisper which said "Damn you!" Then all was silent, and presently Moxon reappeared and said, with a rather sorry smile:

"Pardon me for leaving you so abruptly. I have a machine in there that lost its temper and cut up rough."

Fixing my eyes steadily upon his left cheek, which was traversed by four parallel excoriations showing blood, I said:

"How would it do to trim its nails?" I could have spared myself the jest; he gave it no attention, but seated himself in the chair that he had left and resumed the interrupted monologue as if nothing had occurred:

"Doubtless you do not hold with those (I need not

name them to a man of your reading) who have taught that all matter is sentient, that every atom is a living, feeling, conscious being. *I* do. There is no such thing as dead, inert matter: it is all alive; all instinct with force, actual and potential; all sensitive to the same forces in its environment and susceptible to the contagion of higher and subtler ones residing in such superior organisms as it may be brought into relation with, as those of man when he is fashioning it into an instrument of his will. It absorbs something of his intelligence and purpose—more of them in proportion to the complexity of the resulting machine and that of its work.

"Do you happen to recall Herbert Spencer's definition of 'Life'? I read it thirty years ago. He may have altered it afterward, for anything I know, but in all that time I have been unable to think of a single word that could profitably be changed or added or removed. It seems to me not only the best definition, but the only possible one.

"'Life,' he says, "is a definite combination of heterogeneous changes, both simultaneous and successive, in correspondence with external coexistences and sequences.'"

"That defines the phenomenon," I said, "but gives no hint of its cause."

"That," he replied, "is all that any definition can do. As Mill points out, we know nothing of cause except as an antecedent—nothing of effect except as a consequent. Of certain phenomena, one never occurs without another, which is dissimilar: the first in point of time we call cause, the second, effect. One who had many times seen a rabbit pursued by a dog, and had never seen rabbits and dogs otherwise, would think the rabbit the cause of the dog.

"But I fear," he added, laughing naturally enough, "that my rabbit is leading me a long way from the track of my legitimate quarry: I'm indulging in the pleasure of the chase for its own sake. What I want you to observe is that in Herbert Spencer's definition of 'Life' the activity of a machine is included—there is nothing in the definition that is not applicable to it. According to this sharpest of observers and deepest of thinkers, if a man during his period of activity is alive, so is a machine when in operation. As an inventor and constructor of machines I know that to be true."

Moxon was silent for a long time, gazing absently into the fire. It was growing late and I thought it time to be going, but somehow I did not like the notion of leaving him in that isolated house, all alone except for the presence of some person of whose nature my conjectures could go no further than that it was unfriendly, perhaps malign. Leaning toward him and looking earnestly into his eyes while making a motion with my hand through the door of his workshop, I said:

"Moxon, whom have you in there?"

Somewhat to my surprise he laughed lightly and answered without hesitation:

"Nobody; the incident that you have in mind was caused by my folly in leaving a machine in action with nothing to act upon, while I undertook the interminable task of enlightening your understanding. Do you happen to know that Consciousness is the creature of Rhythm?"

"O bother them both!" I replied, rising and laying hold of my overcoat. "I'm going to wish you good night; and I'll add the hope that the machine which you inadvertently left in action will have her gloves on the next time you think it needful to stop her."

Without waiting to observe the effect of my shot I left the house.

Rain was falling, and the darkness was intense. In the sky beyond the crest of a hill toward which I groped my way along precarious plank sidewalks and across miry, unpaved streets I could see the faint glow of the city's lights, but behind me nothing was visible but a single window of Moxon's house. It glowed with what seemed to me a mysterious and fateful meaning. I knew it was an uncurtained aperture in my friend's "machine-shop," and I had little doubt that he had resumed the studies interrupted by his duties as my instructor in mechanical consciousness and the fatherhood of Rhythm. Odd, and in some degree humorous, as his convictions seemed to me at that time, I could not wholly divest myself of the feeling that they had some tragic relation to his life and character—perhaps to his destiny—although I no longer entertained the notion that they were the vagaries of a disordered mind. Whatever might be thought of his views, his exposition of them was too logical for that. Over and over, his last words came back to me: "Consciousness is the creature of Rhythm." Bald and terse as the statement was, I now found it infinitely alluring. At each recurrence it broadened in meaning and deepened in suggestion. Why, here (I thought) is something upon which to found a philosophy. If Consciousness is the product of Rhythm all things *are* conscious, for all have motion, and all motion is rhythmic. I wondered if Moxon knew the significance and breadth of his thought—the scope of this momentous generalization; or had he arrived at his philosophic faith by the tortuous and uncertain road of observation?

That faith was then new to me, and all Moxon's expounding had failed to make me a convert; but now it seemed as if a great light shone about me, like that which fell upon Saul of Tarsus; and out there in the storm and darkness and solitude I experienced what Lewes calls "the endless variety and excitement of philosophic thought." I exulted in a new sense of knowledge, a new pride of reason. My feet seemed hardly to touch the earth; it was as if I were uplifted and borne through the air by invisible wings.

Yielding to an impulse to seek further light from him whom I now recognized as my master and guide, I had unconsciously turned about, and almost before I was aware of having done so found myself again at Moxon's door. I was drenched with rain, but felt no discomfort. Unable in my excitement to find the doorbell I instinctively tried the knob. It turned and, entering, I mounted the stairs to the room that I had so recently left. All was dark and silent; Moxon, as I had supposed, was in the adjoining room—the "machine-shop." Groping along the wall until found the communicating door I knocked loudly several times, but got no response, which I attributed to the uproar outside, for the wind was blowing a gale and dashing the rain against the thin walls in sheets. The drumming upon the shingle roof spanning the unceiled room was loud and incessant. I had never been invited into the machine-shop—had, indeed, been denied admittance, as had all others, with one exception, a skilled metal worker, of whom no one knew anything except that his name was Haley and his habit silence. But in my spiritual exaltation, discretion and civility were alike forgotten, and I opened the door. What I saw took all philosophical speculation out of me in short order.

Moxon sat facing me at the farther side of a small table upon which a single candle made all the light that was in the room. Opposite him, his back toward me, sat another person. On the table between the two was a chess-board; the men were playing. I knew little of chess, but as only a few pieces were on the board it was obvious that the game was near its close. Moxon was intensely interested—not so much, it seemed to me, in the game as in his antagonist, upon whom he had fixed so intent a look that, standing though I did directly in the line of his vision, I was altogether unobserved. His face was ghastly white, and his eyes glittered like diamonds. Of his antagonist I had only a back view, but that was sufficient; I should not have cared to see his face.

He was apparently not more than five feet in height, with proportions suggesting those of a gorilla—a tremendous breadth of shoulders, thick, short neck and broad, squat head, which had a tangled growth of black hair and was topped with a crimson fez. A tunic of the same colour, belted tightly to the waist, reached the seat—apparently a box—upon which he sat; his legs and feet were not seen. His left forearm appeared to rest in his lap; he moved his pieces with his right hand, which seemed disproportionately long.

I had shrunk back and now stood a little to one side of the doorway and in shadow. If Moxon had looked farther than the face of his opponent he could have observed nothing now, except that the door was open. Something forbade me either to enter or to retire, a feeling—I know not how it came—that I was in the presence of an imminent tragedy and might serve my friend by remaining. With a scarcely conscious rebellion against the indelicacy of the act I remained.

The play was rapid. Moxon hardly glanced at the board before making his moves, and to my unskilled eye seemed to move the piece most convenient to his hand, his motions in doing so being quick, nervous and lacking in precision. The response of his antagonist, while equally prompt in the inception, was made with a slow, uniform, mechanical and, I thought, somewhat theatrical movement of the arm, that was a sore trial to my patience. There was something unearthly about it all, and I caught myself shuddering. But I was wet and cold. Two or three times after moving a piece the stranger slightly inclined his head, and each time I observed that Moxon shifted his king. All at once the thought came to me that the man was dumb. And then that he was a machine—an automaton chess-player! Then I remembered that Moxon had once spoken to me of having invented such a piece of mechanism, though I did not understand that it had actually been constructed. Was all his talk about the consciousness and intelligence of machines merely a prelude to eventual exhibition of this device—only a trick to intensify the effect of its mechanical action upon me in my ignorance of its secret?

A fine end, this, of all my intellectual transports—my "endless variety and excitement of philosophic thought"! I was about to retire in disgust when something occurred to hold my curiosity. I observed a shrug of the thing's great shoulders, as if it were irritated: and so natural was this—so entirely human—that in my new view of the matter it startled me. Nor was that all, for a moment later it struck the table sharply with its clenched hand. At that gesture Moxon seemed even more startled than I: he pushed his chair a little backward, as in alarm.

Presently Moxon, whose play it was, raised his hand high above the board, pounced upon one of his pieces like a sparrow-hawk and with the exclamation "check-mate!" rose quickly to his feet and stepped behind his chair. The automaton sat motionless.

The wind had now gone down, but I heard, at lessening intervals and progressively louder, the rumble and roll of thunder. In the pauses between I now became conscious of a low humming or buzzing which, like the thunder, grew momentarily louder and more distinct. It seemed to come from the body of the automaton, and was unmistakably a whirring of wheels. It gave me the impression of a disordered mechanism which had escaped the repressive and regulating action of some controlling part—an effect such as might be expected if a pawl should be jostled from the teeth of a ratchetwheel. But before I had time for much conjecture as to its nature my attention was taken by the strange motions of the automaton itself. A slight but continuous convulsion appeared to have possession of it. In body and head it shook like a man with palsy or an ague chill, and the motion augmented every moment until the entire figure was in violent agitation. Suddenly it sprang to its feet and with a movement almost too quick for the eye to follow shot forward across table and chair, with both arms thrust forth to their full length—the posture and lunge of a diver. Moxon tried to throw himself backward out of reach, but he was too late: I saw the horrible thing's hand close upon his throat, his own clutch its wrists. Then the table was overturned, and candle thrown to the floor and extinguished, and all was black dark. But the noise of the struggle was dreadfully distinct, and most terrible of all were the raucous, squawking sounds made by the strangled man's efforts to breathe. Guided by the infernal hubbub, I sprang to the rescue of my friend, but had hardly taken a stride in the darkness when the whole room blazed with a blinding white light that burned into my brain and heart and memory a vivid picture of the combatants on the floor, Moxon underneath, his throat still in the clutch of those iron hands, his head forced backward, his eyes protruding, his mouth wide open and his tongue thrust out; and— horrible contrast!—upon the painted face of his assassin an expression of tranquil and profound thought, as in the solution of a problem in chess! This I observed, then all was blackness and silence.

Three days later I recovered consciousness in a hospital. As the memory of that tragic night slowly evolved in my ailing brain I recognized in my attendant Moxon's confidential workman, Haley. Responding to a look he approached, smiling.

"Tell me about it," I managed to say, faintly—"all about it."

"Certainly," he said; "you were carried unconscious from a burning house—Moxon's. Nobody knows how you came to be there. You may have to do a little explaining. The origin of the fire is a bit mysterious, too. My own notion is that the house was struck by lightning."

"And Moxon?"

"Buried yesterday—what was left of him."

Apparently this reticent person could unfold himself on occasion. When imparting shocking intelligence to the sick he was affable enough. After some moments of the keenest mental suffering I ventured to ask another question:

"Who rescued me?"

"Well, if that interests you—I did."

"Thank you, Mr. Haley, and may God bless you for it. Did you rescue, also, that charming product of your skill, the automaton chess-player that murdered its inventor?"

The man was silent a long time, looking away from me. Presently he turned and gravely said:

"Do you know that?"

"I do," I replied; "I saw it done."

That was many years ago. If asked to-day I should answer less confidently.

WHISKABOOM

by Alan Arkin

*Yes, "Whiskaboom" is by that **Alan Arkin** (born 1934):
actor, writer, director, star of stage, screen, and television.
And who, to steal a well-worn phrase, needs no
introduction. (Though it was news to me that he's also a
musician and singer, but I'm yet to catch one of his gigs
in those venues—doesn't anti-trust legislation apply
here?) Back when my eleven-year-old version read the
August 1955 issue of Galaxy, with the terrific story that
follows, I was dazzled and would recall it vividly through
the years from that issue Well-told and well-done, sir!*

Dear Mr. Gretch:

Mrs. Burroughs and I are sending your son Jack to you
because we do not know what else to do with him. As you
can see, we can't keep him with us in his present condition.

Also, Jack owes us two weeks rent and, since Mrs. Burroughs and I are retired, we would appreciate your sending the money. It has been a dry year and our garden has done poorly.

The only reason we put up with your son in the first place was because we are so hard-pressed.

He saw the sign on the porch, rang the bell and paid Mrs. Burroughs a month's rent without even looking at the room. Then he ran out to his car and commenced pulling out suitcases and boxes and dragging them upstairs.

After the third trip, Mrs. Burroughs saw he was having trouble with the stuff and he looked kind of worn out, so she offered to help.

He gave her a hard look, as she described it to me when I got home. He said, "I don't want anyone touching anything. Please don't interfere."

"I didn't mean to interfere," my wife told him. "I only wanted to help."

"I don't want any help," he said quietly, but with a wild look in his eye, and he staggered upstairs with the last of his baggage and locked the door.

When I got home, Mrs. Burroughs told me she thought I ought to take a look at the new boarder. I went up, thinking we'd have a little chat and straighten things out. I could hear him inside, hammering on something.

He didn't hear my first knock or the second. I got sore and nearly banged the door down, at which time he decided to open up.

I charged in, ready to fight a bear. And there was this skinny red-headed son of yours glaring at me.

"That's a lot of hammering you're doing, son," I said.

"That's the only way I can get these boxes open, and don't call me *son*."

"I don't like to disturb you, Mr. Gretch, but Mrs. Burroughs is a little upset over the way you acted today. I think you ought to come down for a cup of tea and get acquainted."

"I know I was rude," he said, looking a little ashamed, "but I have waited for years for a chance to get to work on my own, with no interference. I'll come down tomorrow, when I have got my equipment set up, and apologize to Mrs. Burroughs then."

I asked him what he was working on, but he said he would explain later. Before I got out of the door, he was hammering again. He worked till after midnight.

We saw Jack at mealtimes for the next few days, but he didn't talk much. We learned that he was twenty-six, in spite of his looking like a boy in his teens, that he thought Prof. Einstein the greatest man ever, and that he disliked being called *son*. Of his experiment, he didn't have much to say then. He saw Mrs. Burroughs was a little nervous about his experimenting in the guest room and he assured her it was not dangerous.

Before the week was out, we started hearing the noises. The first one was like a wire brush going around a barrel. It went *whisk, whisk*. Then he rigged up something that went *skaboom* every few seconds, like a loud heartbeat. Once in a while, he got in a sound like a creaky well pump, but mostly it was *skaboom* and *whisk*, which eventually settled down to a steady rhythm, *whiskaboom, whiskaboom*.

It was kind of pleasant.

Neither of us saw him for two days. The noises kept going on. Mrs. Burroughs was alarmed because he did not answer her knock at mealtimes, and one morning she charged upstairs and hollered at him through the door.

"You stop your nonsense this minute and come down to breakfast!"

"I'm not hungry," he called back.

"You open this door!" she ordered and, by George, he did. "Your *whiskaboom* or whatever it is will keep till after breakfast."

He sat at the table, but he was a tired boy. He had a cold, his eyelids kept batting, and I don't believe he could have lifted his coffee cup. He tried to look awake, and then over he went with his face in the oatmeal.

Mrs. Burroughs ran for the ammonia, but he was out cold, so we wiped the oatmeal off his face and carried him upstairs.

My wife rubbed Jack's wrists with garlic and put wet towels on his face, and presently he came to. He looked wildly about the room at his machinery. It was all there, and strange-looking stuff, too.

"Please go away," he begged. "I've got work to do."

Mrs. Burroughs helped him blow his nose. "There'll be no work for you, sonny. Not until you're well. We'll take care of you." He didn't seem to mind being called *sonny*.

He was sick for a week and we tended him like one of our own. We got to know him pretty well. And we also got to know you.

Now, Mr. Gretch, whatever you are doing in your laboratory is your own business. You could be making atomic disintegrators, for all Jack told us. But he does not like or approve of it and he told us about your running battle with him to keep him working on your project instead of his own.

Jack tried to explain his ideas for harnessing time and what he called "the re-integration principle." It was all so much *whiskaboom* to us, so to speak, but he claimed it was for the good of mankind, which was fine with us.

But he said you would not let him work it out because there was less money in it than in your project, and this is why he had to get away and work and worry himself into a collapse.

When he got well, Mrs. Burroughs told him, "From now on, you're going to have three meals a day and eight hours sleep, and in between you can play on your *whiskaboom* all you please."

The *whiskabooming* became as familiar to us as our own voices.

Last Sunday, Mrs. Burroughs and I came home from church, about noon. She went inside through the front door to fix dinner. I walked around the house to look at the garden. And the moment I walked past the front of the house, I got the shock of my life.

The house disappeared!

I was too surprised to stop walking, and a step later I was standing at the back of the house, and it was all there. I took a step back and the whole house vanished again. One more step and I was at the front.

It looked like a real house in front and in back, but

there wasn't any in-between. It was like one of those false-front saloons on a movie lot, but thinner.

I thought of my wife, who had gone into the kitchen and, for all I knew, was as thin as the house, and I went charging in the back door, yelling.

"Are you all right?"

"Of course I'm all right," she said. "What's the matter with you?"

I grabbed her and she was all there, thank heavens. She giggled and called me an old fool, but I dragged her outside and showed her what had happened to our house.

She saw it, too, so I knew I didn't have sunstroke, but she couldn't understand it any better than I.

Right about then, I detected a prominent absence of *whiskabooming*. "Jack!" I hollered, and we hurried back into the house and upstairs.

Well, Mr. Gretch, it was so pitiful, I can't describe it. He was there, but I never saw a more miserable human being. He was not only thin but also flat, like a cartoon of a man who had been steamrollered. He was lying on the bed, holding onto the covers, with no more substance to him than a thin piece of paper. Less.

Mrs. Burroughs took one of his shoulders between her thumb and forefinger, and I took the other, and we held him up. There was a breeze coming through the window and Jack—well, he waved in the breeze.

We closed the window and laid him down again and he tried to explain what had happened. "Professor Einstein wouldn't have liked this!" he moaned. "Something went wrong," he cried, shuddering.

He went on gasping and mumbling, and we gathered that he had hooked up a circuit the wrong way. "I didn't harness the fourth—I chopped off the third dimension! Einstein wouldn't have approved!"

He was relieved to learn that the damage had been confined to himself and the house, so far as we knew. Like the house, Jack had insides, but we don't know where they are. We poured tea down him, and he can eat, after a fashion, but there never is a sign of a lump anywhere.

That night, we pinned him to the bed with clothespins so he wouldn't blow off the bed. Next morning, we rigged a line and pinned him to it so he could sit up.

"I know what to do," he said, "but I would have to go back to the lab. Dad would have to let me have his staff and all sorts of equipment. And he won't do it."

"If he thinks more of his money than he does of his own son," Mrs. Burroughs said, "then he's an unnatural father."

But Jack made us promise not to get in touch with you.

Still, people are beginning to talk. The man from the electric company couldn't find the meter yesterday, because it is attached to the middle of the outside wall and has vanished.

Mr. Gretch, we are parents and we feel that you will not hesitate a moment to do whatever is necessary to get Jack back into shape. So, despite our promise, we are sending Jack to you by registered parcel post, air mail. He doesn't mind the cardboard mailing tube he is rolled up in as he has been sleeping in it, finding it more comfortable than being pinned to the sheets.

Jack is a fine boy, sir, and we hope to hear soon that he is back to normal and doing the work he wants to do.

Very truly yours,
W. Burroughs

P.S. When Jack figures out the re-integration principle, we would appreciate his fixing our house. We get along as usual, but it makes us nervous to live in a house that, strictly speaking, has no insides. W.B.

COMPUTERS DON'T ARGUE

by Gordon R. Dickson

Gordon R. Dickson (1923-2001) may be best known for his celebrated (and unfinished, dammit!) series about the Dorsai interstellar combat troops, but he had a gift for humor, sometimes in fun adventure stories, and also a more satirical, cut-till-it-bleeds type, such as this one. Be careful and don't slip on the blood on the floor on your way in. Of course, the computers are not the ones doing the bleeding . . .

Treasure Book Club
PLEASE DO NOT FOLD, SPINDLE
OR MUTILATE THIS CARD

Mr: Walter A. Child

Balance: $24.98

Dear Customer: Enclosed is your latest book selection. "Kidnapped," by Robert Louis Stevenson.

---

437 Woodlawn Drive
Panduk, Michigan
Nov. 16, 2000

Treasure Book Club
1823 Mandy Street
Chicago, Illinois

Dear Sirs:

I wrote you recently about the computer punch card you sent, billing me for "Kim,' by Rudyard Kipling. I did not open the package containing it until I had already mailed you my check for the amount on the card. On opening the package, I found the book missing half its pages. I sent it back to you, requesting either another copy or my money back. Instead, you have sent me a copy of "Kidnapped," by Robert Louis Stevenson. Will you please straighten this out?

I hereby return the copy of "Kidnapped."

Sincerely yours,
Walter A. Child

Treasure Book Club
SECOND NOTICE
PLEASE DO NOT FOLD, SPINDLE
OR MUTILATE THIS CARD

Mr: Walter A. Child

Balance: $24.98

For "Kidnapped," by Robert Louis Stevenson.
(If remittance has been made for the above, please
disregard this notice.)

---

437 Woodlawn Drive
Panduk, Michigan
Jan. 21, 2001

Treasure Book Club
1823 Mandy Street
Chicago, Illinois

Dear Sirs:

May I direct your attention to my letter of November 16,
2000? You are still continuing to dun me with computer
punch cards for a book I did not order. Whereas, actually,
it is your company that owes me money.

Sincerely yours,
Walter A. Child

Treasure Book Club
1823 Mandy Street
Chicago, Illinois
Feb. 1, 2001

Mr. Walter A. Child
437 Woodlawn Drive
Panduk, Michigan

Dear Mr. Child:

We have sent you a number of reminders concerning an amount owing to us as a result of book purchases you have made from us. This amount, which is $24.98, is now long overdue.

This situation is disappointing to us, particularly since there was no hesitation on our part in extending you credit at the time original arrangements for these purchases were made by you. If we do not receive payment in full by return mail, we will be forced to turn the matter over to a collection agency.

Very truly yours,
Samuel P. Grimes
Collection Mgr.

---

437 Woodlawn Drive
Panduk, Michigan

Feb. 5, 2001

Treasure Book Club
1823 Mandy Street
Chicago, Illinois
Dear Mr. Grimes:

Will you stop sending me punch cards and form letters and make me some kind of a direct answer from a human being?

I don't owe you money. You owe me money. Maybe I should turn your company over to a collection agency.

Walter A. Child

FEDERAL COLLECTION OUTFIT
88 Prince Street Chicago, Illinois
Feb. 28, 2001

Mr. Walter A. Child
437 Woodlawn Drive
Panduk Michigan

Dear Mr. Child:

Your account with the Treasure Book Club, of $24.98 plus interest and charges, has been turned over to our agency for collection. The amount due is now $36.83. Please send your check for this amount or we shall be forced to take immediate action.

FEDERAL COLLECTION OUTFIT
Jacob N. Harshe
Vice President
88 Prince Street Chicago, Illinois
April 8, 2001

Mr. Walter A. Child
437 Woodlawn Drive
Panduk, Michigan

Dear Mr. Child:

You have seen fit to ignore our courteous requests to settle your long overdue account with Treasure Book club, which is now, with accumulated interest and charges, in the amount of $47.53.

If payment in full is not forthcoming by April 15, 2001, we will be forced to turn the matter over to our attorneys for immediate court action.

Jacob N. Harshe
Vice President

MALONEY, MAHONEY,
MACNAMARA and PRUITT, ESQ.
Attorneys at Law
April 22, 2001

Mr. Walter A. Child
437 Woodlawn Drive
Panduk, Michigan

Dear Mr. Child:
Your indebtedness to the Treasure Book Club has been referred to us for legal action to collect.

This indebtedness is now in the amount of $101.56; if you will send us this amount so that we may receive it before May 5, 2001, the matter may be satisfied. However, if we do not receive satisfaction in full by that date, we will take steps to collect through the courts.

I am sure you will see the advantage of avoiding a judgment against you, which as a matter of record would do lasting harm to your credit rating.

Very truly yours,
Hagthorpe M. Pruitt, Jr.
Attorney at law

---

437 Woodlawn Drive
Panduk, Michigan
May 4, 2001

Maloney, Mahoney, MacNamara and Pruitt
89 Prince Street
Chicago, Illinois

Dear Mr. Pruitt:

You don't know what a pleasure it is to me in this matter to get a letter from a live human being to whom I can explain the situation.

This whole matter is silly. I explained it fully in my letters to the Treasure Book Company. But I might as well have been trying to explain to the computer that puts out their punch cards, for all the good it seemed to do. Briefly, what happened was I ordered a copy of "Kim," by Rudyard Kipling, for $24.98. When I opened the package they sent me, I found the book had only half its pages, but I'd previously mailed a check to pay them for the book.

I sent the book back to them, asking either for a whole copy or my money back. Instead, they sent me a copy of "Kidnapped" by Robert Louis Stevenson, which I had not ordered; for which they have been trying to collect from me.

Meanwhile, I am still waiting for the money back that they owe me for the copy of "Kim" that I didn't get. That's the whole story. Maybe you can help me straighten them out.

Relievedly yours,
Walter A. Child

P.S.: I also sent them back their copy of "Kidnapped," as soon as I got it, but it didn't seemed to help. They have never even acknowledged getting it back.

**MALONEY, MAHONEY,
MACNAMARA and PRUITT, ESQ.**
Attorneys at Law
May 9, 2001

Mr. Walter A. Child
437 Woodlawn Drive
Panduk, Michigan

Dear Mr. Child:

I am in possession of no information indicating that any item purchased by you from the Treasure Book Club has been returned.

I would hardly think that, if the case had been as stated, the Treasure Book Club would have retained us to collect the amount owing from you.

If I do not receive your payment in full within three days, by May 12, 2001, we will be forced to take legal action. Very truly yours,

Hagthorpe M. Pruitt, Jr.

COURT OF MINOR CLAIMS
Chicago, Illinois

Mr. Walter A. Child
437 Woodlawn Drive
Panduk Michigan

Be informed that a judgment was taken and entered against you in this court this day of May 26, 2001 in the amount of $135.66 including court costs.

Payment in satisfaction of this judgment may be made to this court or to the adjudged creditor. In the case of payment being made to the creditor, a release should be obtained from the creditor and filed with this court in order to free you of legal obligation in connection with this judgment.

Under the recent Reciprocal Claims Act, if you are a citizen of a different state, a duplicate claim may be automatically entered and judged against you in your own state so that collection may be made there as well as in the State of Illinois.

COURT OF MINOR CLAIMS
Chicago, Illinois
PLEASE DO NOT FOLD, SPINDLE
OR MUTILATE THIS CARD

Judgment was passed this day of May 27, 2001, under Statute $135.66

Against: Child, Walter A. of 347 Woodlawn Drive, Panduk, Michigan
In: Picayune Court, Panduk, Michigan

For Amount: Statute 941

**437 Woodlawn Drive
Panduk, Michigan
May 31, 2001**

Samuel P. Grimes
Vice President, Treasure Book Club
1823 Mandy Street
Chicago, Illinois

Grimes:

This business has gone far enough. I've got to come down to Chicago on business of my own tomorrow. I'll see you then and we'll get this straightened out once and for all, about who owes what to whom, and bow much!

Yours,
Walter A. Child

**From the desk of the Clerk
Picayune Court
June 1, 2001**

Harry:

The attached computer card from Chicago's Minor Claims Court against A. Walter has a 13500-series Statute number on it. That puts it over in Criminal with you, rather than Civil, with me. So I herewith submit it for your computer instead of mine. How's business?

Joe

CRIMINAL RECORDS
Panduk, Michigan
PLEASE DO NOT FOLD, SPINDLE
OR MUTILATE THIS CARD

Convicted: (Child) A. Walter
On: May 26, 2001
Address: 437 Woodlawn Drive
Panduk, Mich.
Crime: Statute: 13566 (Corrected) 13567
Crime: Kidnap
Date: Nov. 16, 2000
Notes, At large. To be picked up at once.

POLICE DEPARTMENT, PANDUK, MICHIGAN.
TO POLICE DEPARTMENT, CHICAGO ILLINOIS.

CONVICTED SUBJECT A. (COMPLETE FIRST
NAME UNKNOWN) WALTER, SOUGHT HERE IN
CONNECTION REF. YOUR NOTIFICATION OF
JUDGMENT FOR KIDNAP OF CHILD NAMED
ROBERT LOUIS STEVENSON, ON NOV. 16, 2000.

INFORMATION HERE INDICATES SUBJECT
FLED HIS RESIDENCE, AT 437 WOODLAND
DRIVE, PANDUK, AND MAY BE AGAIN IN YOUR
AREA.

POSSIBLE CONTACT IN YOUR AREA: THE

TREASURE BOOK CLUB, 1823 MANDY STREET,
CHICAGO, ILLINOIS. SUBJECT NOT KNOWN TO
BE DANGEROUS. PICK UP AND HOLD,
ADVISING US OF CAPTURE . . .

TO POLICE: DEPARTMENT, PANDUK,
MICHIGAN.

REFERENCE YOUR REQUEST TO PICK UP AND
HOLD A. (COMPLETE FIRST NAME UNKNOWN)
WALTER, WANTED IN PANDUK ON STATUTE
1567, CRIME OF KIDNAPPING.

SUBJECT ARRESTED AT OFFICES OF TREASURE
BOOK CLUB, OPERATING THERE UNDER ALIAS
WALTER ANTHONY CHILD AND ATTEMPTING
TO COLLECT $24.98 FROM ONE SAMUEL P.
GRIMES, EMPLOYEE OF THAT COMPANY.

DISPOSAL: HOLDING FOR YOUR ADVICE

POLICE DEPARTMENT PANDUK, MICHIGAN.
TO POLICE DEPARTMENT CHICAGO, ILLINOIS.

REF: A. WALTER (ALIAS WALTER ANTHONY
CHILD) SUBJECT WANTED FOR CRIME OF
KIDNAP, YOUR AREA, REF: YOUR COMPUTER
PUNCH CARD NOTIFICATION OF JUDGMENT,
DATED MAY 27, 2001. COPY OUR CRIMINAL
RECORDS PUNCH CARD HEREWITH
FORWARDED TO YOUR COMPUTER SECTION.

CRIMINAL RECORDS
Chicago, Illinois
PLEASE DO NOT FOLD, SPINDLE
OR MUTILATE THIS CARD

SUBJECT (CORRECTION: OMITTED RECORD
SUPPLIED)

APPLICABLE STATUTE NO. 13567
JUDGMENT NO. 456789
TRIAL RECORD: APPARENTLY MISFILED AND
UNAVAILABLE
DIRECTION: TO APPEAR FOR SENTENCING
BEFORE JUDGE JOHN ALEXANDER MCDIVOT,
COURTROOM A, JUNE 9, 2001

From the Desk of The Honorable Judge
Alexander J. McDivot
June 2, 2001

Dear Tony:

I've got an adjudged criminal coming up before me for
sentencing Thursday morning—but the trial transcript is
apparently misfiled.

I need some kind of information (Ref: A. Walter—
judgment No. 456789, Criminal). For example, what
about the victim of the kidnapping. Was victim harmed?

Jack McDivot

Tonio Malagasi
Records Division
June 3, 2001

Records Search Unit
Re: Ref: judgment No. 456789—was victim harmed?

Records Search Unit
Criminal Records Division
Police Department
Chicago, Ill.
June 3, 2001

To: United States Statistics Office
Attn.: Information Section
Subject: Robert Louis Stevenson
Query: Information concerning

Information Section
U. S. Statistics Office
June 5, 2001

To: Records Search Unit
Criminal Records Division
Police Department
Chicago, Illinois
Subject: Your query re Robert Louis Stevenson (File no. 189623)

Action: Subject deceased. Age at death, 44 yrs. Further information requested?

**Records Search Unit
June 6, 2001**

To: United States Statistics Office
Attn.: Information Division
Subject; RE: File no. 189623
No further information required. Thank you.

**Criminal Records Division Police Department
Chicago, Illinois
June 7, 2001**

To: Tonio Malagasi
Records Division
Re: Ref: judgment No. 456789
Please be advised that victim is dead.
Sincerely, Records Search Unit

**Tony Malagasi
Records Division
June 7, 1966**

To: Judge Alexander J. McDivot Chambers

Dear Jack:

Ref: judgment No. 456789. The victim in this kidnap case was apparently slain.

From the strange lack of background information on the killer and his victim, as well as the victim's age, this smells to me like a gangland killing. This for your information. Don't quote me. It seems to me, though, that Stevenson—the victim has a name that rings a faint bell with me. Possibly, one of the East Coast Mob, since the association comes back to me as something about pirates—possibly New York dockage hijackers and something about buried loot.

As I say, above is only speculation for your private guidance.

Any time I can help . . .

Best,
Tony in Records

––––––––––––––––

MICHAEL R. REYNOLDS
Attorney-at-law
June 8, 2001

49 Water Street
Chicago, Illinois

Dear Tim:

Regrets: I can't make the fishing trip. I've been court-appointed here to represent a man about to be sentenced tomorrow on a kidnapping charge.

Ordinarily, I might have tried to beg off, and McDivot, who is doing the sentencing, would probably have turned me loose. But this is the damndest thing you ever heard of.

The man being sentenced has apparently been not only charged, but adjudged guilty as a result of a comedy of errors too long to go into here. He not only isn't guilty— he's got the best case I ever heard of for damages against one of the larger Book Clubs headquartered here in Chicago. And that's a case I wouldn't mind taking on.

It s inconceivable—but damnably possible, once you stop to think of it in this day and age of machine-made records—that a completely innocent man could be put in this position.

There shouldn't be much to it. I've asked to see McDivot tomorrow before the time for sentencing, and it'll just be a matter of explaining to him. Then I can discuss the damage suit with my freed client at his leisure.

Fishing next weekend?

Yours,
Mike

MICHAEL R. REYNOLDS
Attorney-at-law

49 Water Street
Chicago, Illinois
June 10, 2001

Dear Tim:

In haste—

No fishing this coming week either. Sorry.

You won't believe it. My innocent-as-a-lamb-and-I'm-not kidding client has just been sentenced to death for first-degree murder in connection with the death of his kidnap victim. Yes, I explained the whole thing to McDivot. And when he explained his situation to me, I nearly fell out of my chair.

It wasn't a matter of my not convincing him. It took less than three minutes to show him that my client should never have been within the walls of the County jail for a second. But—get this—McDivot couldn't do a thing about it.

The point is, my man had already been judged guilty according to the computerized records. In the absence of a trial record—of course there never was one (but that's something I'm not free to explain to you now)— the judge has to go by what records are available. And in the case of an adjudged prisoner, McDivot's only legal choice was whether to sentence to life imprisonment, or execution.

The death of the kidnap victim, according to the statute, made the death penalty mandatory. Under the new laws governing length of time for appeal, which has been shortened because of the new system of computerizing records, to force an elimination of unfair delay and mental anguish to those condemned, I have five days in which to file an appeal, and ten to have it acted on.

Needless to say, I am not going to monkey with an appeal. I'm going directly to the Governor for a pardon—after which we will get this farce reversed. McDivot has already written the governor, also, explaining that his sentence was ridiculous, but that he had no choice. Between the two of us, we ought to have a pardon in short order. Then, I'll make the fur fly . . . And we'll get in some fishing.

Best,
Mike

**OFFICE OF THE
GOVERNOR OF ILLINOIS
June 17, 2001**

Mr. Michael R. Reynolds
49 Water Street
Chicago, Illinois

Dear Mr. Reynolds:

In reply to Your query about the request for pardon for Walter A. Child (A. Walter) may I inform you that the Governor is still on his trip with the Midwest Governors' Committee, examining the Wall in Berlin. He should be back next Friday. I will bring your request and letters to his attention the minute he returns.

Very truly yours,
Clara B. Jilks
Secretary to the Governor

**ILLINOIS STATE PRISON
JOLIET, ILL
CELL BLOCK E, Death Row Section
June 27, 2001**

Michael R. Reynolds
49 Water Street
Chicago, Illinois

Dear Mike:
Where is that pardon? My execution date is only five days from now!

Walt

MICHAEL R. REYNOLDS
Attorney-at-law
June 29, 2001

Walter A. Child (A. Walter)
Cell Block E, Death Row Section
Illinois State Penitentiary
Joliet, Illinois

Dear Walt:

The Governor returned, but was called away immediately to the White House in Washington to give his views on interstate sewage.

I am camping on his doorstep and will be on him the moment he arrives here.

Meanwhile, I agree with you about the seriousness of the situation. The warden at the prison there, Mr. Allen Magruder, will bring this letter to you and have a private talk with you. I urge you to listen to what he has to say; and I enclose letters from your family also urging you to listen to Warden Magruder.

Yours,
Mike

**ILLINOIS STATE PRISON
JOLIET, ILL
CELL BLOCK E, Death Row Section
June 30, 2001**

Michael R. Reynolds
49 Water Street
Chicago, Illinois

Dear Mike: (This letter being smuggled out by Warden Magruder)

As I was talking to Warden Magruder in my cell, here, news was brought to him that the Governor has at last returned for a while to Illinois, and will be in his office early tomorrow morning, Friday. So you will have time to get the pardon signed by him and delivered to the prison in time to stop my execution on Saturday.

Accordingly, I have turned down the Warden's kind offer of a chance to escape; since he told me he could by no means guarantee to have all the guards out of my way when I tried it; and there was a chance of my being killed escaping.

But now everything will straighten itself out. Actually, an experience as fantastic as this had to break down sometime under its own weight.

Best,
Walt

FOR THE SOVEREIGN
STATE OF ILLINOIS
Order of Pardon

I, Hubert Daniel Willikens, Governor of the State of Illinois, and invested with the authority and powers appertaining thereto, including the power to pardon those in my judgment wrongfully convicted or otherwise deserving of executive mercy, do this day of July 1, 2001 announce and proclaim that Walter A. Child (A. Walter) now in custody as a consequence of erroneous conviction upon a crime of which he is entirely innocent, is fully and freely pardoned of said crime. And I do direct the necessary authorities having custody of the said Walter A. Child (A. Walter) in whatever place or places he may be held, to immediately free, release, and allow unhindered departure to him . . .

Interdepartmental Routing Service
PLEASE DO NOT FOLD, MUTILATE,
OR SPINDLE THIS CARD

Notice: Failure to route Document properly.

To: Governor Hubert Daniel Willikens
Re: Pardon issued to Walter A. Child, July 1, 2001

Dear State Employee:

You have failed to attach your Routing Number.

PLEASE: Resubmit document with this card and form 876, explaining your authority for placing a TOP RUSH category on this document. Form 876 must be signed by your Departmental Superior.

RESUBMIT ON: Earliest possible date ROUTING SERVICE office is open. In this case, Tuesday, July 5, 2001.

WARNING: Failure to submit form 876 WITH THE SIGNATURE OF YOUR SUPERIOR may make you liable to prosecution for misusing a Service of the State Government. A warrant may be issued for your arrest.

There are NO exceptions. YOU have been WARNED.

THE SNOWBALL EFFECT

by Katherine MacLean

*Nebula Award-winner **Katherine MacLean** (b. 1925) has been writing excellent and distinctive science fiction since the late 1940s. In the early 1950s, when SF writers were finding new topics to play with, she offered this very witty and somewhat scary take on the field of game theory, a seemingly harmless experiment that threatens to go asymptotic. Makes me wonder if something like this might have been going on for some time . . .*

"ALL RIGHT," I said, "what is sociology good for?"

Wilton Caswell, Ph.D. was head of my Sociology Department, and right then he was mad enough to chew nails. On the office wall behind him were three or four framed documents in Latin that were supposed to be signs of great learning, but I didn't care at that moment if he papered the walls with his degrees. I had been appointed dean and president to see to it that the university made money. I had a job to do, and I meant to do it.

He bit off each word with great restraint: "Sociology is the study of social institutions, Mr. Halloway."

I tried to make him understand my position. "Look, it's the big-money men who are supposed to be contributing to the support of this college. To them, sociology sounds like socialism—nothing can sound worse than that—and an institution is where they put Aunt Maggy when she began collecting Wheaties in a stamp album. We can't appeal to them that way. Come on now." I smiled condescendingly, knowing it would irritate him. "What are you doing that's worth anything?"

He glared at me, his white hair bristling and his nostrils dilated like a war horse about to whinny. I can say one thing for them—these scientists and professors always keep themselves well under control. He had a book in his hand and I was expecting him to throw it, but he spoke instead:

"This department's analysis of institutional accretion, by the use of open system mathematics, has been recognized as an outstanding and valuable contribution to—"

The words were impressive, whatever they meant, but this still didn't sound like anything that would pull in money. I interrupted, "Valuable in what way?"

He sat down on the edge of his desk thoughtfully, apparently recovering from the shock of being asked to produce something solid for his position, and ran his eyes over the titles of the books that lined his office walls.

"Well, sociology has been valuable to business in

initiating worker efficiency and group motivation studies, which they now use in management decisions. And, of course, since the depression, Washington has been using sociological studies of employment, labor and standards of living as a basis for its general policies of—"

I stopped him with both raised hands. "Please, Professor Caswell! That would hardly be a recommendation. Washington, the New Deal and the present Administration are somewhat touchy subjects to the men I have to deal with. They consider its value debatable, if you know what I mean. If they got the idea that sociology professors are giving advice and guidance— No, we have to stick to brass tacks and leave Washington out of this. What, specifically, has the work of this specific department done that would make it as worthy to receive money as—say, a heart disease research fund?"

He began to tap the corner of his book absently on the desk, watching me. "Fundamental research doesn't show immediate effects, Mr. Halloway, but its value is recognized."

I smiled and took out my pipe. "All right, tell me about it. Maybe I'll recognize its value."

Prof. Caswell smiled back tightly. He knew his department was at stake. The other departments were popular with donors and pulled in gift money by scholarships and fellowships, and supported their professors and graduate students by research contracts with the government and industry. Caswell had to show a way to make his own department popular—or else. I couldn't fire him directly, of course, but there are ways of doing it indirectly.

He laid down his book and ran a hand over his ruffled hair. "Institutions—organizations, that is—" his voice became more resonant; like most professors, when he had to explain something he instinctively slipped into his platform lecture mannerisms, and began to deliver an essay—"have certain tendencies built into the way they happen to have been organized, which cause them to expand or contract without reference to the needs they were founded to serve."

He was becoming flushed with the pleasure of explaining his subject. "All through the ages, it has been a matter of wonder and dismay to men that a simple organization—such as a church to worship in, or a delegation of weapons to a warrior class merely for defense against an outside enemy—will either grow insensately and extend its control until it is a tyranny over their whole lives, or, like other organizations set up to serve a vital need, will tend to repeatedly dwindle and vanish, and have to be painfully rebuilt.

"The reason can be traced to little quirks in the way they were organized, a matter of positive and negative power feedbacks. Such simple questions as, 'Is there a way a holder of authority in this organization can use the power available to him to increase his power?' provide the key. But it still could not be handled until the complex questions of interacting motives and long-range accumulations of minor effects could somehow be simplified and formulated. In working on the problem, I found that the mathematics of open system, as introduced to biology by Ludwig von Bertalanffy and George Kreezer, could be used as a base that would enable me to develop a specifically social mathematics, expressing the human factors of intermeshing authority and motives in simple formulas.

"By these formulations, it is possible to determine automatically the amount of growth and period of life of any organization. The UN, to choose an unfortunate example, is a shrinker type organization. Its monetary support is not in the hands of those who personally benefit by its governmental activities, but, instead, in the hands of those who would personally lose by any extension and encroachment of its authority on their own. Yet by the use of formula analysis—"

"That's theory," I said. "How about proof?"

"My equations are already being used in the study of limited-size Federal corporations. Washington—"

I held up my palm again. "Please, not that nasty word again. I mean, where else has it been put into operation? Just a simple demonstration, something to show that it works, that's all."

He looked away from me thoughtfully, picked up the book and began to tap it on the desk again. It had some unreadable title and his name on it in gold letters. I got the distinct impression again that he was repressing an urge to hit me with it.

He spoke quietly. "All right, I'll give you a demonstration. Are you willing to wait six months?"

"Certainly, if you can show me something at the end of that time."

Reminded of time, I glanced at my watch and stood up.

"Could we discuss this over lunch?" he asked.

"I wouldn't mind hearing more, but I'm having lunch

with some executors of a millionaire's will. They have to be convinced that by 'furtherance of research into human ills,' he meant that the money should go to research fellowships for postgraduate biologists at the university, rather than to a medical foundation."

"I see you have your problems, too," Caswell said, conceding me nothing. He extended his hand with a chilly smile. "Well, good afternoon, Mr. Halloway. I'm glad we had this talk."

I shook hands and left him standing there, sure of his place in the progress of science and the respect of his colleagues, yet seething inside because I, the president and dean, had boorishly demanded that he produce something tangible.

I frankly didn't give a hoot if he blew his lid. My job isn't easy. For a crumb of favorable publicity and respect in the newspapers and an annual ceremony in a silly costume, I spend the rest of the year going hat in hand, asking politely for money at everyone's door, like a well-dressed panhandler, and trying to manage the university on the dribble I get. As far as I was concerned, a department had to support itself or be cut down to what student tuition pays for, which is a handful of over-crowded courses taught by an assistant lecturer. Caswell had to make it work or get out.

But the more I thought about it, the more I wanted to hear what he was going to do for a demonstration.

At lunch, three days later, while we were waiting for our order, he opened a small notebook. "Ever hear of feedback effects?"

"Not enough to have it clear."

"You know the snowball effect, though."

"Sure, start a snowball rolling downhill and it grows."

"Well, now—" He wrote a short line of symbols on a blank page and turned the notebook around for me to inspect it. "Here's the formula for the snowball process. It's the basic general growth formula—covers everything."

It was a row of little symbols arranged like an algebra equation. One was a concentric spiral going up, like a cross-section of a snowball rolling in snow. That was a growth sign.

I hadn't expected to understand the equation, but it was almost as clear as a sentence. I was impressed and slightly intimidated by it. He had already explained enough so that I knew that, if he was right, here was the growth of the Catholic Church and the Roman Empire, the conquests of Alexander and the spread of the smoking habit and the change and rigidity of the unwritten law of styles.

"Is it really as simple as that?" I asked.

"You notice," he said, "that when it becomes too heavy for the cohesion strength of snow, it breaks apart. Now in human terms—"

The chops and mashed potatoes and peas arrived.

"Go on," I urged.

He was deep in the symbology of human motives and the equations of human behavior in groups. After running through a few different types of grower and shrinker type organizations, we came back to the snowball, and decided to run the test by making something grow.

"You add the motives," he said, "and the equation will translate them into organization."

"How about a good selfish reason for the ins to drag others into the group—some sort of bounty on new members, a cut of their membership fee?" I suggested uncertainly, feeling slightly foolish. "And maybe a reason why the members would lose if any of them resigned, and some indirect way they could use to force each other to stay in."

"The first is the chain letter principle," he nodded. "I've got that. The other. . . ." He put the symbols through some mathematical manipulation so that a special grouping appeared in the middle of the equation. "That's it."

Since I seemed to have the right idea, I suggested some more, and he added some, and juggled them around in different patterns. We threw out a few that would have made the organization too complicated, and finally worked out an idyllically simple and deadly little organization setup where joining had all the temptation of buying a sweepstakes ticket, going in deeper was as easy as hanging around a race track, and getting out was like trying to pull free from a Malayan thumb trap. We put our heads closer together and talked lower, picking the best place for the demonstration.

"Abington?"

"How about Watashaw? I have some student sociological surveys of it already. We can pick a suitable group from that."

"This demonstration has got to be convincing. We'd better pick a little group that no one in his right mind would expect to grow."

"There should be a suitable club—"

Picture Professor Caswell, head of the Department of Sociology, and with him the President of the University, leaning across the table toward each other, sipping coffee and talking in conspiratorial tones over something they were writing in a notebook.

That was us.

"Ladies," said the skinny female chairman of the Watashaw Sewing Circle. "Today we have guests." She signaled for us to rise, and we stood up, bowing to polite applause and smiles. "Professor Caswell, and Professor Smith." (My alias.) "They are making a survey of the methods and duties of the clubs of Watashaw."

We sat down to another ripple of applause and slightly wider smiles, and then the meeting of the Watashaw Sewing Circle began. In five minutes I began to feel sleepy.

There were only about thirty people there, and it was a small room, not the halls of Congress, but they discussed their business of collecting and repairing second hand clothing for charity with the same endless boring parliamentary formality.

I pointed out to Caswell the member I thought would be the natural leader, a tall, well-built woman in a green suit, with conscious gestures and a resonant, penetrating voice, and then went into a half doze while Caswell stayed awake beside me and wrote in his notebook. After a while the resonant voice roused me to attention for a moment. It was the tall woman holding the floor over some collective dereliction of the club. She was being scathing.

I nudged Caswell and murmured, "Did you fix it so

that a shover has a better chance of getting into office than a non-shover?"

"I think there's a way they could find for it," Caswell whispered back, and went to work on his equation again. "Yes, several ways to bias the elections."

"Good. Point them out tactfully to the one you select. Not as if she'd use such methods, but just as an example of the reason why only she can be trusted with initiating the change. Just mention all the personal advantages an unscrupulous person could have."

He nodded, keeping a straight and sober face as if we were exchanging admiring remarks about the techniques of clothes repairing, instead of conspiring.

After the meeting, Caswell drew the tall woman in the green suit aside and spoke to her confidentially, showing her the diagram of organization we had drawn up. I saw the responsive glitter in the woman's eyes and knew she was hooked.

We left the diagram of organization and our typed copy of the new bylaws with her and went off soberly, as befitted two social science experimenters. We didn't start laughing until our car passed the town limits and began the climb for University Heights.

If Caswell's equations meant anything at all, we had given that sewing circle more growth drives than the Roman Empire.

Four months later I had time out from a very busy schedule to wonder how the test was coming along. Passing Caswell's office, I put my head in. He looked up from a student research paper he was correcting.

"Caswell, about that sewing club business—I'm beginning to feel the suspense. Could I get an advance report on how it's coming?"

"I'm not following it. We're supposed to let it run the full six months."

"But I'm curious. Could I get in touch with that woman—what's her name?"

"Searles. Mrs. George Searles."

"Would that change the results?"

"Not in the slightest. If you want to graph the membership rise, it should be going up in a log curve, probably doubling every so often."

I grinned. "If it's not rising, you're fired."

He grinned back. "If it's not rising, you won't have to fire me—I'll burn my books and shoot myself."

I returned to my office and put in a call to Watashaw.

While I was waiting for the phone to be answered, I took a piece of graph paper and ruled it off into six sections, one for each month. After the phone had rung in the distance for a long time, a servant answered with a bored drawl:

"Mrs. Searles' residence."

I picked up a red gummed star and licked it.

"Mrs. Searles, please."

"She's not in just now. Could I take a message?"

I placed the star at the thirty line in the beginning of the first section. Thirty members they'd started with.

"No, thanks. Could you tell me when she'll be back?"

"Not until dinner. She's at the meetin'."

"The sewing club?" I asked.

"No, sir, not that thing. There isn't any sewing club

any more, not for a long time. She's at the Civic Welfare meeting."

Somehow I hadn't expected anything like that.

"Thank you," I said and hung up, and after a moment noticed I was holding a box of red gummed stars in my hand. I closed it and put it down on top of the graph of membership in the sewing circle. No more members. . . .

Poor Caswell. The bet between us was ironclad. He wouldn't let me back down on it even if I wanted to. He'd probably quit before I put through the first slow move to fire him. His professional pride would be shattered, sunk without a trace. I remembered what he said about shooting himself. It had seemed funny to both of us at the time, but. . . . What a mess that would make for the university.

I had to talk to Mrs. Searles. Perhaps there was some outside reason why the club had disbanded. Perhaps it had not just died.

I called back. "This is Professor Smith," I said, giving the alias I had used before. "I called a few minutes ago. When did you say Mrs. Searles will return?"

"About six-thirty or seven o'clock."

Five hours to wait.

And what if Caswell asked me what I had found out in the meantime? I didn't want to tell him anything until I had talked it over with that woman Searles first.

"Where is this Civic Welfare meeting?"

She told me.

Five minutes later, I was in my car, heading for Watashaw, driving considerably faster than my usual speed and keeping a careful watch for highway patrol cars as the speedometer climbed.

The town meeting hall and theater was a big place, probably with lots of small rooms for different clubs. I went in through the center door and found myself in the huge central hall where some sort of rally was being held. A political-type rally—you know, cheers and chants, with bunting already down on the floor, people holding banners, and plenty of enthusiasm and excitement in the air. Someone was making a speech up on the platform. Most of the people there were women.

I wondered how the Civic Welfare League could dare hold its meeting at the same time as a political rally that could pull its members away. The group with Mrs. Searles was probably holding a shrunken and almost memberless meeting somewhere in an upper room.

There probably was a side door that would lead upstairs.

While I glanced around, a pretty girl usher put a printed bulletin in my hand, whispering, "Here's one of the new copies." As I attempted to hand it back, she retreated. "Oh, you can keep it. It's the new one. Everyone's supposed to have it. We've just printed up six thousand copies to make sure there'll be enough to last."

The tall woman on the platform had been making a driving, forceful speech about some plans for rebuilding Watashaw's slum section. It began to penetrate my mind dimly as I glanced down at the bulletin in my hands.

"Civic Welfare League of Watashaw. The United Organization of Church and Secular Charities." That's what it said. Below began the rules of membership.

I looked up. The speaker, with a clear, determined voice and conscious, forceful gestures, had entered the homestretch of her speech, an appeal to the civic pride of all citizens of Watashaw.

"With a bright and glorious future—potentially without poor and without uncared-for ill—potentially with no ugliness, no vistas which are not beautiful—the best people in the best planned town in the country—the jewel of the United States."

She paused and then leaned forward intensely, striking her clenched hand on the speaker's stand with each word for emphasis.

"All we need is more members. Now get out there and recruit!"

I finally recognized Mrs. Searles, as an answering sudden blast of sound half deafened me. The crowd was chanting at the top of its lungs: "Recruit! Recruit!"

Mrs. Searles stood still at the speaker's table and behind her, seated in a row of chairs, was a group that was probably the board of directors. It was mostly women, and the women began to look vaguely familiar, as if they could be members of the sewing circle.

I put my lips close to the ear of the pretty usher while I turned over the stiff printed bulletin on a hunch. "How long has the League been organized?" On the back of the bulletin was a constitution.

She was cheering with the crowd, her eyes sparkling. "I don't know," she answered between cheers. "I only joined two days ago. Isn't it wonderful?"

I went into the quiet outer air and got into my car with my skin prickling. Even as I drove away, I could hear them. They were singing some kind of organization song with the tune of "Marching through Georgia."

Even at the single glance I had given it, the constitution looked exactly like the one we had given the Watashaw Sewing Circle.

All I told Caswell when I got back was that the sewing circle had changed its name and the membership seemed to be rising.

Next day, after calling Mrs. Searles, I placed some red stars on my graph for the first three months. They made a nice curve, rising more steeply as it reached the fourth month. They had picked up their first increase in membership simply by amalgamating with all the other types of charity organizations in Watashaw, changing the club name with each fusion, but keeping the same constitution—the constitution with the bright promise of advantages as long as there were always new members being brought in.

By the fifth month, the League had added a mutual baby-sitting service and had induced the local school board to add a nursery school to the town service, so as to free more women for League activity. But charity must have been completely organized by then, and expansion had to be in other directions.

Some real estate agents evidently had been drawn into the whirlpool early, along with their ideas. The slum improvement plans began to blossom and take on a tinge of real estate planning later in the month.

The first day of the sixth month, a big two page spread appeared in the local paper of a mass meeting which had approved a full-fledged scheme for slum clearance of Watashaw's shack-town section, plus plans for rehousing, civic building, and rezoning. And good prospects for attracting some new industries to the town, industries which had already been contacted and seemed interested by the privileges offered.

And with all this, an arrangement for securing and distributing to the club members alone most of the profit that would come to the town in the form of a rise in the price of building sites and a boom in the building industry. The profit distributing arrangement was the same one that had been built into the organization plan for the distribution of the small profits of membership fees and honorary promotions. It was becoming an openly profitable business. Membership was rising more rapidly now.

By the second week of the sixth month, news appeared in the local paper that the club had filed an application to incorporate itself as the Watashaw Mutual Trade and Civic Development Corporation, and all the local real estate promoters had finished joining en masse. The Mutual Trade part sounded to me as if the Chamber of Commerce was on the point of being pulled in with them, ideas, ambitions and all.

I chuckled while reading the next page of the paper, on which a local politician was reported as having addressed the club with a long flowery oration on their enterprise, charity, and civic spirit. He had been made an honorary member. If he allowed himself to be made a full member with its contractual obligations and its lures, if the politicians went into this, too. . . .

I laughed, filing the newspaper with the other documents on the Watashaw test. These proofs would fascinate any businessman with the sense to see where his bread was buttered. A businessman is constantly dealing with organizations, including his own, and finding them either inert, cantankerous, or both. Caswell's formula could be a handle to grasp them with. Gratitude alone would bring money into the university in carload lots.

The end of the sixth month came. The test was over and the end reports were spectacular. Caswell's formulas were proven to the hilt.

After reading the last newspaper reports, I called him up.

"Perfect, Wilt, perfect! I can use this Watashaw thing to get you so many fellowships and scholarships and grants for your department that you'll think it's snowing money!"

He answered somewhat disinterestedly, "I've been busy working with students on their research papers and marking tests—not following the Watashaw business at all, I'm afraid. You say the demonstration went well and you're satisfied?"

He was definitely putting on a chill. We were friends now, but obviously he was still peeved whenever he was reminded that I had doubted that his theory could work. And he was using its success to rub my nose in the realization that I had been wrong. A man with a string of degrees after his name is just as human as anyone else. I had needled him pretty hard that first time.

"I'm satisfied," I acknowledged. "I was wrong. The formulas work beautifully. Come over and see my file of documents on it if you want a boost for your ego. Now let's see the formula for stopping it."

He sounded cheerful again. "I didn't complicate that organization with negatives. I wanted it to grow. It falls apart naturally when it stops growing for more than two months. It's like the great stock boom before an economic crash. Everyone in it is prosperous as long as the prices just keep going up and new buyers come into the market, but they all knew what would happen if it stopped growing. You remember, we built in as one of the incentives that the members know they are going to lose if membership stops growing. Why, if I tried to stop it now, they'd cut my throat."

I remembered the drive and frenzy of the crowd in the one early meeting I had seen. They probably would.

"No," he continued. "We'll just let it play out to the end of its tether and die of old age."

"When will that be?"

"It can't grow past the female population of the town. There are only so many women in Watashaw, and some of them don't like sewing."

The graph on the desk before me began to look sinister. Surely Caswell must have made some provision for—

"You underestimate their ingenuity," I said into the phone. "Since they wanted to expand, they didn't stick to sewing. They went from general charity to social welfare schemes to something that's pretty close to an incorporated government. The name is now the Watashaw Mutual Trade and Civic Development Corporation, and they're filing an application to change it to Civic Property Pool and Social Dividend, membership contractual, open to all. That social dividend sounds like a Technocrat climbed on the band wagon, eh?"

While I spoke, I carefully added another red star to the curve above the thousand member level, checking with the newspaper that still lay open on my desk. The curve was definitely some sort of log curve now, growing more rapidly with each increase.

"Leaving out practical limitations for a moment, where does the formula say it will stop?" I asked.

"When you run out of people to join it. But after all, there are only so many people in Watashaw. It's a pretty small town."

"They've opened a branch office in New York," I said carefully into the phone, a few weeks later.

With my pencil, very carefully, I extended the membership curve from where it was then.

After the next doubling, the curve went almost straight up and off the page.

Allowing for a lag of contagion from one nation to another, depending on how much their citizens intermingled, I'd give the rest of the world about twelve years.

There was a long silence while Caswell probably drew the same graph in his own mind. Then he laughed weakly. "Well, you asked me for a demonstration."

That was as good an answer as any. We got together and had lunch in a bar, if you can call it lunch. The movement we started will expand by hook or by crook, by seduction or by bribery or by propaganda or by conquest, but it will expand. And maybe a total world government will be a fine thing—until it hits the end of its rope in twelve years or so.

What happens then, I don't know.

But I don't want anyone to pin that on me. From now on, if anyone asks me, I've never heard of Watashaw.

WELL WORTH THE MONEY

by Jody Lynn Nye

Jody Lynn Nye (b. 1957) here combines two of her passions: rip-raoring space adventure and cats. Since a third passion of hers is humor, also going full-throttle, feel free to chuckle as you read this sprightly yarn of interstellar bad guys who picked the wrong ship to mess with. Jody Lynn Nye has penned an impressive number of novels in her career, including her current humorous space adventure series for Baen Books, presently consisting of The View from the Imperium, Fortunes of the Imperium, *and* Rhythm of the Imperium. *For more about her many books and stories, go to jodylynnnye.net.*

((☼))

"WE NEED VOLUNTEERS," the video memo blaring in the IATA employee cafeteria stated, "to crew an exciting but potentially hazardous and rewarding expedition featuring the latest in Drebian/Terran technology. If you are interested in being one of the few, the brave, call extension 6508."

That brief message had begun a dizzying odyssey for Balin Jurgieniewski. He had been with the Intergalactic Assay and Trade Association for a mere five years, four months. His dream of becoming a trade ship captain had been heretofore laughed at, let alone unfulfilled. Men and women with four times his seniority were still without commands of their own. Everyone wanted to be a captain, sailing the stars in the command chair of a powerful vessel, or even one that had the training wheels off. Still, "potentially hazardous" didn't sound nearly as interesting as "rewarding." It wouldn't hurt to find out if their idea of rewarding matched his. He applied for the job.

As the personnel director explained it to him and the two other people who "made the cut" (Jurgieniewski's suspicion was that they were the only ones who applied), Humanity's newest ally and trading partner, the strange, bloblike Drebs, were seeking to pay their debt for goods and services tendered to them by the Terran government by offering it their space travel technology, which lay far beyond its current reach. Naturally, every single company which had ever launched a charge into space was interested. The government threw open the rights at auction.

IATA had been the winner of the sealed bid seeking to gain and manufacture the Drebian starship electronics. The Drebs duly signed, or rather smeared, their symbols on contracts, and the deal was done. All this had been beamed all over the news for months. At last, the first machinery off the line was finished and ready for testing.

Jurgieniewski's first command would be the double shakedown cruise of a newly-refitted vessel, the *Marylou*. The flight to Argylenia was intended at first only to test the new superfast space drive, but IATA's board of directors had, at the last minute, decided to add the Drebs' interactive computer electronics system to the *Marylou*. This had not been leaked to the press, or as far as Jurgieniewski could remember, throughout the rest of IATA's personnel.

Because the knowledge was irreplaceable and the ship wasn't, IATA loaded up three volunteers, chosen only from its rank of junior officers, and sent them on a trading mission to Argylenia, a textile supplier orbiting a blue-white star in Leo Sector.

So if it was potentially a one way trip, why take it? Jurgieniewski had to admit he knew the answers: the money, and the prestige. There was trip pay to be earned, recording fees, specialist fees, and the big one: hazard pay. It was tough for anyone with less than ten years experience to pull down that much credit or accrue the instant seniority that they'd earn for bringing the *Marylou* back successfully. It might, it was hinted to him, get him at least exec officer status, if not a full command, if he, the crew, and the *Marylou* made it back in their several pieces.

Getting to know the ship with her reconstructed innards was a piece of cake. The sky-blue-and-pink blob scientists guided them one by one into the fold-out booth that attached to the left side of the control unit.

"It reads your personality and intellect," the chief Dreb burbled through his translator, "thereby saving time between command and execution. This is particularly of use during a crisis."

As the newly promoted commander, Jurgieniewski went first. At twenty-six, he was the youngest of the three crew members. The whole process consisted of a lot of lights flashing into his eyes, and probes poking into his ears and against his scalp, but beyond slightly disorienting him, didn't feel like much. He shrugged to the other two as he came out. With a wary expression on her face, Diani Marius followed. She was the ship's helm and navigation officer. Okabe Thomas went last. Thomas, the old man of the crew at thirty-four, was known as a trade specialist and diplomat, beside his talents as an engineer. None of them had been with the company more than seven years, and none had immediate family. IATA was taking no chances with survivor benefits or suits for wrongful death.

All three of them acted with great solemnity during the departure ceremony, in which the Drebs and the Humans praised the spirit of cooperation and one another. Carrying the ship's cat, IATA's traditional mascot of good luck that went on every vessel it sent out, they filed on board with the floodlights of the media recorders following them into the *Marylou*'s hatch. They all waved goodbye to the press and their employers. Jurgieniewski felt his heart sink. Fladium Base wasn't much, but it had been his home for years. He might never see it again.

Not everyone shared his anxiety. As soon as the white enameled doors sealed behind them, Thomas let out a whoop and slapped his hands together.

"Oh, friends, is this going to be a blast!" he cried,

grabbing his shipmates in a three-and-a-half-way hug. Kelvin, a black and white female mixed-breed cat, protested and demanded to be put down.

Marius rescued Kelvin from the crush, and put her on the deck. "What are you so thrilled about, Thomas? This thing could blow up on us. We could all die!"

"Not a chance, Helm. Ship?" Thomas said, addressing the air. "Or can I call you Marylou?"

"Working," the computer's pleasant though burbly voice responded.

"Crank this sucker up, and let's get out of here."

"Destination?"

Marius dashed for her console and ran up the coordinates for Argylenia. "Twenty-seven degrees, fifty minutes, right ascendancy ⊠15," she read off.

"Understood. On the command?"

Marius looked at Jurgieniewski. "Given," he said, with some surprise.

Lights on the console shifted from red to green, and gradually up to white. The ship moved under their feet, but so gently that the crewmembers had no trouble getting to their assigned crash couches before the *Marylou* attained acceleration. Jurgieniewski grabbed the cat and stuffed her into her crashbox under the console before he sat down. The huge screen which took up the entire front of the pilot's compartment warmed up to show the field of stars and the stars surrounding Fladium's sun.

"Destination will be reached within thirty-seven days," the *Marylou*'s voice assured them, as they strapped in.

"That's impossible," Marius protested. "It should take at least sixty-two, even at maxiumum acceleration."

Thomas winked at her. "Marylou, honey, give the doubting member of our crew the details of the journey."

Unerringly, the red sensor lights of the Drebian personality monitor went on in front of Marius. Her personal screen filled with mathematical formulae and star maps, reflections of which shone on her face, the expression slowly gaining in enlightenment. "Hot damn, I didn't think a ship this size could do that." She looked up at the others. "Do you mean that's all I have to do?"

Jurgieniewski grinned broadly at his crew, and settled in with his hands tucked behind his head. "I think I'm going to like this ship. She's worth every credit they paid for her."

The galaxy on the big screen streaked into a shock of white, and then all light vanished as the ship bounced into her first jump. When there was nothing more to look at, Jurgieniewski cleared his throat.

"Um, well," he began. "Since we've got five weeks, I want us all to bone up on the features of this ship. We've got reports to send back at regular intervals, and I don't want them to catch us out on a single detail." He tapped the insignia on the shoulder of his dark-blue coverall hopefully. "I want real ones of these when I get home."

"If we get home," Marius said gloomily.

"What are you talking about?" Thomas asked, with his customary cheerful mien. "The *Marylou* will take good care of us. Won't you, sweetheart?" he said to the air.

"Working," the computer voice said. "Affirmative. Honeycakes."

Jurgieniewski pointed toward one of the speakers. "Did you tell her to call you that?" he asked Thomas.

"Naw, but she's picking up on the things I usually say." Thomas thought about it a moment. "I don't think I've said 'honeycakes' yet, though. Not in the computer's presence. I guess the Drebs told the truth when they said that the box reads your mind."

"This is still an experimental vessel," Marius pointed out, resuming the previous argument.

"That's why I want us to know everything there is to know about the *Marylou*," Jurgieniewski assented. "Engine capability, clearance under bridges, armaments . . ."

"Yes, why are we armed?" Thomas said. "We're only going to Argylenia. That's right through well-established, well-patrolled throughways."

"Not this time," Marius said, showing him her terminal. "*Marylou's* redirected us. We go right through a corner of Smoot territory. Computer, put it on the big screen?"

The diagrams appeared, greatly enlarged, with the ship's flight path indicated by a dashed line in red. The Smoot were another bloblike race that Humanity had discovered, but had entirely failed to befriend. The Smoot seemed to be offended by the presence in the universe of a race of vertebrates, which they saw as an offense against their Creator, to be exterminated whenever possible. Thomas's smoky complexion drained to ash, and he swallowed. "Maybe we won't meet any of them."

"Working," *Marylou* said. Thomas's own screen lit up suddenly with another array of formulae, this time referring to the schematics of two powerful, sidemounted laser cannon, and a nose-mounted plasma torpedo launcher. The screen blanked, only to fill again with a list of evasive maneuvers which the *Marylou* was capable of executing, with diagrams, followed by a flashing cursor, and the legend, in block print, "YOUR CHOICE?"

"Whew!" Thomas whistled, and patted the console. "You sure know how to make a fellow feel welcome, honey."

A querelous complaint erupted from underneath the control panel.

"You want to let the cat out, Thomas?" Marius asked.

So far as Jurgieniewski could tell after only a week, the Drebs had done their work with the usual, expected degree of genius. The mind-reading capabilities of the computer were not only complete, but subtle. Every morning when he opened his eyes, a screen went on above his bunk, and beside his elbow, a door slid up to reveal a steaming cup of coffee. On the screen, the *Marylou* reported the ship's status, complete with a tiny diagram of how far they had travelled during his dark shift. Nothing was wrong, or even remotely awry. Jurgieniewski sighed and reached for the cup. The system was flawless. An eight-year-old could run the ship, play a video game, and do his homework all at the same time. Even the coffee was exactly the temperature he liked to drink it, just under boiling but cool enough that it didn't scorch his tongue. He drained his cup, down to the melted sugar on the bottom. *Marylou* seemed to know that he didn't like his sugar mixed in, just dropped straight through, leaving a faint trail of sweetening in the top seven-eighths of the cup. It was absolutely uncanny what tiny details the computer picked up on and exploited. It scared him a little: What if the Marylou decided to take things into her own hands and run the show? He'd look an incredible fool back at IATA HQ.

A duty list popped up on the screen almost before the thought had finished forming. *Marylou* was asking permission to run scheduled system tests, send off personal mail, transmit the daily report to HQ, or do personal system maintenance. At the bottom was the flashing "YOUR CHOICE?"

Jurgicnicwski grinned as he set down the cup. "Thanks, honey. It's nice of you to make me think I'm in charge."

He met Marius and Thomas for breakfast in the small galley. He was undecided whether a hot scrambled egg sandwich or blueberry pancakes would fill the gap in his belly, and decided to let *Marylou* surprise him.

"Hi, gang," he said, sliding into the third chair. The hatch before him whisked open and a plate rose upward. Mmm, he thought, reaching for it. A baked pancake with blueberry filling—now that was a creative way to split the difference. He sent a mental thank you to the ship's computer. He was two or three forkfuls into the steaming cake when he noticed his two crewmembers weren't talking. They were staring into their cups of coffee with thoughtful expressions. "What's the matter?"

"Jurgy," Marius began, still staring at the cup between her fingers as if it troubled her, "don't you feel kind of . . . useless?"

"No," he replied, surprised. He set down the fork. Was this the beginnings of mutiny? What had he done wrong? "I've hardly ever enjoyed a trip more in my life."

"Seriously, Jurgy, there's nothing for us to do."

"That's about it," Thomas said with a sigh. "Ship's too new to have loose bolts, and the Drebs already dusted, oiled, and cleaned up before we took her out. We're just watching her run. I thought it'd be fun, too, but even I'm getting bored."

"Yeah," Marius agreed. "All we do is send out reports and feed Kelvin."

Hearing her name, the cat walked over and rubbed her face against Marius's knee. The navigator reached down and scratched the top of the cat's head.

Jurgieniewski nodded. "All right, we'll come up with something. Meantime, we've survived one whole week in the ship they all thought would blow up on the launch pad. What say we have us a party tonight to celebrate?"

Marius and Thomas perked up. "Now there's a fine concept," Thomas agreed.

The party started at the stroke of third shift. The three humans and the cat assembled in the control room for a round of special meals and entertainments. With all of her talents, the *Marylou*'s Drebian computer had one more heretofore undiscovered skill: she had in her memory banks every bartender's manual ever written.

"Honeycakes, make me up a . . . Viking's Elbow," Thomas commanded, from his launch chair. He had staggered for greater stability when, as he claimed, the deck started to spin.

"Are you still working your way through the alphabet?" Jurgieniewski asked. He was bent raptly over a hand control for the video game *Marylou* had running on the screen. It was a commercial game that Jurgieniewski had spent years learning to win. Tiny spaceships swirled in an attack pattern around a single red ship that dodged and evaded while it shot them down one by one. His running score was in the corner of the three-meter-high image. It was already in the millions, and Jurgieniewski was still hot.

"No, man, I'm going through it again, only backwards this time," Thomas explained. The hatch next to his elbow disgorged a stylized noggin with a dragon-headed stirring rod in it. Thomas discarded the stick, and took a deep drink from the mug.

"Have you tasted this banana mousse?" Marius asked, waving her spoon at the two men. "It's fabulous!"

Kelvin jumped up in her lap and demanded a taste.

"You know, it's too bad Marylou didn't whip up anything special for the cat," Thomas opined, ordering up an Undertaker's Friend. "Hey, baby, make a treat for the cat, huh?"

"Working. Please clarify the command."

"The cat," Thomas repeated. "Give her a plate of tuna sushi, or whatever cats think is party food."

"Working. There is no record for Thecat in these memory circuits."

"Kelvin's our ship's cat. She's right here." Thomas pointed to Kelvin, who was busily lapping up banana cream.

There was some puzzled whirring. The three crewmembers looked at one another, and Jurgieniewski put down the game control. He rose to his feet somewhat unsteadily. "It's not fair we should get everything we want when our little friend gets nothing but Fishy Nibbles," he pronounced. "Let's put her in the personality reader, and *Marylou* can figure out what she wants."

"Great idea," Marius applauded. Kelvin let out an offended yowl at being taken away from her plate when Marius picked her up and carried her over to the expandable booth. Jurgieniewski and Thomas pulled out the folding sides and set the corner braces. The helm officer set the cat inside, and snapped the curtain shut before Kelvin, now confused and frightened, could escape.

"Working," *Marylou* said. The cat's ululations rose to angry growls, and then stopped abruptly. Through the transparent panel, all of them could see Kelvin sitting on the booth's bench with her pupils down to tiny slits and her ears, with the probes sticking out of them, laid flat along her skull. As soon as the lights ceased flashing, Marius snatched the cat out of the booth and stroked her until the fighting ridge went down on the cat's back.

"There, there, kitty, sssshhaa," she said soothingly. The cat's fur smoothed out, and she emitted an interrogative trill. Marius hugged her. "What do you want? Some more mousse? That sounds a little like *mouse*."

For answer, a plate slid out of one of the service hatches at floor level, and Kelvin kicked out of Marius's arms to get to it.

"Tuna sushi," Jurgieniewski nodded, with approval, and went back to his game.

"Bartender," Thomas said, snapping his fingers above his head. "Make me a Tomato Surprise."

Thomas tried to grind the strata of sand out of his eyes long enough to find his morning cup of coffee. He didn't dare sit up lest his brain fall out of his ears before he could nail it in place with a bolt or two of caffeine. "I hope this is strong, baby," he pleaded the computer.

It was strong enough to drag Thomas to his feet and halfway to the bathroom before he knew he'd moved. As he washed up, he realized he was starving. Probably not much of what he'd consumed the night before had significant food value.

"Aw, damn!" he smote himself in the forehead.

Pulling on a coverall, he hurried out into the galley, where Marius was sitting, sipping from a cup of plain black coffee. She glanced up as he dashed in. He glanced past her at Kelvin, who was crouched close to the wall, munching from a bowl.

"Thanks for feeding the cat," he said. "I overslept."

"Didn't do it," Marius said, talking as if forming the words hurt her head. "Maybe Jurgy did it."

Jurgieniewski's eyes were red and half closed as he slid into his chair and received a gigantic beaker of orange juice from the serving hatch. "Not me."

"Then, who?" They all looked at each other. "Did we do what I think I remember us doing last night?" Thomas asked, very carefully. The other two nodded slowly, the full reality of their actions returning to them through the mental haze.

As one, they turned to look at the cat, who had finished her meal and was washing her ear with a diligent paw.

From that day on, the human crew members watched as doors opened for the cat before she reached them.

Kelvin never had to nag any of them for food, and sometimes got portions of the gourmet goodies that were supposed to be held aside for the individual humans who brought them aboard.

"*Marylou*," Jurgieniewski complained, "that spicewurst was special! It took me years to get it."

"It was necessary to the well-being of Crewmember Kelvin," *Marylou* said without a trace of reproach or regret. The commander groaned.

"She got some of my Cornish butter, too," Marius reminded him.

"And the smoked turkey I got from my sister," said Thomas.

"That does it. Override the cat's program, will you, *Marylou*?" Jurgieniewski asked. "Kelvin's not supposed to have things like that. It's probably bad for her."

"Working. Request formulae to judge difference between needs of one Terran crewmember and another."

"Darn those Drebs," Jurgieniewski muttered. "We all look alike to them. How about job orientation? I'm a captain, this is the navigator, and this is the engineer. The cat's only a pet."

"There is no qualification on this ship's complement for a 'pet.' Identify this crewmember," *Marylou* instructed them.

"Her name's Kelvin," Jurgieniewski offered.

"Position?"

He shrugged, and looked at the others for inspiration. "She's the ship's cat."

"There is no entry in ship rosters for 'ship's cat.'"

Thomas's face lit up. "I guess you could call her

Maintenance," he suggested. "She's supposed to handle pest control, even though this thing has never seen a mouse."

The commander could almost hear the mental clicking and whirring as the *Marylou* digested the information. "Working. As a Maintenance worker, Crewmember Kelvin is entitled to statutory three hundred sixty credits per week, retroactive to the beginning of this flight, plus additions for trip pay, hazard pay. . . ."

Jurgieniewski smacked himself in the head and automatically regretted it. "Friends, I think we've created a monster. I'm afraid to try and change it again."

"Me, either," Thomas agreed. "One more slip-up, and that cat'll be an admiral."

"We'll have to straighten this out when we get back," Marius put in. "Anything else we do is going to make matters worse."

"I'm not looking forward to getting back to Fladium and explaining to them why the *cat* is drawing a salary." The brevet commander downed the last of his orange juice and put the empty glass on the serving hatch. It descended out of sight. "Goodbye, field promotion."

"Goodbye, instant seniority," Marius agreed.

"Farewell, smoked turkey," Thomas reminded them. "Still, I can live with it if the rest of you can."

A few days later Jurgieniewski awoke with a snort in the middle of the night, and tried to cry out, but there was something over his mouth. He reached for the light. Marius was sitting on the edge of his bed with her hand plastered over his face to keep him from yelling. He nodded, and she let him go.

"I heard some strange noises in the control room," she whispered.

"Something wrong?" he asked, sitting up.

"No. Come and see."

Curious, he followed her down the narrow, enameled corridor. She paused at the threshold of the main chamber, and gestured to him to look past her.

On the main computer screen, tiny, colorful objects shaped like mice scurried back and forth, or lowered into view like spiders. As soon as one exited, more would appear. The cat, purring as loudly as a drive engine, was bounding all over the room, throwing herself at the screen, pounding the images with her paws. In the corner, the red numbers were mounting. *Marylou* must have been keeping score for her own amusement. The cat, focused on her myriad prey, was having a great time. She never acknowledged the humans in the hallway behind her.

Jurgieniewski glanced at Marius, who was struggling to contain her laughter. "Why doesn't the computer do this kind of stuff for us?" he whispered. "It's terrific! Look at that, a custom video game!"

"Cats have more needs, and they're not particularly ashamed to admit to them," Marius whispered. "I'm only happy that she's been fixed. Can you imagine having the ship decide we have to forego our cargo stop to find a male cat in some other system? Going planet to planet in search of a tom?"

"The company isn't going to like that."

"Look, this is a shakedown cruise," Marius pointed out. "Like you said, when we get home, we can get the alien programmers to delete the cat's personality from the program. Right? How bad could it be for a couple more months?"

On the twentieth day, they entered Smoot-claimed space. Thomas was nervous throughout the first two jumps, as the *Marylou* cut through a couple of barren systems to use the suns as bounce points. Neither was occupied, nor carrying so much as a system beacon. The crew were all keeping their fingers crossed against danger, but all went well.

In the third system, right in the heart of Smoot space, they had hardly exited the jump when the ship began to shake. Jurgieniewski grabbed for his command chair.

"What's happening?" he shouted.

Thomas dashed across, and leaned over his chair arm to his personal screen. "Smoot! We're in deep guano now."

"Is it a tractor beam?" Marius demanded, her inverted triangle of a face pale with fear.

"I don't know," Thomas started to say.

"Is it a weapon?" Jurgieniewski asked. Then he realized his words had made no sense. Only a gutteral groan escaped his throat. He tried to speak again, but nothing at all came out. He was pondering the strangeness, when his knees and spine folded up, depositing him on the floor.

"What's happening to me?" he tried to scream. His body, out of his control, slumped against the side of the command chair. Thomas, his eyes wide with fear, collapsed over the arm of his chair like a curtain on a hanger. Jurgieniewski was completely aware of everything that was happening to him, including how much his leg, which struck the side of the couch, was hurting. He suspected the shin was broken from striking the metal pedestal. He screamed at his muscles to move him, to obey his commands. The only voluntary muscles which responded were in his eye sockets. Out of the corner of his left eye, he saw Marius, slumped against the wall with her hands splayed out to either side of her, like a discarded rag doll. The vibration stopped. The *Marylou's* main viewscreen lit up to show a red and white painted vessel, long and sinuously flexible like a snake. It was a Smoot destroyer. Jurgieniewski was terrified.

In a few moments, the Smoots would move in on them, take them aboard, and finish them off. There were legends told of the tortures the invertebrate monsters inflicted on Terran spacers, yanking the bones out of prisoners one at a time until they died in agony. He could see by the sweat breaking out on their faces that the others were thinking of those stories, too. All they could do was wait and hope it would be over quickly.

From behind him, out of his range of vision, came a tremendous hiss, modulating into a fearsome growl. Poor Kelvin, Jurgieniewski thought. She's only a cat, and she's going to die, too.

Kelvin advanced into his peripheral vision. She was walking sideways, with her fur stuck up all along her spine in a fighting ridge, terminating in a tail fluffed like a bottle brush. He was struck by the heartbreaking futility of the tiny creature in her attempt to make herself look as large as possible so as to scare off a foe a thousand times her size.

"Eeeerrrrooooooooonnnnggggghhhh," the cat growled, her voice advancing angrily up and down the scales. Her eyes fixed on the red, snakelike shape hanging in the center of the screen, and her enlarged tail switched back and forth.

A lot of good that would do, Jurgieniewski thought, closing his eyes and letting them roll back in his head. He felt as if he could cry. In a minute, the Smoot would start blasting at the ship's system pods with lasers until nothing but life support remained. And then, the Smoot would have their fun with him. He willed his flaccid muscles to respond, to do anything at all. Drool ran out of a corner of his mouth onto his lap, and he realized his jaw was hanging open. What an undignified way to die.

The Smoot opened fire. Out of a turret on the top of the snake's head came a dot of fire, growing and growing in his field of vision until it smashed into the side of the *Marylou*. Thomas was thrown off his crash couch onto the floor, and Jurgieniewski's head bounced painfully against the frame of his chair.

The cat slid backwards along the floor. Kelvin's growl rose several decibels, and she advanced on the screen with redoubled fury.

"Working," the computer's voice said suddenly. "Defense systems armed and ready." At the top of his range of vision, Jurgieniewski's personal screen spread with the menu of defense diagrams, and the blinking words, "YOUR CHOICE?"

He wanted to scream, "We're incapacitated, you dumb computer! Do something yourself!"

Kelvin hunkered down before the screen, the very tip

of her black and white tail twitching rapidly back and forth as she gathered herself to spring. To Jurgieniewski, it was the very height of burlesque. They were about to die, and the cat was chasing images on the computer as if it was a video game.

The Smoot snake shot out of its stationary pose, and swung in a wide arc, choosing the next target with care. It had all the time in the universe on its side.

The movement set off the cat's springs like pulling a trigger. She bounded up at the screen and batted one-two punches at the head of the snake with either paw.

"Working," *Marylou* said.

The cat dropped to the floor, and gathered her haunches again. Astoundingly, where the cat had struck, two laser bolts lanced out of the *Marylou*'s own battery, and smacked into the side of the Smoot ship, knocking it first one way, then the other. The view changed, dropping down below the ecliptic plane of the Smoot ship. Jurgieniewski was dumbfounded. It had to be a fluke.

The Smoot shifted just as rapidly, diving toward the viewscreen. Those blobs must have been furious, thinking that their prey was already helpless, and finding there was someone aboard who was still capable of fighting. They'd have gone crazy if they could see their opponent. Jurgieniewski wished he could grin.

Kelvin was ready for it as soon as it turned, delivering a fierce roundhouse, and galloping backwards and to the right as soon as the blow struck, avoiding the burning light which made her pupils shrink to slits. *Marylou* followed her moves, pounding the Smoot's engine compartment with a full-strength bolt, and veering sideways. Good tactical maneuvering, Jurgieniewski mentally complimented the cat.

He counted six laser emplacements on the snake's back. The *Marylou* was badly outgunned. Still, they had maneuverability on their side. If they could inflict enough small wounds, it might take all the fight out of the Smoot, allowing them a chance to get away.

Jurgieniewski was overwhelmed with a wave of embarrassment. They weren't fighting this battle. Their lives depended on a five-kilo feline who liked to sharpen her claws on his pants leg. Still, it was a chance.

"Win this for us, kitty, and you can have every last scrap of my Sinosian spicewurst," Jurgieniewski vowed, "and wash it down with Thomas's smoked turkey. I'll make it up to him."

To a slightly blurring eye, the Smoot ship did resemble a living creature. As it rounded on them, moving into position for its next shot, Jurgieniewski could almost see it narrowing its eyes and twitching its pointed tail.

There was some movement in the rear section. It attracted Kelvin, who pounced at it, smacking the tail with one paw, and bounding immediately back to one-two the head as it turned toward them. Automatically, the *Marylou*'s battery fired three shots.

The Smoot fired back, but Kelvin dodged easily out of the way of the hot, yellow light of the fireball. Her next move surprised him. She jumped up on top of the console, trying to get above the Smoot. *Marylou* shifted upward along the z-axis and slid through space until the top of the snake was in view at the very bottom of the screen. Kelvin dove off the console onto the snake's back, pummeling and biting her intangible foe. The head and tail angled upward, guns firing at them, but Jurgieniewski could see that the Smoot was suffering some internal distress. The first fireball knocked into the *Marylou*'s side, but the second missed by a million klicks. It was never followed by a third. Kelvin's attack must have hit squarely over the power plant. The snake blew into two pieces, each of which exploded silently but magnificently in the black, star-strewn sky.

Kelvin turned away from the screen, head and tail high, and walked majestically over to Thomas's crash couch. She bounded upward, settled herself with one leg over her head, and began to wash. The service hatch in the console opened up to disgorge a saucerful of rank-smelling fish. Jurgieniewski couldn't possibly begrudge it to her.

It was hours before the paralysis of the Smoot ray wore off. As soon as their tongues and palates could move again, the three humans burst out talking about the unbelievable feat they had just witnessed. For the rest of the journey, every time the cat walked into the room, they petted and praised her. On Argylenia, the three of them took her into every gourmet shop in the main city, buying her a kilo of whatever seemed to interest her.

"This cat's a hero," Thomas explained to the dumbfounded shopkeepers, who were taken aback at selling their most prized delicacies to a ship's pet. "If I told you why, you'd never believe me. Just let her have what she wants."

The IATA brass were waiting for the *Marylou* when

she docked at Fladium Station with their hold full of textiles. Jurgieniewski felt as if he could drop to the metal walkway and kiss it. Beyond the decontamination barrier, he could see dozens of reporters waiting. He exchanged glances with the other two. Kelvin, curled up in Marius's arms, never bothered to look up.

"What are you going to say?" Thomas asked, nodding sideways at the cat.

"I don't know yet," he admitted.

"The brave crew returns!" The vice president who had seen them off came out of the V.I.P. waiting room with his arms outstretched. "Congratulations, one and all."

There was a clamour from the press, but the vice president whisked the crew into the lounge, and locked the door. Following his gesture, the three sat down. Marius put the cat on the table between them.

"Well done," the executive said, nodding to them all. "We want to let the press in to talk to you in a little while, but not until we've cleared your story. For example, there's a few of facets of your reports which we are finding it hard to believe. And there's the matter of an item or two of expenditure which is even more difficult to justify. Are we to understand that we're paying a regular salary to a cat?"

"She saved our lives," Jurgieniewski explained, meeting the vice president's disbelieving scrutiny with a bland expression. "Everything in the reports I sent you is true. Review the ship's log if you want, but if you ask me, you won't question it."

"Kelvin here was a functioning member of the crew, and I think she deserves every minim," Marius added.

"Yes, but paying three hundred sixty credits weekly to a *cat*? Plus hazard pay?" The vice president shook his head. Kelvin watched him without blinking, but her tail tip twitched.

"Look at it this way, sir," Thomas put in, smoothly, and Jurgieniewski remembered that he had had diplomatic training. He leaned forward confidingly. "Notwithstanding the fact that Kelvin blew up a Smoot warship all by herself, could you ask for better publicity for the utility and easy operation of the Drebian system, if a mere cat can use it? Think of the numbers! The press'll love it!"

"As a matter of advertisement," the vice president mused, scrubbing his chin with the tips of his fingers, "I suppose it would be just about priceless."

"And what a spokesperson you could offer them, too," Jurgieniewski said. Kelvin rolled over and presented her belly to the vice president to be scratched.

The man laughed, and reached out to fluff the cat's fur. "I suppose we're getting off lightly. For a human model, I'd have to pay thousands. But what about the three of you? If we publicize that the cat ran the ship, won't you feel foolish?"

Jurgieniewski gathered nods of approbation from the other two, and drew a deep breath. "Not if it'll help the company, sir."

The vice president mused, staring at a wall as Kelvin squirmed happily under his fingertips. "Captain," he said at last, rising to his feet and gathering up the cat, "I like your loyalty. Come out with me to see the media. I'm sure you'd like to tell them the adventures the four of you had on your ship." The emphasis fell heavily on the last two words, and Jurgieniewski caught his breath. Marius and Thomas looked hopeful. The vice president didn't miss their expressions.

"I presume you're happy with your crew complement as well?" he asked casually.

"Yes, sir," Jurgieniewski said, with unconcealed joy. He gave the cat a quick scratch on the head. "I ordered another spicewurst for you this morning," he told Kelvin in a low murmur just before the door opened.

"What's that, captain?"

"Oh, nothing, sir. Nothing." Grasping Marius's and Thomas's hands in a triumphant squeeze, he followed the IATA executive out of the lounge to where the press were waiting.

TIC TOC

by Sarah Hoyt

Sarah A. Hoyt (November 8, 1962) grew up in Portugal with a changing background of changing governments of varying shades of varying Marxistity (is that a word?) before moving to the U.S.A. in 1985 to get married to Robert Hoyt, also an SF writer and mathematician. A naturalized citizen since 1988. The couple have two sons, both presently in college. Here she considers a possible explanation for the sharp decline in the quality of occupants of the Oval Office since the Reagan administration. In fact, it makes you wonder if something like this is actually going on behind closed doors. I also wonder if the author was thinking of a certain character in Baum's novels of Oz when she wrote this one. Sarah is currently writing the Darkship series for Baen Books, so far including Darkship Thieves, Darkship Renegades, *and* Through Fire, *with* Darkship Revenge *coming in 2017.*

((◎))

WHEN I CAME into the oval office, the president was in pieces on the floor, and Jack, his shirt sleeves rolled up almost to his armpits ,was doing something in the presidential chest region with a 12-volt battery checker. What he thought that would tell him I'll never know. Honestly, these days we're reduced to hiring incompetents. Incompetents who can keep their mouth shut, but incompetents, nonetheless.

He heard my entrance, and rocked back to sit on his heels and look up at me, "Thank God you're here."

"Yeah," I said. And turned around to lock the door. "And thank God none of the security detail came in with me. Or someone who doesn't know what's supposed to be going on. Honestly, Jack, what were you thinking, leaving the door unlocked." As I spoke, I took off my coat and threw it over the back of a chair.

I was removing my tie—I can never work in a tie—when Jack said, "I'm sorry, I'm just so—I don't know what the hell to do."

That much I could tell of course. "Well," I said, looking at the circuits and wires, the transistors and the other pieces of cobbled-together technology on the floor. "It's always a good idea not to completely take apart a piece that goes back to the late eighties. We almost didn't get it over Y2K."

I started arranging things from memory, and he said, "If you ask me, it hasn't been functioning even close to properly since." He sniffed, with the easy disdain of someone who really has no understanding of technology or technological limitations. "All those horrible words it kept making up. *Misunderestimating,* indeed."

I ignored him. What I wanted to say was *Listen, buttercup, they achieved AI in the eighties. The eighties for crying out loud. People were still watching movies on VCR tapes, and they created a decent enough AI, plausible enough to pass as the president of the United States of America.*

I didn't because Jack was secure in his position, and I didn't intend to challenge him. For one, because he clearly had strong allies at the top.

And as I thought that, the genius I'd first met when I'd come to Washington, DC to help with the inauguration of George H. W. Bush came in. The direction he came in from, he used the entrance in the presidential restroom. Or else, he was hiding under a table. I'd like to say that's preposterous, but with geniuses you never know and this man was a genius.

No, you'd never know his name. He's a functionary, deep in the bowels of the federal government, and anyone who doesn't know him will think he's just a cog in the machine. And he's not an inventor. He has no name on any patents. But he stepped in, in 1985, and saved us from national disaster, which seemed inevitable. He organized the research teams, he appropriated money—I believe from the department of agriculture—and in the end, before that fateful day in January, we had us a brand new president, and not one that would hold the line on taxes, whether the fool those blessed idiots had elected at the ballot box had read his lips or not.

There were departments and people hanging on the line who'd have been unemployed if he'd not come through.

We called him Mr. Smith.

I was trying to fit all the parts of the president in the frame. We'd had to change the frame pretty drastically since the last one, since the new one was much shorter and broader, and I had to figure out how to put some things so it wouldn't rattle.

And I'd just found a piece of wire that looked forcibly torn, and a circuit that was cracked through, when Mr. Smith said, "How bad is it?"

I held on to the broken portion. "I don't know. How did this happen?"

Mr. Smith didn't say anything, but Jack did. Of course Jack did. I wondered if he was Mr. Smith's illegitimate son. Surely anyone else would long since have been dismissed from the presidential maintenance corps.

"It was the same thing as the two other times," he said. "One of the scientists who escaped tried to destroy it."

Silence was suddenly absolute in the oval office. I almost dropped the pieces, and controlled myself only with an effort of will. "The scientists?" I said, almost casually. "The ones who . . . created him?" I worked quickly, busily, making it obvious I knew the entrails of the president, and they couldn't dispense with me.

I'd never thought of what had happened to the scientists who'd created the creature. I assumed they'd been told that it was nothing but a sort of body double, to fill in for the great man—I gave a wry look at the eviscerated robot—or woman, should the time come, and that they'd retired somewhere, in the belief they'd done nothing but allow protocol to go on.

But the words *scientists who escaped* put a cold shiver up my spine.

Okay, I'm not stupid. I should have thought of this earlier. After all, through the presidential robot and the presidential maintenance corps, Mr. Smith controlled Washington, DC and, arguably, through Washington, DC the world itself. Surely someone wouldn't risk that on the memories and good behavior of a bunch of pointy heads, who, after all, might have got doddery and started speaking in their old age.

I knew of the scientists, and I knew of the attacks on the president, but I'd never connected the two. I'd figured the other attacks had been normal assassins.

"In prison, were they?" I continued, carefully reassembling the creature. I showed Jack some of the broken pieces, "I'm going to need more of these. They should be in the supply closet."

Jack rushed out, and Mr. Smith snorted. "Please. We're neither dumber nor more cruel than we have to be." He could have fooled me, having taken one of my most promising young electronics technicians, caught under the presidential desk making some adjustments during the tenure of William Jefferson Clinton, and destroyed her life with carefully concocted tales and blue dresses and public humiliation. But I wasn't in a position to talk. "They are given the . . . ah . . . presidential treatment."

I nodded. That made sense. For the duration of their tenure, the presidents were sent to a small island in the pacific. Very well outfitted, very peaceful, very guarded.

All communication with the world outside was stopped. And before they returned, they were treated by the best hypnotists in the world, so they remembered being president.

Sometimes, in the cases where that applied, their wives were sent with them so they wouldn't discover the truth. It's amazing the number of cases in which that wasn't necessary.

"How in hell do they manage to get here, then?"

"Oh, come on," Mr. Smith had a hoarse voice, the sort of voice that would sound good in someone commanding a vast network of shady underworld figures. "These are geniuses." He sighed. "Fucking geniuses."

"Yes, sir."

I could feel him smile, without seeing it. Part of the trick to dealing with people like Mr. Smith is to make sure they know you're a coward. If you weren't a coward, you could endanger them and that could be a problem. "Almost as bad as fucking cowboys." Mr. Smith's hatred for Reagan was legendary. I'd often wondered if that was what had impelled him to start the project. Because he said the world couldn't be subjected to the whims of the dear little voters, or whom they took it in their grubby heads to choose for the presidency. There had been balance and equilibrium during the cold war, and a certain amount the fear to keep the rubes in line.

"So? Contrived credentials? What? How do they get in?"

"The one who did this during Clinton's tenure, just came in, with a tour group. Then detached and came here and did . . . well, you remember that mess, right?"

I remembered that mess. It had been . . . interesting. We'd actually had to have some parts fabricated, and until they were available had had to rely on Chinese knockoffs. Though the fact that for that time the robot had gone around propositioning anything that moved and looked vaguely female hadn't hurt. Even if it had given Mr. Smith the idea for how to dispose of Monica.

"After that," Mr. Smith rasped on. "We stopped all traffic in front of the white house. But this one came in through the kitchens. He masqueraded as a second sous chef and waited his turn." He sighed. "Honestly, it's getting harder and harder. We're better at vetting, and we look through all resumes, from the secret service to the most junior janitor, but these guys have gotten better, too. There are plastic surgery techniques, and this last one took over the real identity of someone with a long career in political kitchens. Fortunately it was the last one. There were four of them and all four have now . . . been stopped."

I nodded sympathetically. I was going to guess the only reason I hadn't been given the presidential treatment was that I was the last person alive who knew how to repair the damn thing when it got blasted. Because sometime in the oughts Jack had gotten clever and shredded the scientists' notes. Thank heavens for an eidetic memory, or we'd have been in serious trouble then.

Jack came back in with the circuit boards, and I examined them before I put them back in, because you never knew what Jack was going to bring you, precisely. But they were the right pieces, and I was assembling it, when the door opened and one of the secret service guys stepped in.

I barely had the time to roll out of the way as he opened fire. I'd expected screams, or perhaps a call for help. I did not expect shooting. He had a silencer on, and he'd closed the door behind him, and he was shooting at the robot.

Bullets burned a path through the just-reassembled circuits, and Jack screamed like a little girl, and Mr. Smith took a glock from his coat pocket and shot the man.

Before he had even fallen, I'd made it to the door, and locked it. Jack had, of course, left it quite unlocked. Leading to the present disaster.

Mr. Smith and Jack were standing over the man. "Damn it," Mr. Smith said. "I thought the one this morning was the last one of them."

I bit my lip. I couldn't smell blood. And the man had been shot through the heart. I should have been able to smell blood. As Jack said, "Another body to dispose of," I stepped close, and looked at the wound. There was no blood, and a faint plume of smoke rose from the charred coat. I got hold of the torn edges, and pulled. It tore completely, revealing the same sort of synthetic skin we use for the president. Yes, I know it looks like the real thing. It looks like the real thing enough to fool reporters who take beach shots. But it doesn't fool the experts. I tore at the skin, to reveal the ceramic structure beneath and the pieces inside it.

What Mr. Smith had shot was the connections that went between the central processor, in the chest, and the unit's limbs and brain. The central processor was still ticking. "Tic, toc," I said, in a tone that came out wry and almost mocking. Jack swore. Mr. Smith held his breath for a few minutes.

"Are you sure the one this morning was human?"

Mr. Smith grunted. "Very. And I was sure he was the last."

"Are you sure the one before that was human?"

Mr. Smith looked at Jack. Jack nodded. But this was Jack, okay? You couldn't trust him to close the door, much less to— It occurred to me I didn't know what they meant by disposing of the scientists. Did they shoot them, as they had shot this robot? Did they just send them back to confinement? No. That wouldn't warrant that "last" thing. I felt a cold finger up my spine.

There were other things, too, things that I thought Mr. Smith hadn't put together, all of it adding up to a feeling of wrongness in the back of my mind.

I said, in as cheery a voice as I could manage, "Well, well, now we have a whole lot of new circuit boards."

Jack helped me crack the ceramic structure and get at the insides.

And man, were there circuit boards. There were things I didn't have a name for, though I could guess at their function from where they were. Whoever had done this was a genius, years—decades—ahead of everyone else in robotics, and had gained a decade for each of the years since the president had been assembled.

I used them. Oh, I know what you're going to say. You're going to say I didn't check for pre-programming, for possible malware, and that I was responsible for what happened to Baltimore. Maybe I was. But I'm telling you that right then and there I had no other choice.

Mr. Smith was watching me, and I could see him weighing my usefulness. I suspected if he could find another person who could repair the president I would be done for. I was the living definition of knowing too much.

And I could hear Jack nattering, and I was afraid of what he would do next, and how heinous it would be, and most of all, most of all, I was aware of those other secret service guys out there. Outside the door. I'd caught a glimpse of them, there, when the shooter had come in and shot.

Was it possible that they hadn't seen? Was it possible they didn't recognize the sound of silenced shots?

Impossible. So there were two theories: either they were in on the conspiracy, which was possible, since I'd never known how far Mr. Smith's power extended, or—

It was the or that made my hands rush, as I packed the pieces in, making the whole as functional as possible as quickly as possible.

Repairing the skin was more difficult, as we were almost out of the special glue we used. Having a much darker president had played havoc with our supplies, as the entire skin had needed to be replaced twice, instead of just the patches to change shape and size. Once when he was sworn in, and once when his successor was.

Fortunately the current president had long ago left any standards of beauty or even of normal appearance behind, so no one would notice creases or slightly infelicitous joining.

When we were done, Mr. Smith brought out a suit, and we dressed the robot.

After which I collected my thirty pieces of silver and left, quickly.

It wasn't silver, of course, and it was considerably more than thirty. Betraying the national conscience and the Constitution was very well paid.

It had never troubled me before. Look, someone has to be on top. Someone has to govern. And stability is better than instability. And one thing Mr. Smith was right on the money about was that the people the voters kept choosing kept getting stranger and stranger.

For the first time, as I got out the gate of the White House on that lovely spring morning, I wondered if that was because the voters sensed nothing ever changed, nothing real, and were trying to get out of the bind they were in without knowing it.

The cherry trees were in blossom all over town. I walked a lot. I had a strange feeling that if I were to take a cab, or my car, or even public transport . . .

I walked till sunset, and then I found a place to change my clothes and someone who could change my appearance with makeup before I could change it more permanently.

The thing I'd noticed, see, as I walked past those secret service men who hadn't reacted to shots, is that there was a faint whirring sound.

Now, some pumps that replace hearts make that noise. But would six secret service guards, in the prime of their life and condition, all have had their hearts replaced with mechanical pumps?

Once my appearance was changed enough, I took a train west. I won't say the possibility of needing to do this had never occurred to me.

Years ago, I bought a small car repair shop in the middle of nowhere, Kansas.

I do well. I mean, not well as I did when I maintained the presidential robot, but well enough. And the changes to my appearance are now permanent, and barring disaster, I'll never be picked up by those I know must be looking for me.

I'm surprised, honestly, it's been this many years. I wonder if Mr. Smith has figured out how to repair the thing himself.

Or if he's just been lucky.

Clearly the scientists decided it was worth their lives to try to take down Mr. Smith and his clique in Washington. I thought the door guards came from them.

But as the years go by, sometimes I wonder if it was just a rival clique, hoping to take over with their own robot.

And sometimes, as I sit in front of the shop and watch the flag fly over city hall, I wonder if it's my duty to get back there. To destroy the robot myself. All the robots. To restore the republic to the control of the voters, because, silly and blinkered though they are, they have to be better than the Mr. Smiths of the world. Or at least there's so many of them that it makes it impossible for a single set of corrupt interests to control the nation.

I haven't worked up my nerve for it, yet.

DAY OF TRUCE

by Clifford D. Simak

*Multiple Hugo and Nebula Award-winner **Clifford D. Simak** (1904-1988) was one of the most popular writers who were part of Astounding's "Golden Age" in the 1940s, notably for his series of stories that became the classic novel* City, *and continued to contribute memorable stories and novels to the new postwar magazines from the 1950s until the day his pen was silenced. He was sometimes called SF's "pastoral" author, known for writing autumn-tinted stories set in bucolic landscapes. Like many generalizations, that one has a great many exceptions, such as this one. After all, he not only received the Grand Master Nebula Award from the Science Fiction Writers of America for a lifetime of distinguished writing, but also the Horror Writers Association's award named after Bram Stoker, the author of* Dracula, *for much less cozy work*

((I))

THE EVENING WAS QUIET. There was no sign of

the Punks. Silence lay heavily across the barren and eroded acres of the subdivision and there was nothing moving—not even one of the roving and always troublesome dog packs.

It was too quiet, Max Hale decided.

There should have been some motion and some noise. It was as if everyone had taken cover against some known and coming violence—another raid, perhaps. Although there was only one place against which a raid could possibly be aimed. Why should others care, Max wondered; why should they cower indoors, when they had long since surrendered?

Max stood upon the flat lookout-rooftop of the Crawford stronghold and watched the streets to north and west. It was by one of these that Mr. Crawford would be coming home. No one could guess which one, for he seldom used the same road. It was the only way one could cut down the likelihood of ambush or of barricade. Although ambush was less frequent now. There were fewer fences, fewer trees and shrubs; there was almost nothing behind which one could hide. In this barren area it called for real ingenuity to effect an ambuscade. But, Max reminded himself, no one had ever charged the Punks with lack of ingenuity.

Mr. Crawford had phoned that he would be late and Max was getting nervous. In another quarter hour, darkness would be closing in. It was bad business to be abroad in Oak Manor after dark had fallen. Or, for that matter, in any of the subdivisions. For while Oak Manor might be a bit more vicious than some of the others of them, it still was typical.

He lifted his glasses again and swept the terrain slowly. There was no sign of patrols or hidden skulkers. There must be watchers somewhere, he knew. There were always watchers, alert to the slightest relaxation of the vigilance maintained at Crawford stronghold.

Street by street he studied the sorry houses, with their broken window panes and their peeling paint, still marked by the soap streaks and the gouges and the red-paint splashes inflicted years before. Here and there dead trees stood stark, denuded of their branches. Browned evergreens, long dead, stood rooted in the dusty yards— yards long since robbed of the grass that once had made them lawns.

And on the hilltop, up on Circle Drive, stood the ruins of Thompson stronghold, which had fallen almost five years before. There was no structure standing. It had been leveled stone by stone and board by board. Only the smashed and dying trees, only the twisted steel fence posts marked where it had been.

Now Crawford stronghold stood alone in Oak Manor. Max thought of it with a glow of pride and a surge of painful memory. It stood because of him, he thought, and he would keep it standing.

In this desert it was the last oasis, with its trees and grass, with its summer houses and trellises, with the massive shrubbery and the wondrous sun dial beside the patio, with its goldfish-and-lily pond and the splashing fountain.

"Max," said the walkie-talkie strapped across his chest.

"Yes, Mr. Crawford."

"Where are you located, Max?"

"Up on the lookout, sir."

"I'll come in on Seymour Drive," said Mr. Crawford's voice. "I'm about a mile beyond the hilltop. I'll be coming fast."

"The coast seems to be quite clear, sir."

"Good. But take no chances with the gates."

"I have the control box with me, sir. I can operate from here. I will keep a sharp lookout."

"Be seeing you," said Crawford.

Max picked up the remote control box and waited for his returning master.

The car came over the hill and streaked down Seymour Drive, made its right-hand turn on Dawn, roared toward the gates.

When it was no more than a dozen feet away, Max pushed the button that unlocked the gates. The heavy bumper slammed into them and pushed them open. The buffers that ran along each side of the car held them aside as the machine rushed through. When the car had cleared them, heavy springs snapped them shut and they were locked again.

Max slung the control-box strap over his shoulder and went along the rooftop catwalk to the ladder leading to the ground.

Mr. Crawford had put away the car and was closing the garage door as Max came around the corner of the house.

"It does seem quiet," said Mr. Crawford. "Much quieter, it would seem to me, than usual."

"I don't like it, sir. There is something brewing."

"Not very likely," said Mr. Crawford. "Not on the eve of Truce Day."

"I wouldn't put nothing past them dirty Punks," said Max.

"I quite agree," said Mr. Crawford, "but they'll be coming here tomorrow for their day of fun. We must treat them well for, after all, they're neighbors and it is a custom. I would hate to have you carried beyond the bounds of propriety by overzealousness."

"You know well and good," protested Max, "I would never do a thing. I am a fighter, sir, but I fight fair and honorable."

Mr. Crawford said, "I was thinking of the little gambit you had cooked up last year."

"It would not have hurt them, sir. Leastwise, not permanently. They might never have suspected. Just a drop or two of it in the fruit punch was all we would have needed. It wouldn't have taken effect until hours after they had left. Slow-acting stuff, it was."

"Even so," said Mr. Crawford sternly, "I am glad I found out in time. And I don't want a repeat performance, possibly more subtle, to be tried this year. I hope you understand me."

"Oh, certainly, sir," said Max. "You can rely upon it, sir."

"Well, good night, then. I'll see you in the morning."

It was all damn foolishness, thought Max—this business of a Day of Truce. It was an old holdover from the early days when some do-gooder had figured maybe there would be some benefit if the stronghold people and the Punks could meet under happy circumstance and spend a holiday together.

It worked, of course, but only for the day. For twenty-four hours there were no raids, no flaming arrows, no bombs across the fence. But at one second after midnight, the feud took up again, as bitter and relentless as if had ever been.

It had been going on for years. Max had no illusions about how it all would end. Some day Crawford stronghold would fall, as had all the others in Oak Manor. But until that day, he pledged himself to do everything he could. He would never lower his guard nor relax his vigilance. Up to the very end he would make them smart for every move they made.

He watched as Mr. Crawford opened the front door and went across the splash of light that flowed out from the hall. Then the door shut and the house stood there, big and bleak and black, without a sliver of light showing anywhere. No light ever showed from the Crawford house. Well before the fall of night he always threw the lever on the big control board to slam steel shutters closed against all the windows in the place. Lighted windows made too good a nighttime target.

Now the raids always came at night. There had been a time when some had been made in daylight, but that was too chancy now. Year by year, the defenses had been built up to a point where an attack in daylight was plain foolhardiness.

Max turned and went down the driveway to the gates. He drew on rubber gloves and with a small flashlight examined the locking mechanism. It was locked. It had never failed, but there might come a time it would. He never failed to check it once the gates had closed.

He stood beside the gates and listened. Everything was quiet, although he imagined he could hear the faint singing of the electric current running through the fence. But that, he knew, was impossible, for the current was silent.

He reached out with a gloved hand and stroked the fence. Eight feet high, he told himself, with a foot of barbed wire along the top of it, and every inch of it alive with the surging current.

And inside of it, a standby, auxiliary fence into which current could be introduced if the forward fence should fail.

A clicking sound came padding down the driveway and Max turned from the gate.

"How you, boy," he said.

It was too dark for him to see the dog, but he could hear it snuffling and snorting with pleasure at his recognition.

It came bumbling out of the darkness and pushed against his legs. He squatted down and put his arms about it. It kissed him sloppily.

"Where are the others, boy?" he asked, and it wriggled in its pleasure.

Great dogs, he thought. They loved the people in the stronghold almost to adoration, but had an utter hatred for every other person. They had been trained to have.

The rest of the pack, he knew, was aprowl about the yard, alert to every sound, keyed to every presence. No one could approach the fence without their knowing it. Any stranger who got across the fence they would rip to bits.

He stripped off the rubber gloves and put them in his pocket.

"Come on, boy," he said.

He turned off the driveway and proceeded across the yard—cautiously, for it was uneven footing. There was no inch of it that lay upon the level. It was cleverly designed so that any thrown grenade or Molotov cocktail would roll into a deep and narrow bomb trap.

There had been a time, he recalled, when there had been a lot of these things coming over the fence. There were fewer now, for it was a waste of effort. There had been a time, as well, when there had been flaming arrows, but these had tapered off since the house had been fireproofed.

He reached the side yard and stopped for a moment, listening, with the dog standing quietly at his side. A slight wind had come up and the trees were rustling. He lifted his head and stared at the delicate darkness of them, outlined against the lighter sky.

Beautiful things, he thought. It was a pity there were not more of them. Once this area had been named Oak Manor for the stately trees that grew here. There, just ahead of him, was the last of them—a rugged old patriarch with its massive crown blotting out the early stars.

He looked at it with awe and appreciation—and with apprehension, too. It was a menace. It was old and brittle and it should be taken down, for it leaned toward the fence and some day a windstorm might topple it across the wire. He should have mentioned it long ago to Mr. Crawford, but he knew the owner held this tree in a sentimental regard that matched his own. Perhaps it could be made safe by guywires to hold it against the wind, or at least to turn its fall away from the fence should it be broken or uprooted. Although it seemed a sacrilege to anchor it with guywires, an insult to an ancient monarch.

He moved on slowly, threading through the bomb traps, with the dog close at his heels, until he reached the patio and here he stopped beside the sun dial. He ran his hand across its rough stone surface and wondered why Mr. Crawford should set such a store by it. Perhaps because it was a link to the olden days before the Punks and raids. It was an old piece that had been brought from a monastery garden somewhere in France. That in itself, of course, would make it valuable. But perhaps Mr. Crawford saw in it another value, far beyond the fact that it was hundreds of years old and had come across the water.

Perhaps it had grown to symbolize for him the day now past when any man might have a sun dial in his garden, when he might have trees and grass without fighting for them, when he might take conscious pride in the unfenced and unmolested land that lay about his house.

Bit by bit, through the running years, those rights had been eroded.

((II))

FIRST it had been the little things—the casual,

thoughtless trampling of the shrubbery by the playing small fry, the killing of the evergreens by the rampaging packs of happy dogs that ran with the playing small fry. For each boy, the parents said, must have himself a dog.

The people in the first place had moved from the jam-packed cities to live in what they fondly called the country, so that they could keep a dog or two and where their children would have fresh air and sunlight and room in which to run.

But too often this country was, in reality, no more than another city, with its houses cheek by jowl—each set on acre or half-acre lots, but still existing cheek by jowl.

Of course, a place to run. The children had. But no more than a place to run. There was nothing more to do. Run was all they could do—up and down the streets, back and forth across the lawns, up and down the driveways, leaving havoc in their trail. And in time the toddlers grew up and in their teen-age years they still could only run. There was no place for them to go, nothing they might do. Their mothers foregathered every morning at the coffee klatches and their fathers sat each evening in the backyards drinking beer. The family car could not be used because gasoline cost money and the mortgages were heavy and the taxes terrible and the other costs were high.

So to find an outlet for their energies, to work off their unrealized resentments against having nothing they could do, these older fry started out, for pure excitement only, on adventures in vandalism. There was a cutting of the backyard clotheslines, a chopping into bits of watering hoses left out overnight, a breaking and ripping up of the patios, ringing of the doorbells, smashing of the windows, streaking of the siding with a cake of soap, splashing with red paint.

Resentments had been manufactured to justify this vandalism and now the resentments were given food to grow upon. Irate owners erected fences to keep out the children and the dogs, and this at once became an insult and a challenge.

And that first simple fence, Max told himself, had been the forerunner of the eight-foot barrier of electricity which formed the first line of defense in the Crawford stronghold. Likewise, those small-time soap-cake vandals, shrieking their delight at messing up a neighbor's house, had been the ancestors of the Punks.

He left the patio and went down the stretch of backyard, past the goldfish-and-lily pond and the tinkling of the fountain, past the clump of weeping willows, and so out to the fence.

"Psst!" said a voice just across the fence.

"That you, Billy?"

"It's me," said Billy Warner.

"All right. Tell me what you have."

"Tomorrow is Truce Day and we'll be visiting…"

"I know all that," said Max.

"They're bringing in a time bomb."

"They can't do that," said Max, disgusted. "The cops will frisk them at the gates. They would spot it on them."

"It'll be all broken down. Each one will have a piece. Stony Stafford hands out the parts tonight. He has a crew that has been practicing for weeks to put a bomb together fast—even in the dark, if need be."

"Yeah," said Max, "I guess they could do it that way. And once they get it put together?"

"The sun dial," Billy said. "Underneath the sun dial."

"Well, thanks," said Max. "I am glad to know. It would break the boss' heart should something happen to the sun dial."

"I figure," Billy said, "this might be worth a twenty."

"Yes," Max agreed. "Yes, I guess it would."

"If they ever knew I told, they'd take me out and kill me."

"They won't ever know," said Max. "I won't ever tell them."

He pulled his wallet from his pocket, turned on the flash and found a pair of tens.

He folded the bills together, lengthwise, twice. Then he shoved them through an opening in the fence.

"Careful, there," he cautioned. "Do not touch the wire."

Beyond the fence he could see the faint, white outline of the other's face. And a moment later, the hand that reached out carefully and grabbed the corner of the folded bills.

Max did not let loose of the money immediately. They stood, each of them, with their grip upon the bills.

"Billy," said Max, solemnly, "you would never kid me, would you? You would never sell me out. You would never feed me erroneous information."

"You know me, Max," said Billy. "I've played square with you. I'd never do a thing like that."

Max let go of the money and let the other have it.

"I am glad to hear you say that, Billy. Keep on playing

square. For the day you don't, I'll come out of here and hunt you down and cut your throat myself."

But the informer did not answer. He was already moving off, out into the deeper darkness.

Max stood quietly, listening. The wind still blew in the leaves and the fountain kept on splashing, like gladsome silver bells.

"Hi, boy," Max said softly, but there was no snuffling answer. The dog had left him, was prowling with the others up and down the yard.

Max turned about and went up the yard toward the front again, completing his circuit of the house. As he rounded the corner of the garage, a police car was slowing to a halt before the gates.

He started down the drive, moving ponderously and deliberately.

"That you, Charley?" he called softly.

"Yes, Max," said Charley Pollard. "Is everything all right?"

"Right as rain," said Max.

He approached the gates and saw the bulky loom of the officer on the other side.

"Just dropping by," said Pollard. "The area is quiet tonight. We'll be coming by one of these days to inspect the place. It looks to me you're loaded."

"Not a thing illegal," Max declared. "All of it's defensive. That is still the rule."

"Yes, that is the rule," said Pollard, "but it seems to me that there are times you become a mite too enthusiastic. A full load in the fence, no doubt."

"Why, certainly," said Max. "Would you have it otherwise?"

"A kid grabs hold of it and he could be electrocuted, at full strength."

"Would you rather I had it set just to tickle them?"

"You're playing too rough, Max."

"I doubt it rather much," said Max. "I watched from here, five years ago, when they stormed Thompson stronghold. Did you happen to see that?"

"I wasn't here five years ago. My beat was Farview Acres."

"They took it apart," Max told him. "Stone by stone, brick by brick, timber by timber. They left nothing standing. They left nothing whole. They cut down all the trees and chopped them up. They uprooted all the shrubs. They hoed out all the flower beds. They made a desert of it. They reduced it to their level. And I'm not about to let it happen here, not if I can help it. A man has got the right to grow a tree and a patch of grass. If he wants a flower bed, he has a right to have a flower bed. You may not think so, but he's even got the right to keep other people out."

"Yes," said the officer, "all you say is true. But these are kids you are dealing with. There must be allowances. And this is a neighborhood. You folks and the others like you wouldn't have this trouble if you only tried to be a little neighborly."

"We don't dare be neighborly," said Max. "Not in a place like this. In Oak Manor, and in all the other manors and all the other acres and the other whatever-you-may-call-thems, neighborliness means that you let people overrun you. Neighborliness means you give up your right to live your life the way you want to live it. This kind of neighborliness is rooted way back in those days when the kids made a path across your lawn as a shortcut to the school bus and you couldn't say a thing for fear that they would sass you back and so create a scene. It started when your neighbor borrowed your lawn mower and forgot to bring it back and when you went to get it you found that he had broken it. But he pretended that he hadn't and, for the sake of neighborliness, you didn't have the guts to tell him that he had and to demand that he pay the bill for the repairing of it."

"Well, maybe so," said Pollard, "but it's gotten out of hand. It has been carried too far. You folks have got too high and mighty."

"There's a simple answer to everything," Max told him stoutly. "Get the Punks to lay off us and we'll take down the fence and all the other stuff."

Pollard shook his head. "It has gone too far," he said. "There is nothing anyone can do."

He started to go back to the car, then turned back.

"I forgot," he said. "Tomorrow is your Truce Day. Myself and a couple of the other men will be here early in the morning."

Max didn't answer. He stood in the driveway and watched the car pull off down the street. Then he went up the driveway and around the house to the back door.

Nora had a place laid at the table for him and he sat down heavily, glad to be off his feet. By this time of the evening he was always tired. Not as young, he thought, as he once had been.

"You're late tonight," said the cook, bringing him the food. "Is everything all right?"

"I guess so. Everything is quiet. But we may have trouble tomorrow. They're bringing in a bomb."

"A bomb!" cried Nora. "What will you do about it? Call in the police, perhaps."

Max shook his head. "No, I can't do that. The police aren't on our side. They'd take the attitude we'd egged on the Punks until they had no choice but to bring in the bomb. We are on our own. And, besides, I must protect the lad who told me. If I didn't, the Punks would know and he'd be worthless to me then. He'd never get to know another thing. But knowing they are bringing something in, I can watch for it."

He still felt uneasy about it all, he realized. Not about the bomb itself, perhaps, but something else, something that was connected with it. He wondered why he had this feeling. Knowing about the bomb, he all but had it made. All he'd have to do would be to locate it and dig it out from beneath the sun dial. He would have the time to do it. The day-long celebration would end at six in the evening and the Punks could not set the bomb to explode earlier than midnight. Any blast before midnight would be a violation of the truce.

He scooped fried potatoes from the dish onto his plate and speared a piece of meat. Nora poured his coffee and, pulling out a chair, sat down opposite him.

"You aren't eating?" he asked.

"I ate early, Max."

He ate hungrily and hurriedly, for there still were

things to do. She sat and watched him eat. The clock on the kitchen wall ticked loudly in the silence.

Finally she said: "It is getting somewhat grim, Max."

He nodded, his mouth full of food and unable to speak.

"I don't see," said the cook, "why the Crawfords want to stay here. There can't be much pleasure in it for them. They could move into the city and it would be safer there. There are the juvenile gangs, of course, but they mostly fight among themselves. They don't make life unbearable for all the other people."

"It's pride," said Max. "They won't give up. They won't let Oak Manor beat them. Mr. and Mrs. Crawford are quality. They have some steel in them."

"They couldn't sell the place, of course," said Nora. "There would be no one to buy it. But they don't need the money. They could just walk away from it."

"You misjudge them, Nora. The Crawfords in all their lives have never walked away from anything. They went through a lot to live here. Sending Johnny off to boarding school when he was a lad, since it wouldn't have been safe for him to go to school with the Punks out there. I don't suppose they like it. I don't see how they could. But they won't be driven out. They realize someone must stand up to all that trash out there, or else there's no hope."

Nora sighed. "I suppose you're right. But it is a shame. They could live so safe and comfortable and normal if they just moved to the city."

He finished eating and got up.

"It was a good meal, Nora," he said. "But then you always fix good meals."

"Ah, go on with you," said Nora.

He went into the basement and sat down before the short-wave set. Systematically, he started putting in his calls to the other strongholds. Wilson stronghold, over in Fair Hills, had had a little trouble early in the evening— a few stink bombs heaved across the fence—but it had quieted down. Jackson stronghold did not answer. While he was trying to get through to Smith stronghold in Harmony Settlement, Curtis stronghold in Lakeside Heights began calling him. Everything was quiet, John Hennessey, the Curtis custodian told him. It had been quiet for several days.

He stayed at the radio for an hour and by that time had talked with all the nearby strongholds. There had been scattered trouble here and there, but nothing of any consequence. Generally it was peaceful.

He sat and thought about the time bomb and there was still that nagging worry. There was something wrong, he knew, but he could not put his finger on it.

Getting up, he prowled the cavernous basement, checking the defense material—extra sections of fencing, piles of posts, pointed stakes, rolls of barb wire, heavy flexible wire mesh and all the other items for which some day there might be a need. Tucked into one corner, hidden, he found the stacked carboys of acid he had secretly cached away. Mr. Crawford would not approve, he knew, but if the chips ever should be down, and there was need to use those carboys, he might be glad to have them.

He climbed the stairs and went outside to prowl

restlessly about the yard, still upset by that nagging something about the bomb he could not yet pin down.

The moon had risen. The yard was a place of interlaced light and shadow, but beyond the fence the desert acres that held the other houses lay flat and bare and plain, without a shadow on them except the shadows of the houses.

Two of the dogs came up and passed the time of night with him and then went off into the shrubbery.

He moved into the backyard and stood beside the sun dial.

The wrongness still was there. Something about the sun dial and the bomb—some piece of thinking that didn't run quite true.

He wondered how they knew that the destruction of the sun dial would be a heavy blow to the owner of the stronghold. How could they possibly have known?

The answer seemed to be that they couldn't. They didn't. There was no way for them to know. And even if, in some manner, they had learned, a sun dial most certainly would be a piddling thing to blow up when that single bomb could be used so much better somewhere else.

Stony Stafford, the leader of the Punks, was nobody's fool. He was a weasel—full of cunning, full of savvy. He'd not mess with any sun dial when there was so much else that a bomb could do so much more effectively.

And as he stood there beside the sun dial, Max knew where that bomb would go—knew where he would plant it were he in Stafford's place.

At the roots of that ancient oak which leaned toward the fence.

He stood and thought about it and knew that he was right.

Billy Warner, he wondered. Had Billy double-crossed him?

Very possibly he hadn't. Perhaps Stony Stafford might have suspected long ago that his gang harbored an informer and, for that reason, had given out the story of the sun dial rather than the oak tree. And that, of course, only to a select inner circle which would be personally involved with the placing of the bomb.

In such a case, he thought, Billy Warner had not done too badly.

Max turned around and went back to the house, walking heavily. He climbed the stairs to his attic room and went to bed. It had been, he thought just before he went to sleep, a fairly decent day.

((III))

THE POLICE showed up at eight o'clock. The carpenters came and put up the dance platform. The musicians appeared and began their tuning up. The caterers arrived and set up the tables, loading them with food and two huge punch bowls, standing by to serve.

Shortly after nine o'clock the Punks and their girls began to straggle in. The police frisked them at the gates and found no blackjacks, no brass knuckles, no bicycle chains on any one of them.

The band struck up. The Punks and their girls began to dance. They strolled through the yard and admired the flowers, without picking any of them. They sat on the grass and talked and laughed among themselves. They gathered at the overflowing boards and ate. They laughed and whooped and frolicked and everything was fine.

"You see?" Pollard said to Max. "There ain't nothing wrong with them. Give them a decent break and they're just a bunch of ordinary kids. A little hell in them, of course, but nothing really bad. It's your flaunting of this place in their very faces that makes them the way they are."

"Yeah," said Max.

He left Pollard and drifted down the yard, keeping as inconspicuous as he could. He wanted to watch the oak, but he knew he didn't dare to. He knew he had to keep away from it, should not even glance toward it. If he should scare them off, then God only knew where they would plant the bomb. He thought of being forced to hunt wildly for it after they were gone and shuddered at the thought.

There was no one near the bench at the back of the yard, near the flowering almond tree, and he stretched out on it. It wasn't particularly comfortable, but the day was warm and the air was drowsy. He dropped off to sleep.

When he woke he saw that a man was standing on the gravel path just beyond the bench.

He blinked hard and rubbed his eyes.

"Hello, Max," said Stony Stafford.

"You should be up there dancing, Stony."

"I was waiting for you to wake up," said Stony. "You are a heavy sleeper. I could of broke your neck."

Max sat up. He rubbed a hand across his face.

"Not on Truce Day, Stony. We all are friends on Truce Day."

Stony spat upon the gravel path.

"Some other day," he said.

"Look," said Max, "why don't you just run off and forget about it? You'll break your back if you try to crack this place. Pick up your marbles, Stony, and go find someone else who's not so rough to play with."

"Some day we'll make it," Stony said. "This place can't stand forever."

"You haven't got a chance," said Max.

"Maybe so," said Stony. "But I think we will. And before we do, there is just one thing I want you to know. You think nothing will happen to you even if we do. You think that all we'll do is just rip up the place, not harming anyone. But you're wrong, Max. We'll do it the way it is supposed to be with the Crawfords and with Nora. We won't hurt them none. But we'll get you, Max. Just because we can't carry knives or guns doesn't mean there aren't other ways. There'll be a stone fall on you or a timber hit you. Or maybe you'll stumble and fall into the fire. There are a lot of ways to do it and we plan to get you plenty."

"So," said Max, "you hate me. It makes me feel real bad."

"Two of my boys are dead," said Stony. "There are others who are crippled pretty bad."

"There wouldn't be nothing happen to them, Stony, if you didn't send them up against the fence."

He looked up and saw that hatred that lay in Stony

Stafford's eyes, but washing across the hatred was a gleam of triumph.

"Good-by, dead man," said Stony.

He turned and stalked away.

Max sat quietly on the bench, remembering that gleam of triumph in Stony Stafford's eyes. And that meant he had been right. Stony had something up his sleeve and it could be nothing else but the bomb beneath the oak.

The day wore on. In the afternoon, Max went up to the house and into the kitchen. Nora fixed him a sandwich, grumbling.

"Why don't you go out and eat off the tables?" she demanded. "There is plenty there."

"Just as soon keep out of their way," said Max. "I have to fight them all the rest of the year. I don't see why I should pal up with them today."

"What about the bomb?"

"Shhh," said Max. "I know where it is."

Nora stood looking out the window. "They don't look like bad kids," she said. "Why can't we make a peace of some sort with them?"

Max grunted. "It's gone too far," he said.

Pollard had been right, he thought. It was out of hand. Neither side could back down now.

The police could have put a stop to it to start with, many years ago, if they had cracked down on the vandals instead of adopting a kids-will-be-kids attitude and shrugging it all off as just an aggravated case of quarreling in the neighborhood. The parents could have stopped it by paying some attention to the kids, by giving them something that would have stopped their running wild. The community could have put a stop to it by providing some sort of recreational facilities.

But no one had put a stop to it. No one had even tried.

And now it had grown to be a way of life and it must be fought out to the bitter end.

Max had no illusions as to who would be the winner.

Six o'clock came and the Punks started drifting off. By six thirty the last of them had gone. The musicians packed up their instruments and left. The caterers put away their dishes and scooped up the leftovers and the garbage and drove away. The carpenters came and got their lumber. Max went down to the gates and checked to see that they were locked.

"Not a bad day," said Pollard, speaking through the gates to Max. "They really aren't bad kids, if you'd just get to know them."

"I know them plenty now," said Max.

He watched the police car drive off, then turned back up the driveway.

He'd have to wait a while, he knew, until the dusk could grow a little deeper, before he started looking for the bomb. There would be watchers outside the fence. It would be just as well if they didn't know that he had found it. It might serve a better purpose if they could be left to wonder if it might have been a dud. For one thing, it would shake their confidence. For another, it would protect young Billy Warner. And while Max could feel no admiration for the kid, Billy had been useful in the past and still might be useful in the future.

He went down to the patio and crawled through the masking shrubbery until he was only a short distance from the oak.

He waited there, watching the area out beyond the fence. There was as yet no sign of life out there. But they would be out there watching. He was sure of that.

The dusk grew deeper and he knew he could wait no longer. Creeping cautiously, he made his way to the oak. Carefully, he brushed away the grass and leaves, face held close above the ground.

Halfway around the tree, he found it—the newly upturned earth, covered by a sprinkling of grass and leaves, and positioned neatly between two heavy roots.

He thrust his hand against the coolness of the dirt and his fingers touched the metal. Feeling it, he froze, then very slowly, very gently, pulled his hand away.

He sat back on his heels and drew in a measured breath.

The bomb was there, all right, just as he had suspected. But set above it, protecting it, was a contact bomb. Try to get the time bomb out and the contact bomb would be triggered off.

He brushed his hands together, wiping off the dirt.

There was, he knew, no way to get out the bombs. He had to let them stay. There was nothing he could do about it.

No wonder Stony's eyes had shown a gleam of triumph. For there was more involved than just a simple time bomb. This was a foolproof setup. There was nothing that could be done about it. If it had not been for the roots, Max thought, he might have taken a chance on working from one side and digging it all out. But with the heavy roots protecting it, that was impossible.

Stony might have known that he knew about it and then had gone ahead, working out a bomb set that no one would dare to mess around with.

It was exactly the sort of thing that would be up Stony's alley. More than likely, he was setting out there now, chuckling to himself.

Max stayed squatted, thinking.

He could string a line of mesh a few feet inside the tree, curving out to meet the auxiliary fence on either side. Juice could be fed into it and it might serve as a secondary defense. But it was not good insurance. A determined rush would carry it, for at best it would be flimsy. He'd not be able to install it as he should, working in the dark.

Or he could rig the tree with guywires to hold it off the fence when it came crashing down. And that, he told himself, might be the thing to do.

He got up and went around the house, heading for the basement to look up some wire that might serve to hold the tree.

He remembered, as he walked past the short wave set, that he should be sitting in on the regular evening check among the nearby strongholds. But it would have to wait tonight.

He walked on and then stopped suddenly as the thought came to him. He stood for a moment, undecided, then swung around and went back to the set.

He snapped on the power and turned it up.

He'd have to be careful what he said, he thought, for

there was the chance the Punks might be monitoring the channels.

John Hennessey, custodian of the Curtis stronghold, came in a few seconds after Max had started calling.

"Something wrong, Max?"

"Nothing wrong, John. I was just wondering—do you remember telling me about those toys that you have?"

"Toys?"

"Yeah. The rattles."

He could hear the sound of Hennessey sucking in his breath.

Finally he said: "Oh, those. Yes, I still have them."

"How many would you say?"

"A hundred, probably. Maybe more than that."

"Could I borrow them?"

"Sure," said Hennessey. "Would you want them right away?"

"If you could," said Max.

"Okay. You'll pick them up?"

"I'm a little busy."

"Watch for me," said Hennessey. "I'll box them up and be there in an hour."

"Thanks, John," said Max.

Was it wrong? he wondered. Was it too much of a chance?

Perhaps he didn't have the right to take any chance at all.

But you couldn't sit forever, simply fending off the Punks. For if that was all you did, they'd keep on coming back. But hit back hard at them and they might get a belly full. You might end it once for all. The trouble was, he thought, you could strike back so seldom. You could never act except defensively, for if you took any other kind of action, the police were down on you like a ton of bricks.

He licked his lips.

It was seldom one had a chance like this—a chance to strike back lustily and still be legally defensive.

((IV))

HE GOT UP QUICKLY and walked to the rear of the basement, where he found the heavy flexible mesh. He carried out three rolls of it and a loop of heavy wire to hang it on. He'd have to use some trees to stretch out the wire. He really should use some padding to protect the trees against abrasion by the wire, but he didn't have the time.

Working swiftly, he strung the wire, hung the mesh upon it, pegged the bottom of the mesh tight against the ground, tied the ends of it in with the auxiliary fence.

He was waiting at the gates when the truck pulled up. He used the control box to open the gates and the truck came through. Hennessey got out.

"Outside is swarming with Punks," he told Max. "What is going on?"

"I got troubles," said Max.

Hennessey went around to the back of the truck and lowered the tail gate. Three large boxes, with mesh inserts, rested on the truck bed.

"They're in there?" asked Max.

Hennessey nodded. "I'll give you a hand with them."

Between them they lugged the boxes to the mesh curtain, rigged behind the oak.

"I left one place unpegged," said Max. "We can push the boxes under."

"I'll unlock the lids first," said Hennessey. "We can reach through with the pole and lift the lids if they are unlocked. Then use the pole again to tip the boxes over."

They slid the boxes underneath the curtain, one by one. Hennessey went back to the truck to get the pole. Max pegged down the gap.

"Can you give me a bit of light?" asked Hennessey. "I know the Punks are waiting out there. But probably they'd not notice just a squirt of it. They might think you were making just a regular inspection of the grounds."

Max flashed the light and Hennessey, working with the pole thrust through the mesh, flipped back the lids. Carefully, he tipped the boxes over. A dry slithering and frantic threshing sounds came out of the dark.

"They'll be nasty customers," said Hennessey. "They'll be stirred up and angry. They'll do a lot of circulating, trying to get settled for the night and that way, they'll get spread out. Most of them are big ones. Not many of the small kinds."

He put the pole over his shoulder and the two walked back to the truck.

Max put out his hand and the two men shook.

"Thanks a lot, John."

"Glad to do it, Max. Common cause, you know. Wish I could stay around . . ."

"You have a place of your own to watch."

They shook hands once again and Hennessey climbed into the cab.

"You better make it fast the first mile or so," said Max. "Our Punks may be laying for you. They might have recognized you."

"With the bumpers and the power I have," said Hennessey, "I can get through anything."

"And watch out for the cops. They'd raise hell if they knew we were helping back and forth."

"I'll keep an eye for them."

Max opened the gates and the truck backed out, straightened in the road and swiftly shot ahead.

Max listened until it was out of hearing, then checked to see that the gates were locked.

Back in the basement he threw the switch that fed current into the auxiliary fence—and now into the mesh as well.

He sighed with some contentment and climbed the stairs out to the yard.

A sudden flash of light lit up the grounds. He spun swiftly around, then cursed softly at himself. It was only a bird hitting the fence in flight. It happened all the time. He was getting jittery and there was no need of it. Everything was under control—reasonably so.

He climbed a piece of sloping ground and stood behind the oak. Staring into the darkness, it seemed to him that he could see shadowy forms out beyond the fence.

They were gathering out there and they would come swarming in as soon as the tree went down, smashing the fences. Undoubtedly they planned to use the tree as a bridge over the surging current that still would flow in the smashed-down fence.

Maybe it was taking too much of a chance, he thought. Maybe he should have used the guy-wires on the tree. That way there would have been no chance at all. But, likewise, there would have been no opportunity.

They might get through, he thought, but he'd almost bet against it.

He stood there, listening to the angry rustling of a hundred rattlesnakes, touchy and confused, in the area beyond the mesh.

The sound was a most satisfying thing.

He moved away, to be out of the line of blast when the bomb exploded, and waited for the day of truce to end.

A SUBWAY NAMED MOBIUS

by A. J. Deutsch

A. J. Deutsch *(1918-1969), full name Armin Joseph Deutsch, as far as I can find, only wrote this one SF story—and it's a classic! In his day job, Dr. Deutsch was an astronomer, who received his PhD from the University of Chicago, and, according to Wikipedia.org, "He is noted for the concept of Doppler tomography, which he presented at a symposium at Mount Wilson Observatory in 1958." He served as associate editor for the* Annual Review of Astronomy and Astrophysics *prior to 1966. From 1964 until 1967 he served as a councillor for the American Astronomical Society. In 1996, "A Slubway Named Mobius" was made into an Argentinian movie,* Moebius, *which combined the disappearing trains with people the Argentinian government was making disappear at the same time. That's according to the speakers and a flyer accompanying a New York showing of the movie— the movie soundtrack was in the original language without subtitles and I only grok English. While* *this was his only SF story I know about, he published a number of papers and books in the field of astronomy. And besides, he has a crater on the far side of the Moon named after him. Top that!*

IN A COMPLEX and ingenious pattern, the subway had spread out from a focus at Park Street. A shunt connected the Lechmere line with the Ashmont for trains southbound, and with the Forest Hills line for those northbound. Harvard and Brookline had been linked with a tunnel that passed through Kenmore Under, and during rush hours every other train was switched through the Kenmore Branch back to Egleston. The Kenmore Branch joined the Maverick Tunnel near Fields Corner. It climbed a hundred feet in two blocks to connect Copley Over with Scollay Square; then it dipped down again to join the Cambridge line at Boylston. The Boylston shuttle had finally tied together the seven principal lines on four different levels. It went into service, you remember, on March 3rd. After that, a train could travel from any one station to any other station in the whole system.

There were two hundred twenty-seven trains running the subways every weekday, and they carried about a million and a half passengers. The Cambridge-Dorchester train that disappeared on March 4th was Number 86. Nobody missed it at first. During the evening rush, the traffic was a little heavier than usual on that line. But a crowd is a crowd. The ad posters at the Forest Hills yards looked for 86 about 7:30, but neither of them mentioned its absence until three days later. The controller at the Milk Street Cross-Over called the Harvard checker for an extra train after the hockey game that night, and the Harvard checker relayed the call to the yards. The dispatcher there sent out 87, which had been put to bed at ten o'clock, as usual. He didn't notice that 86 was missing.

It was near the peak of the rush the next morning that Jack O'Brien, at the Park Street Control, called Warren Sweeney at the Forest Hills yards and told him to put another train on the Cambridge run. Sweeney was short, so he went to the board and scanned it for a spare train and crew. Then, for the first time, he noticed that Gallagher had not checked out the night before. He put the tag up and left a note. Gallagher was due on at ten. At ten-thirty, Sweeney was down looking at the board again, and he noticed Gallagher's tag still up, and the note where he had left it. He groused to the checker and asked if Gallagher had come in late. The checker said he hadn't seen Gallagher at all that morning. Then Sweeney wanted to know who was running 86? A few minutes later he found that Dorkin's card was still up, although it was Dorkin's day off. It was 11:30 before he finally realized that he had lost a train.

Sweeney spent the next hour and a half on the phone, and he quizzed every dispatcher, controller, and checker on the whole system. When he finished his lunch at 1:30, he covered the whole net again. At 4:40, just before he left for the day, he reported the matter, with some indignation, to Central Traffic. The phones buzzed through the tunnels and shops until nearly midnight before the general manager was finally notified at his home.

It was the engineer on the main switchbank who, late in the morning of the 6th, first associated the missing train with the newspaper stories about the sudden rash of missing persons. He tipped off the Transcript, and by the end of the lunch hour three papers had Extras on the streets. That was the way the story got out.

Kelvin Whyte, the General Manager, spent a good part of that afternoon with the police. They checked Gallagher's wife, and Dorkin's. The motorman and the conductor had not been home since the morning of the 4th. By midafternoon, it was clear to the police that three hundred and fifty Bostonians, more or less, had been lost with the train. The System buzzed, and Whyte nearly expired with simple exasperation. But the train was not found.

Roger Tupelo, the Harvard mathematician, stepped into the picture the evening of the 6th. He reached Whyte by phone, late, at his home, and told him he had some ideas about the missing train. Then he taxied to Whyte's home in Newton and had the first of many talks with Whyte about Number 86.

Whyte was an intelligent man, a good organizer, and not without imagination. "But I don't know what you're talking about!" he expostulated.

Tupelo was resolved to be patient. "This is a very hard thing for anybody to understand, Mr. Whyte," he said. "I can see why you are puzzled. But it's the only explanation. The train has vanished, and the people on it. But the

System is closed. Trams are conserved. It's somewhere on the System!"

Whyte's voice grew louder again. "And I tell you, Dr. Tupelo, that train is not on the System! It is not! You can't overlook a seven-car train carrying four hundred passengers. The System has been combed. Do you think I'm trying to hide the train?"

"Of course not. Now look, let's be reasonable. We know the train was en route to Cambridge at 8:40 A.M. on the 4th. At least twenty of the missing people probably boarded the train a few minutes earlier at Washington, and forty more at Park Street Under. A few got off at both stations. And that's the last. The ones who were going to Kendall, to Central, to Harvard—they never got there. The train did not get to Cambridge."

"I know that, Dr. Tupelo," Whyte said savagely. "In the tunnel under the River, the train turned into a boat. It left the tunnel and sailed for Africa." "No, Mr. Whyte. I'm trying to tell you. It hit a node."

Whyte was livid. "What is a node!" he exploded. "The System keeps the tracks clear. Nothing on the tracks but trains, no nodes left lying around—"

"You still don't understand. A node is not an obstruction. It's a singularity. A pole of high order."

Tupelo's explanations that night did not greatly clarify the situation for Kelvin Whyte. But at two in the morning, the general manager conceded to Tupelo the privilege of examining the master maps of the System. He put in a call first to the police, who could not assist him with his first attempt to master topology, and then, finally, to Central Traffic. Tupelo taxied down there alone, and pored over the maps till morning. He had coffee and a snail, and then went to Whyte's office.

He found the general manager on the telephone. There was a conversation having to do with another, more elaborate inspection of the Dorchester-Cambridge tunnel under the Charles River. When the conversation ended, Whyte slammed the telephone into its cradle and glared at Tupelo. The mathematician spoke first.

"I think probably it's the new shuttle that did this," he said.

Whyte gripped the edge of his desk and prowled silently through his vocabulary until he had located some civil words. "Dr. Tupelo," he said, "I have been awake all night going over your theory. I don't understand it all. I don't know what the Boylston shuttle has to do with this."

"Remember what I was saying last night about the connective properties of networks?" Tupelo asked quietly.

"Remember the Mobius band we made—the surface with one face and one edge? Remember this—?" and he removed a little glass Klein bottle from his pocket and placed it on the desk.

Whyte sat back in his chair and stared wordlessly at the mathematician. Three emotions marched across his face in quick succession—anger, bewilderment, and utter dejection. Tupelo went on.

"Mr. Whyte, the System is a network of amazing topological complexity. It was already complex before the Boylston shuttle was installed, and of a high order of connectivity. But this shuttle makes the network absolutely unique. I don't fully understand it, but the situation seems to be something like this; the shuttle has made the connectivity of the whole System of an order so high that I don't know how to calculate it. I suspect the connectivity has become infinite."

The general manager listened as though in a daze. He kept his eyes glued to the little Klein bottle.

"The Mobius band," Tupelo said, "has unusual properties because it has a singularity. The Klein bottle, with two singularities, manages to be inside of itself. The topologists know surfaces with as many as a thousand singularities, and they have properties that make the Mobius band and the Klein bottle both look simple. But a network with infinite connectivity must have an infinite number of singularities. Can you imagine what the properties of that network could be?"

After a long pause, Tupelo added; "I can't either. To tell the truth, the structure of the System, with the Boylston shuttle, is completely beyond me. I can only guess."

Whyte swiveled his eyes up from the desk at a moment when anger was the dominant feeling within him.

"And you call yourself a mathematician, Professor Tupelo!" he said. Tupelo almost laughed aloud. The incongruous, the absolute foolishness of the situation, all but overwhelmed him. He smiled thinly, and said: "I'm no topologist. Really, Mr. Whyte, I'm a tyro in the field— not much better acquainted with it than you are. Mathematics is a big pasture. I happen to be an algebraist."

His candor softened Whyte a little. "Well, then," he ventured, "if you don't understand it, maybe we should call in a topologist. Are there any in Boston?"

"Yes and no," Tupelo answered. "The best in the world is at Tech."

Whyte reached for the telephone. "What's his name?" he asked. "I'll call him."

"Merritt Turnbull. He can't be reached. I've tried for three days."

"Is he out of town?" Whyte asked. "We'll send for him—emergency."

"I don't know. Professor Turnbull is a bachelor. He lives alone at the Brattle Club. He has not been seen since the morning of the 4th."

Whyte was uncommonly perceptive. "Was he on the train?" he asked tensely.

"I don't know," the mathematician replied. "What do you think?"

There was a long silence. Whyte looked alternately at Tupelo and at the glass object on the desk. "I don't understand it," he said finally. "We've looked everywhere on the System. There was no way for the train to get out."

"The train didn't get out. It's still on the System," Tupelo said.

"Where?"

Tupelo shrugged. "The train has no real 'where.' The whole System is without real 'whereness.' It's double-valued, or worse."

"How can we find it?"

"'I don't think we can," Tupelo said.

There was another long silence. Whyte broke it with a loud exclamation. He rose suddenly, and sent the Klein bottle flying across the room. "You are crazy, professor!"

he shouted. Between midnight tonight and 6.00 A.M. tomorrow, we'll get every train out of the tunnels. I'll send in three hundred men, to comb every inch of the tracks— every inch of the one hundred eighty-three miles. We'll find the train! Now, please excuse me." He glared at Tupelo.

Tupelo left the office. He felt tired, completely exhausted. Mechanically, he walked along Washington Street toward the Essex Station. Halfway down the stairs, he stopped abruptly, looked around him slowly. Then he ascended again to the street and hailed a taxi. At home, he helped himself to a double shot. He fell into bed.

At 3:30 that afternoon he met his class in "Algebra of Fields and Rings." After a quick supper at the Crimson Spa, he went to his apartment and spent the evening in a second attempt to analyze the connective properties of the System. The attempt was vain, but the mathematician came to a few important conclusions. At eleven o'clock he telephoned Whyte at Central Traffic.

"I think you might want to consult me during tonight's search," he said. "May I come down?"

The general manager was none too gracious about Tupelo's offer of help.

He indicated that the System would solve this little problem without any help from harebrained professors who thought that whole subway trains could jump off into the fourth dimension. Tupelo submitted to Whyte's unkindness, then went to bed. At about 4:00 A.M. the telephone awakened him. His caller was a contrite Kelvin Whyte.

"Perhaps I was a bit hasty last night, professor," he

stammered. "You may be able to help us after all. Could you come down to the Milk Street Cross-Over?"

Tupelo agreed readily. He felt none of the satisfaction he had anticipated. He called a taxi, and in less than half an hour was at the prescribed station. At the foot of the stairs, on the upper level, he saw that the tunnel was brightly lighted, as during normal operation of the System. But the platforms were deserted except for a tight little knot of seven men near the far end. As he walked towards the group, he noticed that two were policemen. He observed a one-car train on the track beside the platform. The forward door was open, the car brightly lit, and empty. Whyte heard his footsteps and greeted him sheepishly.

"Thanks for coming down, professor," he said, extending his hand. "Gentlemen, Dr. Roger Tupelo, of Harvard.

Dr. Tupelo, Mr. Kennedy, our chief engineer; Mr. Wilson, representing the Mayor; Dr. Gannot, of Mercy Hospital." Whyte did not bother to introduce the motorman and the two policemen.

"How do you do," said Tupelo. "Any results, Mr. Whyte?"

The general manager exchanged embarrassed glances with his companions. "Well . . . yes, Dr. Tupelo," he finally answered. "1 think we do have some results, of a kind."

"Has the train been seen?"

"Yes," said Whyte. "That is, practically seen. At least, we know it's somewhere in the tunnels." The six others nodded their agreement.

Tupelo was not surprised to learn that the train was still on the System. After all, the System was closed.

"Would you mind telling me just what happened?" Tupelo insisted.

"I hit a red signal," the motorman volunteered. "Just outside the Copley junction."

"The tracks have been completely cleared of all trains," Whyte explained, "except for this one. We've been riding it, all over the System, for four hours now. When Edmunds, here, hit a red light at the Copley junction, he stopped, of course. I thought the light must be defective, and told him to go ahead. But then we heard another train pass the junction."

"Did you see it?" Tupelo asked.

"We couldn't see it. The light is placed just behind a curve. But we all heard it. There's no doubt the train went through the junction. And it must be Number 86, because our car was the only other one on the tracks."

"What happened then?"

"Well, then the light changed to yellow, and Edmunds went ahead."

"Did he follow the other train?"

"No. We couldn't be sure which way it was going. We must have guessed wrong."

"How long ago did this happen?" "At 1:38, the first time—"

"Oh," said Tupelo, "then it happened again later?"

"Yes. But not at the same spot, of course. We hit another red signal near South Station at 2:15. And then at 3:28—"

Tupelo interrupted the general manager. "Did you see the train at 2:15?"

"We didn't even hear it, that time. Edmunds tried to

catch it, but it must have turned off onto the Boylston shuttle."

"What happened at 3.28?"

"Another red light. Near Park Street. We heard it up ahead of us."

"But you didn't see it?"

"No. There is a little slope beyond the light. But we all heard it. The only thing I don't understand, Dr. Tupelo, is how that train could run the tracks for nearly five days without anybody seeing—"

Whyte's words trailed off into silence, and his right hand went up in a peremptory gesture for quiet. In the distance, the low metallic thunder of a fast-rolling train swelled up suddenly into a sharp, shrill roar of wheels below. The platform vibrated perceptibly as the train passed.

"Now we've got it!" Whyte exclaimed. "Right past the men on the platform below!" He broke into a run towards the stairs to the lower level. All the others followed him, except Tupelo. He thought he knew what was going to happen. It did. Before Whyte reached the stairs, a policeman bounded up to the top.

"Did you see it, now?" he shouted.

Whyte stopped in his tracks, and the others with him.

"Did you see that train?" the policeman from the lower level asked again, as two more men came running up the stairs.

"What happened?" Wilson wanted to know.

"Didn't you see it?" snapped Kennedy.

"Sure not," the policeman replied. "It passed through up here." "It did not," roared Whyte. "Down there!"

The six men with Whyte glowered at the three from the lower level. Tupelo walked to Whyte's elbow. "The train can't be seen, Mr. Whyte," he said quietly.

Whyte looked down at him in utter disbelief. "You heard it yourself. It passed right below—

"Can we go to the car, Mr. Whyte?" Tupelo asked. "I think we ought to talk a little."

Whyte nodded dumbly, then turned to the policemen and the others who had been watching at the lower level, "You really didn't see it?" he begged them.

"We heard it," the policemen answered. "It passed up here, going that way, I think," and he gestured with his thumb.

"Get back downstairs, Maloney," one of the policemen with Whyte commanded. Maloney scratched his head, turned, and disappeared below. The two other men followed him. Tupelo led the original group to the car beside the station platform. They went in and took seats, silently. Then they all watched the mathematician and waited.

"You didn't call me down here tonight just to tell me you'd found the missing train," Tupelo began, looking at Whyte. "Has this sort of thing happened before?"

Whyte squirmed in his seat and exchanged glances with the chief engineer. "Not exactly like this," he said, evasively, "but there have been some funny things."

"Like what?" Tupelo snapped.

"Well, like the red lights. The watchers near Kendall found a red light at the same time we hit the one near South Station."

"Go on."

"Mr. Sweeney called me from Forest Hills at Park Street-Under. He heard the train there just two minutes after we heard it at the Copley junction.Twenty-eight track miles away."

"As a matter of fact, Dr. Tupelo," Wilson broke in, "several dozen men have seen lights go red, or have heard the train, or both, inside of the last four hours. The thing acts as though it can be in several places at once."

"It can," Tupelo said,

"We keep getting reports of watchers seeing the thing," the engineer added. "Well, not exactly seeing it, either, but everything except that. Sometimes at two or even three places, far apart, at the same time. It's sure to be on the tracks. Maybe the cars are uncoupled."

"Are you really sure it's on the tracks, Mr. Kennedy?" Tupelo asked.

"Positive," the engineer said. "The dynamometers at the power house show that it's drawing power. It's been drawing power all night. So at 3:30 we broke the circuits. Cut the power."

"What happened?"

"Nothing," Whyte answered. "Nothing at all. The power was off for twenty minutes. During that time, not one of the two hundred fifty men in the tunnels saw a red light or heard a train. But the power wasn't on for five minutes before we had two reports again—one from Arlington, the other from Egleston."

There was a long silence after Whyte finished speaking. In the tunnel below, one man could be heard calling something to another. Tupelo looked at his watch. The time was 5:20.

"In short, Dr. Tupelo," the general manager finally said, "we are compelled to admit that there may be something in your theory." The others nodded agreement.

"Thank you, gentlemen," Tupelo said.

The physician cleared his throat. "Now about the passengers," he began. "Have you any idea what—?"

"None," Tupelo interrupted.

"What should we do, Dr. Tupelo?" the mayor's representative asked. "I don't know. What can you do?"

"As I understand it from Mr. Whyte," Wilson continued, "the train has . . . , well, it has jumped into another dimension. It isn't really on the System at all. It's just gone. Is that right?"

"In a manner of speaking."

"And this . . . er . . . peculiar behavior has resulted from certain mathematical properties associated with the new Boylston shuttle?"

"Correct."

"And there is nothing we can do to bring the train back to . . . uh . . . this dimension?"

"I know of nothing."

Wilson took the bit in his teeth. "In this case, gentlemen," he said, "our course is clear. First, we must close off the new shuttle, so this fantastic thing can never happen again. Then, since the missing train is really gone, in spite of all these red lights and noises, we can resume normal operation of the System. At least there will be no danger of collision—which has worried you so much, Whyte. As for the missing train and the people on it—" He gestured them into infinity. "Do you agree, Dr. Tupelo?" he asked the mathematician.

Tupelo shook his head slowly. "Not entirely, Mr. Wilson," he responded. "Now, please keep in mind that I don't fully comprehend what has happened. It's unfortunate that you won't find anybody who can give a good explanation. The one man who might have done so is Professor Turnbull, of Tech, and he was on the train. But in any case, you will want to check my conclusions against those of some competent topologists. I can put you in touch with several.

"Now, with regard to the recovery of the missing train, I can say that I think this is not hopeless. There is a finite probability, as I see it, that the train will eventually pass from the nonspatial part of the network, which it now occupies, back to the spatial part. Since the nonspatial part is wholly inaccessible, there is unfortunately nothing we can do to bring about this transition, or even to predict when or how it will occur. But the possibility of the transition will vanish if the Boylston shuttle is taken out. It is just this section of track that gives the network its essential singularities. If the singularities are removed, the train can never reappear. Is this clear?"

It was not clear, of course, but the seven listening men nodded agreement. Tupelo continued.

"As for the continued operation of the System while the missing train is in the nonspatial part of the network, I can only give you the facts as I see them and leave to your judgment the difficult decision to be drawn from them. The transition back to the spatial part is unpredictable, as I have already told you. There is no way to know when it will occur, or where. In particular, there is a fifty percent probability that, if and when the train reappears, it will be running on the wrong track. Then there will be a collision, of course."

The engineer asked: "To rule out this possibility, Dr. Tupelo, couldn't we leave the Boylston shuttle open, but send no trains through it? Then, when the missing train reappears on the shuttle, it cannot meet another train."

"That precaution would be ineffective, Mr. Kennedy," Tupelo answered. "You see, the train can reappear anywhere on the System. It is true that the System owes its topological complexity to the new shuttle. But, with the shuttle in the System, it is now the whole System that possesses infinite connectivity. In other words, the relevant topological property is a property derived from the shuttle, but belonging to the whole System. Remember that the train made its first transition at a point between Park and Kendall, more than three miles away from the shuttle.

"There is one question more you will want answered. If you decide to go on operating the System, with the Boylston shuttle left in until the train reappears, can this happen again, to another train? I am not certain of the answer, but I think it is: No. I believe an exclusion principle operates here, such that only one train at a time can occupy the nonspatial network."

The physician rose from his seat. "Dr. Tupelo," he began, timorously, "when the train does reappear, will the passengers—?"

"I don't know about the people on the train," Tupelo cut in. "The topological theory does not consider such matters." He looked quickly at each of the seven tired, querulous faces before him. "I am sorry, gentlemen," he added, somewhat more gently. "I simply do not know." To Whyte, he added: "I think I can be of no more help tonight. You know where to reach me." And, turning on his heel, he left the car and climbed the stairs. He found dawn spilling over the street, dissolving the shadows of night.

That impromptu conference in a lonely subway car was never reported in the papers. Nor were the full results of the night-long vigil over the dark and twisted tunnels. During the week that followed, Tupelo participated in four more formal conferences with Kelvin Whyte and certain city officials. At two of these, other topologists were present. Ornstein was imported to Boston from Philadelphia, Kashta from Chicago, and Michaelis from Los Angeles. The mathematicians were unable to reach a consensus. None of the three would fully endorse Tupelo's conclusions, although Kashta indicated that there might be something to them. Ornstein averred that a finite network could not possess infinite connectivity, although he could not prove this proposition and could not actually calculate the connectivity of the System. Michaelis expressed his opinion that the affair was a hoax and had nothing whatever to do with the topology of the System. He insisted that if the train could not be found on the System then the System must be open, or at least must once have been open.

But the more deeply Tupelo analyzed the problem, the more fully he was convinced of the essential correctness of his first analysis. From the point of view of topology, the System soon suggested whole families of multiple-valued networks, each with an infinite number of infinite discontinuities. But a definitive discussion of these new spatio-hyperspatial networks somehow eluded him. He gave the subject his full attention for only a week. Then his other duties compelled him to lay the analysis aside. He resolved to go back to the problem later in the spring, after courses were over.

Meanwhile, the System was operated as though nothing untoward had happened. The general manager and the mayor's representative had somehow managed to forget the night of the search, or at least to reinterpret what they had seen and not seen. The newspapers and the public at large speculated wildly, and they kept continuing pressure on Whyte. A number of suits were filed against the System on behalf of persons who had lost a relative. The State stepped into the affair and prepared its own thorough investigation. Recriminations were sounded in the halls of Congress. A garbled version of Tupelo's theory eventually found its way into the press. He ignored it, and it was soon forgotten.

The weeks passed, and then a month. The State's investigation was completed. The newspaper stories moved from the first page to the second; to the twenty-third; and then stopped. The missing persons did not return. In the large, they were no longer missed.

One day in mid-April, Tupelo traveled by subway again, from Charles Street to Harvard. He sat stiffly in the front of the first car, and watched the tracks and gray tunnel walls hurl themselves at the train. Twice the train stopped for a red light, and Tupelo found himself wondering whether the other train was really just ahead, or just beyond space. He half-hoped, out of curiosity, that his exclusion principle was wrong, that the train might make the transition. But he arrived at Harvard on time. Only he among the passengers had found the trip exciting.

The next week he made another trip by subway, and again the next. As experiments, they were unsuccessful, and much less tense than the first ride in mid-April. Tupelo began to doubt his own analysis. Sometime in May, he reverted to the practice of commuting by subway between his Beacon Hill apartment and his office at Harvard. His mind stopped racing down the knotted gray caverns ahead of the train. He read the morning newspaper, or the abstracts in Reviews of Modern Mathematics,

Then there was one morning when he looked up from the newspaper and sensed something. He pushed panic back on its stiff, quivering spring, and looked quickly out the window at his right. The lights of the car showed the black and gray lines of wall-spots streaking by. The tracks ground out their familiar steely dissonance. The train rounded a curve and crossed a junction that he remembered. Swiftly, he recalled boarding the train at Charles, noting the girl on the ice-carnival poster at Kendall, meeting the southbound train going into Central.

He looked at the man sitting beside him, with a lunch pail on his lap. The other seats were filled, and there were a dozen or so straphangers. A mealy-faced youth near the front door smoked a cigarette, in violation of the rules. Two girls behind him across the aisle were discussing a club meeting. In the seat ahead, a young woman was scolding her little son. The man on the aisle, in the seat ahead of that, was reading the paper. The Transit-Ad above him extolled Florida oranges.

He looked again at the man two seats ahead and fought down the terror within. He studied that man. What was it? Brunette, graying hair; a roundish head; wan complexion; rather flat features; a thick neck, with the hairline a little low, a little ragged; a gray, pin-stripe suit. While Tupelo watched, the man waved a fly away from his left ear. He swayed a little with the train. His newspaper was folded vertically down the middle. His newspaper! It was last March's!

Tupelo's eyes swiveled to the man beside him. Below his lunch pail was a paper. Today's. He turned in his seat and looked behind him. A young man held the Transcript open to the sports pages. The date was March 4th. Tupelo's eyes raced up and down the aisle. There were a dozen passengers carrying papers ten weeks old.

Tupelo lunged out of his seat. The man on the aisle muttered a curse as the mathematician crowded in front of him. He crossed the aisle in a bound and pulled the cord above the windows. The brakes sawed and screeched at the tracks, and the train ground to a stop. The startled passengers eyed Tupelo with hostility.

At the rear of the car, the door flew open and a tall, thin man in a blue uniform burst in. Tupelo spoke first.

"Mr. Dorkin?" he called, vehemently.

The conductor stopped short and groped for words.

"There's been a serious accident, Dorkin," Tupelo said, loudly, to carry over the rising swell of protest from the pas-sangers. "Get Gallagher back here right away!"

Dorkin reached up and pulled the cord four times. "What happened?" he asked.

Tupelo ignored the question, and asked one of his own. "Where have you been, Dorkin?

The conductor's face was blank. "In the next car, but—

Tupelo cut him off. He glanced at his watch, then shouted at the passengers. "It's ten minutes to nine on May 17th!"

The announcement stilled the rising clamor for a moment. The passengers exchanged bewildered glances.

"Look at your newspapers!" Tupelo shouted. "Your newspapers!"

The passengers began to buzz. As they discovered each other's papers, the voices rose. Tupelo took Dorkin's arm and led him to the rear of the car. "What time is it?" he asked.

"8:21," Dorkin said, looking at his watch.

"Open the door," said Tupelo, motioning ahead. "Let me out. Where's the phone?"

Dorkin followed Tupelo's directions. He pointed to a niche in the tunnel wall a hundred yards ahead. Tupelo vaulted to the ground and raced down the narrow lane between the cars and the wall. "Central Traffic!" he barked at the operator. He waited a few seconds, and saw that a train had stopped at the red signal behind his train. Flashlights were advancing down the tunnel. He saw Gallagher's legs running down the tunnel on the other side of 86. "Get me Whyte!" he commanded, when Central Traffic answered. "Emergency!"

There was a delay. He heard voices rising from the

train beside him. The sound was mixed—anger, fear, hysteria.

"Hello!" he shouted. "Hello! Emergency! Get me Whyte!"

"I'll take it," a man's voice said at the other end of the line. "Whyte's busy!"

"Number 86 is back," Tupelo called. "Between Central and Harvard now. Don't know when it made the jump. I caught it at Charles ten minutes ago, and didn't notice it till a minute ago."

The man at the other end gulped bard enough to carry over the telephone. "The passengers?" he croaked.

"All right, the ones that are left," Tupelo said. "Some must have got off already at Kendall and Central."

"Where have they been?"

Tupelo dropped the receiver from his ear and stared at it, his mouth wide open. Then he slammed the receiver onto the hook and ran back to the open door.

Eventually, order was restored, and within a half hour the train proceeded to Harvard. At the station, the police took all passengers into protective custody. Whyte himself arrived at Harvard before the train did. Tupelo found him on the platform.

Whyte motioned weakly towards the passengers. "They're really all right?" he asked.

"Perfectly," said Tupelo. "Don't know they've been gone."

"Any sign of Professor Turnbull?" asked the general manager. "I didn't see him. He probably got off at Kendall, as usual."

"Too bad," said Whyte. "I'd like to see him!"

"So would I!" Tupelo answered. "By the way, now is the time to close the Boylston shuttle."

"Now is too late," Whyte said. "Train 143 vanished twenty-five minutes ago between Egleston and Dorchester."

Tupelo stared past Whyte, and down and down the tracks. "We've got to find Turnbull," Whyte said.

Tupelo looked at Whyte and smiled thinly.

"Do you really think Turnbull got off this train at Kendall?"

"Of course!" answered Whyte. "Where else?"

EXPERIMENT

by Fredric Brown

Fredric Brown (1906-1972) was a legend in the fields of mystery (after a decade of writing stories for the mystery pulps, his first mystery novel, The Fabulous Clipjoint, *won the Mystery Writers of America's Edgar Award) and science fiction (beginning in the 1930s, before anyone much considered SF deserving of awards. His SF novels included the hilarious* Martians Go Home *and the hard-boiled and deadly serious* The Lights in the Sky are Stars. *And then, there's* What Mad Universe, *which almost defies categorization. One his specialties was the short-short story, which took up to four pages, usually hitting with an unforeseen surprise ending. Here are two examples of the master craftsman's artistry*

"Experiment," which follows this intro, packs cosmic concepts almost into a one-liner. When this appeared in Galaxy *magazine, the editorial introduction described it as short and sharp—like a hypodermic. Ah, yes!*

"THE FIRST TIME MACHINE, gentlemen," Professor Johnson proudly informed his two colleagues. "True, it is a small-scale experimental model. It will operate only on objects weighing less than three pounds, five ounces and for distances into the past and future of twelve minutes or less. But it works."

The small-scale model looked like a small scale—a postage scale—except for two dials in the part under the platform.

Professor Johnson held up a small metal cube. "Our experimental object," he said, "is a brass cube weighing one pound, two point three ounces. First, I shall send it five minutes into the future."

He leaned forward and set one of the dials on the time machine. "Look at your watches," he said.

They looked at their watches. Professor Johnson placed the cube gently on the machine's platform. It vanished.

Five minutes later, to the second, it reappeared.

Professor Johnson picked it up. "Now five minutes into the past." He set the other dial. Holding the cube in his hand he looked at his watch. "It is six minutes before three o'clock. I shall now activate the mechanism—by placing the cube on the platform—at exactly three o'clock. Therefore, the cube should, at five minutes before three, vanish from my hand and appear on the platform, five minutes before I place it there."

"How can you place it there, then?" asked one of his colleagues.

"It will, as my hand approaches, vanish from the platform and appear in my hand to be placed there. Three o'clock. Notice, please."

The cube vanished from his hand.

It appeared on the platform of the time machine.

"See? Five minutes before I shall place it there, it is there!"

His other colleague frowned at the cube. "But," he said, "what if, now that it has already appeared five minutes before you place it there, you should change your mind about doing so and not place it there at three o'clock? Wouldn't there be a paradox of some sort involved?"

"An interesting idea," Professor Johnson said. "I had not thought of it, and it will be interesting to try. Very well, I shall not . . ."

There was no paradox at all. The cube remained.

But the entire rest of the Universe, professors and all, vanished.

ANSWER

by Fredric Brown

Fredric Brown gets in another good, solid whack *at the reader's ,mental stability, in a story which has taken on an independent life of its own (somewhat like the centerpiece of the story) and has been plagiar-, er, "retold" in various versions, including a distorted version in no less than* Life *magazine when it published an article on computers in the early 1960s. Naturally, no credit was given to Mr. Brown. Here is the downright diabolical original. Accept no substitutes!*

DWAR EV ceremoniously soldered the final connection with gold. The eyes of a dozen television cameras watched him and the subether bore throughout the universe a dozen pictures of what he was doing.

He straightened and nodded to Dwar Reyn, then moved to a position beside the switch that would complete the contact when he threw it. The switch that would connect, all at once, all of the monster computing machines of all the populated planets in the universe—ninety-six billion planets—into the supercircuit that would connect them all into one supercalculator, one cybernetics machine that would combine all the knowledge of all the galaxies.

Dwar Reyn spoke briefly to the watching and listening trillions. Then after a moment's silence he said, "Now, Dwar Ev."

Dwar Ev threw the switch. There was a mighty hum, the surge of power from ninety-six billion planets. Lights flashed and quieted along the miles-long panel.

Dwar Ev stepped back and drew a deep breath. "The honor of asking the first question is yours, Dwar Reyn."

"Thank you," said Dwar Reyn. "It shall be a question which no single cybernetics machine has been able to answer."

He turned to face the machine. "Is there a God?"

The mighty voice answered without hesitation, without the clicking of a single relay.

"Yes, *now* there is a God."

Sudden fear flashed on the face of Dwar Ev. He leaped to grab the switch.

A bolt of lightning from the cloudless sky struck him down and fused the switch shut.

MANNERS OF THE AGE

by H. B. Fyfe

Horace Browne Fyfe, Jr. (1918-1997) seems to have eluded the biographers of science fiction, and, once again, I wish I had more information about this much-too-overlooked writer. The skimpy mentions that his first story was "Locked Out" in 1940, his career was interrupted by army service in WWII, and afterwards he wrote a series about the Bureau of Slick Tricks, in which clever humans outwit dim-witted aliens. In 1962 he published his only novel, D-99, which continues in much the same vein as the Slick Tricks series Another source mentions that he was a laboratory assistant and draftsman. Other sources give little more than bibliographical information. "Manners of the Age," originally in Galaxy, hilariously and ingeniously explored the possibility of a world where people communicate almost exclusively by electronic means and hardly ever see each other in person, with resultant behavior that will be all too familiar to anyone who's observed the temper tantrums, bullying, and flame wars that are appallingly common on the Internet.

THE RED TENNIS ROBOT scooted desperately across the court, its four wide-set wheels squealing. For a moment, Robert's hard-hit passing shot seemed to have scored. Then, at the last instant, the robot whipped around its single racket-equipped arm. Robert sprawled headlong in a futile lunge at the return.

"Game and set to Red Three," announced the referee box from its high station above the net.

"Ah, shut up!" growled Robert, and flung down his racket for one of the white serving robots to retrieve.

"Yes, Robert," agreed the voice. "Will Robert continue to play?" Interpreting the man's savage mumble as a negative, it told his opponent, "Return to your stall, Red Three!"

Robert strode off wordlessly toward the house. Reaching the hundred-foot-square swimming pool, he hesitated uncertainly.

"Weather's so damned hot," he muttered. "Why didn't the old-time scientists find out how to do something about that while there were still enough people on Earth to manage it?"

He stripped off his damp clothing and dropped it on the "beach" of white sand. Behind him sounded the steps of a humanoid serving robot, hastening to pick it up. Robert plunged deep into the cooling water and let himself float lazily to the surface.

Maybe they did, he thought. *I could send a robot over to the old city library for information. Still, actually doing anything would probably take the resources of a good many persons—and it isn't so easy to find people now that Earth is practically deserted.*

He rolled sideward for a breath and began to swim slowly for the opposite side of the pool, reflecting upon the curious culture of the planet. Although he had accepted this all his life, it really was remarkable how the original home of the human race had been forsaken for fresher worlds among the stars. Or was it more remarkable that a few individuals had asserted their independence by remaining?

Robert was aware that the decision involved few difficulties, considering the wealth of robots and other automatic machines. He regretted knowing so few humans, though they were really not necessary. If not for his hobby of televising, he would probably not know any at all.

"Wonder how far past the old city I'd have to go to meet someone in person," he murmured as he pulled himself from the pool. "Maybe I ought to try accepting that televised invitation of the other night."

Several dark usuform robots were smoothing the sand on this beach under the direction of a blue humanoid supervisor. Watching them idly, Robert estimated that it must be ten years since he had seen another human face to face. His parents were dim memories. He got along very well, however, with robots to serve him or to obtain occasional information from the automatic scanners of the city library that had long ago been equipped to serve such a purpose.

"Much better than things were in the old days," he

told himself as he crossed the lawn to his sprawling white mansion. "Must have been awful before the population declined. Imagine having people all around you, having to listen to them, see them, and argue to make them do what you wanted!"

The heel of his bare right foot came down heavily on a pebble, and he swore without awareness of the precise meaning of the ancient phrases. He limped into the baths and beckoned a waiting robot as he stretched out on a rubbing table.

"Call Blue One!" he ordered.

The red robot pushed a button on the wall before beginning the massage. In a few moments, the major-domo arrived.

"Did Robert enjoy the tennis?" it inquired politely.

"I did *not!*" snapped the man. "Red Three won—and by too big a score. Have it geared down a few feet per second."

"Yes, Robert."

"And have the lawn screened again for pebbles!"

As Blue One retired he relaxed, and turned his mind to ideas for filling the evening. He hoped Henry would televise: Robert had news for him.

After a short nap and dinner, he took the elevator to his three-story tower and turned on the television robot. Seating himself in a comfortable armchair, he directed the machine from one channel to another. For some time, there was no answer to his perfunctory call signals, but one of his few acquaintances finally came on.

"Jack here," said a quiet voice that Robert had long suspected of being disguised by a filter microphone.

"I haven't heard you for some weeks," he remarked, eying the swirling colors on the screen.

He disliked Jack for never showing his face, but curiosity as to what lay behind the mechanical image projected by the other's transmitter preserved the acquaintance.

"I was . . . busy," said the bodiless voice, with a discreet hint of a chuckle that Robert found chilling.

He wondered what Jack had been up to. He remembered once being favored with a televised view of Jack's favorite sport—a battle between companies of robots designed for the purpose, horribly reminiscent of human conflicts Robert had seen on historical films.

He soon made an excuse to break off and set the robot to scanning Henry's channel. He had something to tell the older man, who lived only about a hundred miles away and was as close to being his friend as was possible in this age of scattered, self-sufficient dwellings.

"I don't mind talking to *him*," Robert reflected. "At least he doesn't overdo this business of individual privacy."

He thought briefly of the disdainful face—seemingly on a distant station—which had merely examined him for several minutes one night without ever condescending to speak. Recalling his rage at this treatment, Robert wondered how the ancients had managed to get along together when there were so many of them. They must have had some strict code of behavior, he supposed, or they never would have bred so enormous a population.

"I must find out about that someday," he decided. "How did you act, for instance, if you wanted to play tennis but someone else just refused and went to eat dinner? Maybe that was why the ancients had so many murders."

He noticed that the robot was getting an answer from Henry's station, and was pleased. He could talk as long as he liked, knowing Henry would not resent his cutting off any time he became bored with the conversation.

The robot focused the image smoothly. Henry gave the impression of being a small man. He was gray and wrinkled compared with Robert, but his black eyes were alertly sharp. He smiled his greeting and immediately launched into a story of one of his youthful trips through the mountains, from the point at which it had been interrupted the last time they had talked.

Robert listened impatiently.

"Maybe I have some interesting news," he remarked as the other finished. "I picked up a new station the other night."

"That reminds me of a time when I was a boy and—"

Robert fidgeted while Henry described watching his father build a spare television set as a hobby, with only a minimum of robot help. He pounced upon the first pause.

"A new station!" he repeated. "Came in very well, too. I can't imagine why I never picked it up before."

"Distant, perhaps?" asked Henry resignedly.

"No, not very far from me, as a matter of fact."

"You can't always tell, especially with the ocean so close. Now that there are so few people, you'd think there'd be land enough for all of them; but a good many spend all their lives aboard ship-robots."

"Not this one," said Robert. "She even showed me an outside view of her home."

Henry's eyebrows rose. "She? A woman?"

"Her name is Marcia-Joan."

"Well, well," said Henry. "Imagine that. Women, as I recall, usually do have funny names."

He gazed thoughtfully at his well-kept hands.

"Did I ever tell you about the last woman I knew?" he asked. "About twenty years ago. We had a son, you know, but he grew up and wanted his own home and robots."

"Natural enough," Robert commented, somewhat briefly since Henry *had* told him the story before.

"I often wonder what became of him," mused the older man. "That's the trouble with what's left of Earth culture—no families any more."

Now he'll tell about the time he lived in a crowd of five, thought Robert. *He, his wife, their boy and the visiting couple with the fleet of robot helicopters.*

Deciding that Henry could reminisce just as well without a listener, Robert quietly ordered the robot to turn itself off.

Maybe I will make the trip, he pondered, on the way downstairs, *if only to see what it's like with another person about.*

At about noon of the second day after that, he remembered that thought with regret.

The ancient roads, seldom used and never repaired, were rough and bumpy. Having no flying robots, Robert was compelled to transport himself and a few mechanical servants in ground vehicles. He had—idiotically, he now realized—started with the dawn, and was already tired.

Consequently, he was perhaps unduly annoyed when two tiny spy-eyes flew down from the hills to hover above his caravan on whirring little propellers. He tried to glance up pleasantly while their lenses televised pictures to their base, but he feared that his smile was strained.

The spy-eyes retired after a few minutes. Robert's vehicle, at his voiced order, turned onto a road leading between two forested hills.

Right there, he thought four hours later, *was where I made my mistake. I should have turned back and gone home!*

He stood in the doorway of a small cottage of pale blue trimmed with yellow, watching his robots unload baggage. They were supervised by Blue Two, the spare for Blue One.

Also watching, as silently as Robert, was a pink-and-blue striped robot which had guided the caravan from the entrance gate to the cottage. After one confused protest in a curiously high voice, it had not spoken.

Maybe we shouldn't have driven through that flower bed, thought Robert. *Still, the thing ought to be versatile enough to say so. I wouldn't have such a gimcrack contraption!*

He looked up as another humanoid robot in similar colors approached along the line of shrubs separating the main lawns from that surrounding the cottage.

"Marcia-Joan has finished her nap. You may come to the house now."

Robert's jaw hung slack as he sought for a reply. His face flushed at the idea of a robot's offering *him* permission to enter the house.

Nevertheless, he followed it across the wide lawn and between banks of gaily blossoming flowers to the main house. Robert was not sure which color scheme he disliked more, that of the robot or the unemphatic pastel tints of the house.

The robot led the way inside and along a hall. It pulled back a curtain near the other end, revealing a room with furniture for human use. Robert stared at the girl who sat in an armchair, clad in a long robe of soft, pink material.

She looked a few years younger than he. Her hair and eyes were also brown, though darker. In contrast to Robert's, her smooth skin was only lightly tanned, and she wore her hair much longer. He thought her oval face might have been pleasant if not for the analytical expression she wore.

"I am quite human," he said in annoyance. "Do you have a voice?"

She rose and walked over to him curiously. Robert saw that she was several inches shorter than he, about the height of one of his robots. He condescended to bear her scrutiny.

"You look just as you do on the telescreen," she marveled.

Robert began to wonder if the girl were feeble-minded. How else should he look?

"I usually swim at this hour," he said to change the subject. "Where is the pool?"

Marcia-Joan stared at him.

"Pool of what?" she asked.

Sensing sarcasm, he scowled. "Pool of water, of course! To swim in. What did you think I meant—a pool of oil?"

"I am not acquainted with your habits," retorted the girl.

"None of that stupid wit!" he snapped. "Where is the pool?"

"Don't shout!" shouted the girl. Her voice was high and unpleasantly shrill compared with his. "I don't have a pool. Who wants a swimming pool, anyway?"

Robert felt his face flushing with rage.

So she won't tell me! he thought. All right, I'll find it myself. Everybody has a pool. And if she comes in, I'll hold her head under for a while!

Sneering, he turned toward the nearest exit from the house. The gaily striped robot hastened after him.

The door failed to swing back as it should have at Robert's approach. Impatiently, he seized the ornamental handle. He felt his shoulder grasped by a metal hand.

"Do not use the front door!" said the robot.

"Let go!" ordered Robert, incensed that any robot should presume to hinder him.

"Only Marcia-Joan uses this door," said the robot, ignoring Robert's displeasure.

"I'll use it if I like!" declared Robert, jerking the handle.

The next moment, he was lifted bodily into the air. By the time he realized what was happening, he was carried, face down, along the hall. Too astonished even to yell, he caught a glimpse of Marcia-Joan's tiny feet beneath the hem of her pink robe as his head passed the curtained doorway.

The robot clumped on to the door at the rear of the house and out into the sunshine. There, it released its grip.

When Robert regained the breath knocked out of him

by the drop, and assured himself that no bones were broken, his anger returned.

"I'll find it, wherever it is!" he growled, and set out to search the grounds.

About twenty minutes later, he was forced to admit that there really was no swimming pool. Except for a brook fifty yards away, there was only the tiled bathroom of the cottage to bathe in.

"Primitive!" exclaimed Robert, eyeing this. "Manually operated water supply, too! I must have the robots fix something better for tomorrow."

Since none of his robots was equipped with a thermometer, he had to draw the bath himself. Meanwhile, he gave orders to Blue Two regarding the brook and a place to swim. He managed to fill the tub without scalding himself mainly because there was no hot water. His irritation, by the time he had dressed in fresh clothes and prepared for another talk with his hostess, was still lively.

"Ah, you return?" Marcia-Joan commented from a window above the back door.

"It is time to eat," said Robert frankly.

"You are mistaken."

He glanced at the sunset, which was already fading.

"It is time," he insisted. "I always eat at this hour."

"Well, I don't."

Robert leaned back to examine her expression more carefully. He felt very much the way he had the day the water-supply robot for his pool had broken down and, despite Robert's bellowed orders, had flooded a good part of the lawn before Blue One had disconnected it. Some instinct warned him, moreover, that bellowing now would be as useless as it had been then.

"What *do* you do now?" he asked.

"I dress for the evening."

"And when do you eat?"

"After I finish dressing."

"I'll wait for you," said Robert, feeling that that much tolerance could do no particular harm.

He encountered the pink-and-blue robot in the hall, superintending several plain yellow ones bearing dishes and covered platters. Robert followed them to a dining room.

"Marcia-Joan sits there," the major-domo informed him as he moved toward the only chair at the table.

Robert warily retreated to the opposite side of the table and looked for another chair. None was visible.

Of course, he thought, trying to be fair. *Why should anybody in this day have more than one chair? Robots don't sit.*

He waited for the major-domo to leave, but it did not. The serving robots finished laying out the dishes and retired to posts along the wall. Finally, Robert decided that he would have to make his status clear or risk going hungry.

If I sit down somewhere, he decided, *it may recognize me as human. What a stupid machine to have!*

He started around the end of the table again, but the striped robot moved to intercept him. Robert stopped.

"Oh, well," he sighed, sitting sidewise on a corner of the table.

The robot hesitated, made one or two false starts in

different directions, then halted. The situation had apparently not been included among its memory tapes. Robert grinned and lifted the cover of the nearest platter.

He managed to eat, despite his ungraceful position and what he considered the scarcity of the food. Just as he finished the last dish, he heard footsteps in the hall.

Marcia-Joan had dressed in a fresh robe, of crimson. Its thinner material was gathered at the waist by clasps of gleaming gold. The arrangement emphasized bodily contours Robert had previously seen only in historical films.

He became aware that she was regarding him with much the same suggestion of helpless dismay as the major-domo.

"Why, you've eaten it all!" she exclaimed.

"All?" snorted Robert. "There was hardly any food!"

Marcia-Joan walked slowly around the table, staring at the empty dishes.

"A few bits of raw vegetables and the tiniest portion of protein-concentrate I ever saw!" Robert continued. "Do you call that a dinner to serve a guest?"

"And I especially ordered two portions—"

"Two?" Robert repeated in astonishment. "You must visit me sometime. I'll show you—"

"What's the matter with my food?" interrupted the girl. "I follow the best diet advice my robots could find in the city library."

"They should have looked for human diets, not song-birds'."

He lifted a cover in hopes of finding some overlooked morsel, but the platter was bare.

"No wonder you act so strangely," he said. "You must

be suffering from malnutrition. I don't wonder with a skimpy diet like this."

"It's very healthful," insisted Marcia-Joan. "The old film said it was good for the figure, too."

"Not interested," grunted Robert. "I'm satisfied as I am."

"Oh, yes? You look gawky to me."

"*You* don't," retorted Robert, examining her disdainfully. "You are short and stubby and too plump."

"*Plump?*"

"Worse, you're actually fat in lots of places I'm not."

"At least not between the ears!"

Robert blinked.

"Wh-wh-WHAT?"

"And besides," she stormed on, "those robots you brought are painted the most repulsive colors!"

Robert closed his mouth and silently sought the connection.

Robots? he thought. *Not fat, but repulsive colors, she said. What has that to do with food? The woman seems incapable of logic.*

"And furthermore," Marcia-Joan was saying, "I'm not sure I care for the looks of you! Lulu, put him out!"

"Who's Lulu?" demanded Robert.

Then, as the major-domo moved forward, he understood.

"What a silly name for a robot!" he exclaimed.

"I suppose you'd call it Robert. Will you go now, or shall I call more robots?"

"I am not a fool," said Robert haughtily. "I shall go. Thank you for the disgusting dinner."

"Do not use the front door," said the robot. "Only Marcia-Joan uses that. All robots use other doors."

Robert growled, but walked down the hall to the back door. As this swung open to permit his passage, he halted.

"It's dark out there now," he complained over his shoulder. "Don't you have any lights on your grounds? Do you want me to trip over something?"

"Of course I have ground lights!" shrilled Marcia-Joan. "I'll show you—not that I care if you trip or not."

A moment later, lights concealed among the trees glowed into life. Robert walked outside and turned toward the cottage.

I should have asked her what the colors of my robots had to do with it, he thought, and turned back to re-enter.

He walked right into the closed door, which failed to open before him, though it had operated smoothly a moment ago.

"Robots not admitted after dark," a mechanical voice informed him. "Return to your stall in the shed."

"Whom do you think you're talking to?" demanded Robert. "I'm not one of your robots!"

There was a pause.

"Is it Marcia-Joan?" asked the voice-box, after considerable buzzing and whirring.

"No, I'm Robert."

There was another pause while the mechanism laboriously shifted back to its other speech tape. Then: "Robots not admitted after dark. Return to your stall in the shed."

Robert slowly raised both hands to his temples. Lingeringly, he dragged them down over his cheeks and under his chin until at last the fingers interlaced over his tight lips. After a moment, he let out his breath between his fingers and dropped his hands to his sides.

He raised one foot to kick, but decided that the door looked too hard.

He walked away between the beds of flowers, grumbling.

Reaching the vicinity of the cottage, he parted the tall shrubs bordering its grounds and looked through carefully before proceeding. Pleased at the gleam of water, he called Blue Two.

"Good enough! Put the other robots away for the night. They can trim the edges tomorrow."

He started into the cottage, but his major-domo warned, "Someone comes."

Robert looked around. Through thin portions of the shrubbery, he caught a glimpse of Marcia-Joan's crimson robe, nearly black in the diffused glow of the lights illuminating the grounds.

"Robert!" called the girl angrily. "What are your robots doing? I saw them from my upstairs window—"

"Wait there!" exclaimed Robert as she reached the shrubs.

"What? Are you trying to tell me where I can go or not go? I—YI!"

The shriek was followed by a tremendous splash. Robert stepped forward in time to be spattered by part of the flying spray. It was cold.

Naturally, being drawn from the brook, he reflected. *Oh, well, the sun will warm it tomorrow.*

There was a frenzy of thrashing and splashing in the

dimly lighted water at his feet, accompanied by coughs and spluttering demands that he "do something!"

Robert reached down with one hand, caught his hostess by the wrist, and heaved her up to solid ground.

"My robots are digging you a little swimming hole," he told her. "They brought the water from the brook by a trench. You can finish it with concrete or plastics later; it's only fifteen by thirty feet."

He expected some sort of acknowledgment of his efforts, and peered at her through the gloom when none was forthcoming. He thus caught a glimpse of the full-swinging slap aimed at his face. He tried to duck.

There was another splash, followed by more floundering about.

"Reach up," said Robert patiently, "and I'll pull you out again. I didn't expect you to like it this much."

Marcia-Joan scrambled up the bank, tugged viciously at her sodden robe, and headed for the nearest pathway without replying. Robert followed along.

As they passed under one of the lights, he noticed that the red reflections of the wet material, where it clung snugly to the girl's body, were almost the color of some of his robots.

The tennis robot, he thought, *and the moving targets for archery—in fact, all the sporting equipment.*

"You talk about food for the figure," he remarked lightly. "You should see yourself now! It's really funny, the way—"

He stopped. Some strange emotion stifled his impulse to laugh at the way the robe clung.

Instead, he lengthened his stride, but he was still a few

feet behind when she charged through the front entrance of the house. The door, having opened automatically for her, started to swing closed. Robert sprang forward to catch it.

"Wait a minute!" he cried.

Marcia-Joan snapped something that sounded like "Get out!" over her shoulder, and squished off toward the stairs. As Robert started through the door to follow, the striped robot hastened toward him from its post in the hall.

"Do not use the front door!" it warned him.

"Out of my way!" growled Robert.

The robot reached out to enforce the command. Robert seized it by the forearm and put all his weight into a sudden tug. The machine tottered off balance. Releasing his grip, he sent it staggering out the door with a quick shove.

A hasty glance showed Marcia-Joan flapping wetly up the last steps. Robert turned to face the robot.

"Do not use that door!" he quoted vindictively, and the robot halted its rush indecisively. "Only Marcia-Joan uses it."

The major-domo hesitated. After a moment, it strode off around the corner of the house. First darting one more look at the stairs, Robert thrust his head outside and shouted: "Blue Two!"

He held the door open while he waited. There was an answer from the shrubbery. Presently, his own supervisor hurried up.

"Fetch the emergency toolbox!" Robert ordered. "And bring a couple of others with you."

"Naturally, Robert. I would not carry it myself."

A moment after the robot had departed on the errand, heavy steps sounded at the rear of the hall. Marcia-Joan's robot had dealt with the mechanism of the back door.

Robert eyed the metal mask as the robot walked up to him. He found the color contrast less pleasant than ever.

"I am not using the door," he said hastily. "I am merely holding it open."

"Do you intend to use it?"

"I haven't decided."

"I shall carry you out back," the robot decided for him.

"No, you don't!" exclaimed Robert, leaping backward.

The door immediately began to swing shut as he passed through.

Cursing, he lunged forward. The robot reached for him.

This time, Robert missed his grip. Before he could duck away, his wrist was trapped in a metal grasp.

The door will close, he despaired. *They'll be too late*.

Then, suddenly, he felt the portal drawn back and heard Blue Two speak.

"What does Robert wish?"

"Throw this heap out the door!" gasped Robert.

Amid a trampling of many feet, the major-domo was raised bodily by Blue Two and another pair of Robert's machines and hustled outside. Since the grip on Robert's wrist was not relaxed, he involuntarily accompanied the rush of metal bodies.

"Catch the door!" he called to Blue Two.

When the latter sprang to obey, the other two took the action as a signal to drop their burden. The pink-and-blue robot landed full length with a jingling crash. Robert was free.

With the robots, he made for the entrance. Hearing footsteps behind him as the major-domo regained its feet, he slipped hastily inside.

"Pick up that toolbox!" he snapped. "When that robot stops in the doorway, knock its head off!"

Turning, he held up a finger.

"Do not use the front door!"

The major-domo hesitated.

The heavy toolbox in the grip of Blue Two descended with a thud. The pink-and-blue robot landed on the ground a yard or two outside the door as if dropped from the second floor. It bounced once, emitted a few sparks and pungent wisps of smoke, lay still.

"Never mind, that's good enough," said Robert as Blue Two stepped forward. "One of the others can drag it off to the repair shop. Have the toolbox brought with us."

"What does Robert wish now?" inquired Blue Two, trailing the man toward the stairway.

"I'm going upstairs," said Robert. "And I intend to be prepared if any more doors are closed against me!"

He started up, the measured treads of his own robots sounding reassuringly behind him. . . .

It was about a week later that Robert sat relaxed in the armchair before his own telescreen, facing Henry's wizened visage.

The elder man clucked sympathetically as he re-examined the scratches on Robert's face and the bruise under his right eye.

"And so you left there in the morning?"

"I certainly did!" declared Robert. "We registered a marriage record at the city library by television, of course, but I don't care if I never see her again. She needn't even tell me about the child, if any. I simply can't stand that girl!"

"Now, now," Henry said.

"I mean it! Absolutely no consideration for my wishes. Everything in the house was run to suit her convenience."

"After all," Henry pointed out, "it is her house."

Robert glared. "What has that to do with it? I don't think I was as unreasonable as she said in smashing that robot. The thing just wouldn't let me alone!"

"I guess," Henry suggested, "it was conditioned to obey Marcia-Joan, not you."

"Well, that shows you! Whose orders are to count, anyway? When I tell a robot to do something, I expect it done. How would you like to find robots trying to boss you around?"

"Are you talking about robots," asked Henry, "or the girl?"

"Same thing, isn't it? Or it would be if I'd decided to bring her home with me."

"Conflict of desires," murmured Henry.

"Exactly! It's maddening to have a perfectly logical action interfered with because there's another person present to insist—insist, mind you—on having her way."

"And for twenty-odd years, you've had your own way in every tiny thing."

Somewhere in the back of Robert's lurked a feeling that Henry sounded slightly sarcastic.

"Well, why shouldn't I?" he demanded. "I noticed that in every disagreement, my view was the right one."

"It was?"

"Of course it was! What did you mean by that tone?"

"Nothing. . . ." Henry seemed lost in thought. "I was just wondering how many 'right' views are left on this planet. There must be quite a few, all different, even if we have picked up only a few by television. An interesting facet of our peculiar culture—every individual omnipotent and omniscient, *within his own sphere.*"

Robert regarded him with indignant incredulity.

"You don't seem to understand my point," he began again. "I told her we ought to come to my house, where things are better arranged, and she simply refused. Contradicted me! It was most—"

He broke off.

"The *impudence* of him!" he exclaimed. "Signing off when I wanted to talk!"

THE DWINDLING SPHERE

by Willard E. Hawkins

Willard E. Hawkins (1897-1970) was not a prolific author, but this story of his, from the March 1940 issue of Astounding, makes me want to check out his other works. For this story alone, probably the ultimate environmental SF story, Hawkins should not be forgotten, and I wish I had more information about him.

**EXTRACTS FROM THE DIARY OF
FRANK BAXTER, B.S., M.Sc.**

June 23, 1945. I thought today I was on the track of something, but the results, while remarkable in their way, were disappointing. The only thing of importance I can be said to have demonstrated is that, with my new technique of neutron bombardment, it is unnecessary to confine experiments to the heavier elements. This broadens the field of investigation enormously. Substituted a lump of common coal for uranium in today's experiment, and it was reduced to a small cinder. Probably oxidized, owing to a defect in the apparatus or in my procedure.

However, it seems remarkable that, despite the almost instantaneous nature of the combustion, there was no explosion. Nor, as far as I could detect, was any heat generated. In fact, I unthinkingly picked up the cinder— a small, smooth buttonlike object—and it was scarcely warm.

June 24, 1945. Repeated yesterday's experiment carefully checking each step, with results practically identical to yesterday's. Can it be that I am on the verge of success? But that is absurd. If—as might be assumed from the evidence—my neutron bombardment started a self-perpetuating reaction which continued until every atom in the mass had been subjected to fission, enormous energy would have been generated. In fact, I would no longer be here, all in one piece, to tell about it. Even the combustion of my lump of coal at such a practically instantaneous rate would be equivalent to exploding so much dynamite.

It is very puzzling, for the fact remains that the lump has been reduced to a fraction of its original weight and size. There is, after all, only one possible answer: the greater part of its mass must have been converted into energy. The question, then, is what became of the energy?

June 28, 1945. Have been continuing my experiments, checking and rechecking. I have evidently hit upon some new principle in the conversion of matter into energy. Here are some of the results thus far:

Tried the same experiment with a chunk of rock—identical result. Tried it with a lump of earth, a piece of wood, and a brass doorknob. Only difference in results was the size and consistency of the resulting cinder. Have weighed the substance each time, then the residue after neutron bombardment. The original substance seems to be reduced to approximately one twentieth of its original mass, although this varies somewhat according to the strength of the magnetic field and various adjustments in the apparatus. These factors also seem to affect the composition of the cinder.

The essence of the problem, however, has thus far baffled me. Why is it that I cannot detect the force generated? What is its nature? Unless I can solve this problem the whole discovery is pointless.

I have written to my old college roommate, Bernard Ogilvie, asking him to come and check my results. He is a capable engineer and I have faith in his honesty and common sense—even though he appears to have been lured away from scientific pursuits by commercialism.

July 15, 1945. Ogilvie has been here now for three days. He is greatly excited, but I am sorry that I sent for him. He has given me no help at all on my real problem, in fact, he seems more interested in the by-products than in the experiment itself. I had hoped he would help me to solve the mystery of what becomes of the energy generated by my process. Instead, he appears to be fascinated by those little chunks of residue—the cinders.

When I showed that it was possible, by certain adjustments in the apparatus, to control their texture and substance, he was beside himself with excitement. The result is that I have spent all my time since his arrival in making these cinders. We have produced them in consistency ranging all the way from hard little buttons to a mushy substance resembling cheese.

Analysis shows them to be composed of various elements, chiefly carbon and silica. Ogilvie appears to think there has been an actual transmutation of elements into this final result. I question it. The material is simply a form of ash—a residue.

We have enlarged the apparatus and installed a hopper into which we shovel rock, debris—in fact, anything that comes handy, including garbage—and other waste. If my experiment after all proves a failure, I shall at least have the ironic satisfaction of having produced an ideal incinerator. Ogilvie declares there is a fortune in that alone.

July 20, 1945. Bernard Ogilvie has gone. Now I can get down to actual work again. He took with him a quantity of samples and plans for the equipment. Before he left, he revealed what is on his mind. He thinks my process may revolutionize the plastics industry. What a waste of time to have called him in. A fine mind spoiled by commercialism. With an epochal discovery in sight, all he can think of is that here is an opportunity to convert raw material which costs practically nothing into commercial gadgets. He thinks the stuff can be molded and shaped— perhaps through a matrix principle incorporated right in the apparatus.

Partly, I must confess, to get rid of him, I signed the agreement he drew up. It authorizes him to patent the process in my name, and gives me a major interest in all subsidiary "devices and patents" that may be developed by his engineers. He himself is to have what he calls the promotion rights, but there is some sort of a clause whereby the control reverts wholly to me or to my heirs at his death. Ogilvie says it will mean millions to both of us.

He undoubtedly is carried away by his imagination. What could I do with such an absurd sum of money? However, a few thousand dollars might come in handy for improved equipment. I must find a means of capturing and controlling that energy.

EXTRACTS FROM THE DIARY OF QUENTIN BAXTER, PRESIDENT OF PLASTOSCENE PRODUCTS, INC.

August 3, 2065. I have made a discovery today which moved me profoundly—so profoundly that I have opened this journal so that my own thoughts and reactions may be likewise recorded for posterity. Diary keeping has heretofore appeared to me as a rather foolish vanity—it now appears in an altogether different light.

The discovery, which so altered my viewpoint, was of a diary kept by my great-grandfather, Frank Baxter, the actual inventor of plastoscene.

I have often wondered what sort of a man this ancestor

of mine could have been. History tells us almost nothing about him. I feel that I know him as intimately as I know my closest associates. And what a different picture this diary gives from the prevailing concept!

Most of us have no doubt thought of the discoverer of the plastoscene principle as a man who saw the need for a simple method of catering to humanity's needs—one which would supplant the many laborious makeshifts of his day—and painstakingly set out to evolve it.

Actually, the discovery appears to have been an accident. Frank Baxter took no interest in its development— regarded it as of little account. Think of it! An invention more revolutionary than the discovery of fire, yet its inventor failed entirely to grasp its importance! To the end of his days it was to him merely a by-product. He died considering himself a failure, because he was unable to attain the goal he sought, the creation of atomic power.

In a sense, much of the credit apparently belongs to his friend Bernard Ogilvie, who grasped the possibilities inherent in the new principle. Here again, what a different picture the diary gives from that found in our schoolbooks! The historians would have us regard Frank Baxter as a sort of mastermind, Bernard Ogilvie as his humble disciple and Man Friday.

Actually, Ogilvie was a shrewd promoter who saw the possibilities of the discovery and exploited them—not especially to benefit humanity, but for personal gain. We must give him credit, however, for a scrupulous honesty, which was amazing for his time. It would have been easy for him to take advantage of the impractical, dreamy scientist. Instead, he arranged that the inventor of the process should reap its rewards, and it is wholly owing to his insistence that control reverted to our family, where it has remained for more than a century.

All honor to these two exceptional men!

Neither, it is true, probably envisioned the great changes that would be wrought by the discovery. My ancestor remained to the end of his days dreamy and aloof, concerned solely with his futile efforts to trap the energy, which he was sure he had released. The wealth, which rolled up for him through Plastoscene Products, Inc.—apparently the largest individual fortune of his time—was to him a vague abstraction. I find a few references to it in his diary, but they are written in a spirit of annoyance. He goes so far as to mention once— apparently exasperated because the responsibilities of his position called him away from his experiments for a few hours—that he would like to convert the millions into hard currency and pour them into a conversion hopper, where at least they might be turned into something useful.

It is strange, by the way, that the problem he posed has never been demonstrably solved. Scientists still are divided in their allegiance to two major theories—one that the force generated by this conversion of elements escapes into the fourth dimension; the other that it is generated in the form of radiations akin to cosmic rays, which are dissipated with a velocity approaching the infinite. These rays do not affect ordinary matter, according to the theory, because they do not impinge upon it, but instead pass through it, as light passes through a transparent substance.

August 5, 2065. I have read and reread my grandfather's diary and confess that I more and more find in him a kindred spirit. His way of life seems to me infinitely more appealing than that which inheritance has imposed upon me. The responsibilities resting on my shoulders, as reigning head of the Baxter dynasty, become exceedingly onerous at times. I even find myself wondering whether plastoscene has, after all, proved such an unmixed blessing for mankind.

Perhaps the greatest benefits may lie in the future. Certainly each stage in its development has been marked by economic readjustments—some of them well-nigh world shattering. I have often been glad that I did not live through those earlier days of stress, when industry after industry was wiped out by the remorseless juggernaut of technological progress. When, for example, hundreds of thousands were thrown out of employment in the metal mining and refining and allied industries. It was inevitable that plastoscene substitutes, produced at a fraction of the cost from common dirt of the fields, should wipe out this industry—but the step could have been taken, it seems to me, without subjecting the dispossessed workers and employers to such hardship, thereby precipitating what amounted to a civil war. When we pause to think of it, almost every article in common use today represents one or more of those industries which was similarly wiped out, and on which vast numbers of people depended for their livelihood.

We have, at length, achieved a form of stable society— but I, for one, am not wholly satisfied with it. What do we have? —A small owning class—a cluster of corporations grouped around the supercorporation, Plastoscene Products, Inc., of which I am—heaven help me!—the hereditary ruler. Next, a situation-holding class, ranging from scientists, executives and technicians down to the mechanical workers. Here again—because there are so few situations open, compared with the, vast reservoir of potential producers—the situation holders have developed what amounts to a system of hereditary succession. I am told that it is almost impossible for one whose father was not a situation holder even to obtain the training necessary to qualify him for any of the jealously guarded positions.

Outside of this group is that great, surging mass, the major part of human society. These millions, I grant, are fed and clothed and housed and provided with a standard of living, which their ancestors would have regarded as luxurious. Nevertheless, their lot is pitiful. They have no incentives; their status is that of a subject class. Particularly do I find distasteful the law, which makes it a crime for any member of this enforced leisure group to be caught engaging in useful labor. The appalling number of convictions in our courts for this crime shows that there is in mankind an instinct to perform useful service, which cannot be eradicated merely by passing laws.

The situation is unhealthy as well from another standpoint. To me it seems a normal thing that society should progress. Yet we cannot close our eyes to the fact that the most highly skilled scientific minds the world has ever known have failed to produce a worthwhile advance in technology for over a quarter of a century. Has science become sterile? No. In fact, every schoolboy knows the answer.

Our scientists do not dare to announce their discoveries. I am supposed to shut my eyes to what I know—that every vital discovery along the lines of technology has been suppressed. The plain, blunt truth is that we dare not introduce any technical advance, which would eliminate more situation holders. A major discovery—one that reduced an entire class of situation holders to enforced leisure—would precipitate another revolution.

Is human society, as a result of its greatest discovery, doomed to sterility?

October 17, 2089. It has been nearly a quarter of a century since I first read the diary of my great-grandfather, Frank Baxter. I felt an impulse to get it out to show to my son, and before I realized it I had reread the volume in its entirety. It stirred me even more than it did back in my younger days. I must preserve its crumbling pages in facsimile, on permanent plastoscene parchment, so that later descendants—finding our two journals wrapped together will thrill as I have thrilled to that early record of achievement.

The reading has crystallized thoughts long dormant in my mind. I am nearing the end of the trail. Soon I will turn over the presidency of Plastoscene Products, Inc. to my son—if he desires it. Perhaps he will have other ideas. He is now a full-fledged Pl. T.D. Doctor of Plastoscene Technology. It may be that power and position will mean as little to him as they have come to mean to me. I shall send for him tomorrow.

October 18, 2089. I have had my discussion with Philip,

but I fear I bungled matters. He talked quite freely of his experiments. It seems that he has been working along the line of approach started by Levinson some years ago. As we know, the plastoscene principle in use involves the making of very complex adjustments. That is to say, if we wish to manufacture some new type of object—say a special gyroscope bearing—the engineer in charge first sets the machine to produce material of a certain specific hardness and temper, then he adjusts the controls which govern size and shape, and finally, having roughly achieved the desired result, he refines the product with micrometer adjustments—but largely through the trial-and-error method—until the quality, dimensions and so on meet the tests of his precision instruments. If the object involved is complex— involving two or more compounds, for example—the adjustments are correspondingly more difficult. We have not succeeded in producing palatable foodstuffs, though our engineers have turned out some messes, which are claimed to have nourishing qualities. I suspect that the engineers have purposely made them nauseating to the taste.

True, once the necessary adjustments have been made, they are recorded on microfilm. Thereafter, it is only necessary to feed this film into the control box, where the electric eye automatically makes all the adjustments for which the skill of the technician was initially required. Levinson, however, proposed to reproduce natural objects in plastoscene by photographic means.

It is this process which Philip apparently has perfected. His method involves a three-dimensional "scanning" device, which records the texture, shape and the exact molecular structure of the object to be reproduced. The record is made on microfilm, which then needs only to be passed through the control box to re-create the object as many times as may be required.

"Think of the saving of effort!" Philip remarked enthusiastically. "Not only can objects of the greatest intricacy be reproduced without necessity of assembling, but even natural foods can be created in all their flavor and nourishing quality. I have eaten synthetic radishes—I have even tasted synthetic chicken that could not be told from the original which formed its matrix."

"You mean," I demanded in some alarm, "that you can reproduce life?"

His face clouded. "No. That is a quality that seems to elude the scanner. But I can reproduce the animal, identical with its live prototype down to the last nerve tip and hair, except that it is inert—lifeless. The radishes I spoke of will not grow in soil—they cannot reproduce themselves—but chemically and in cell structure they image the originals."

"Philip," I declared, "this is an amazing achievement! It removes the last limitation upon the adaptability of plastoscene. It means that we can produce not merely machine parts but completely assembled machines. It means that foodstuffs can be—"

I stopped, brought to myself by his sudden change in expression.

"True, Father," he observed coldly, "except that it happens to be a pipe dream. I did not expect that you would be taken in by my fairy tale. I have an engagement and must go."

He hurried from the room before I could get my wits about me.

October 23, 2089. Philip has been avoiding me, but I managed at last to corner him.

I began this time by mentioning that it would soon be necessary for me to turn over the burden of Plastoscene Products, Inc. to him as my logical successor.

He hesitated, and then blurted, "Father, I know this is going to hurt you, but I don't want to carry on the succession. I prefer to remain just a cog in the engineering department."

"Responsibility," I reminded him, "is something that cannot be honorably evaded."

"Why should it be my responsibility?" he demanded vehemently. "I didn't ask to be your son."

"Nor," I countered, "did I ask to be my father's son, nor the great-grandson of a certain inventor who died in the twentieth century. Philip, I want you to do one thing for me. Take this little book, read it, then bring it back and tell me what you think of it." I handed him Frank Baxter's diary.

October 24, 2089. Philip brought back the diary today. He admitted that he had sat up all night reading it. "But I'm afraid the effect isn't what you expected," he told me frankly. "Instead of instilling the idea that we Baxters have a divine mission to carry on the dynasty, it makes me feel that our responsibility is rather to undo the damage already caused by our meddling. That old fellow back there—Frank Baxter—didn't intend to produce this hideous stuff."

"Hideous stuff?" I demanded.

"Don't be shocked, Father," he said, a trifle apologetically. "I can't help feeling rather deeply about this. Perhaps you think we're better off than people in your great-grandfather's time. I doubt it. They had work to do. There may have been employment problems, but it wasn't the enforced idleness of our day. Look at Frank Baxter—he could work and invent things with the assurance that he was doing something to advance mankind. He wasn't compelled to cover up his discoveries for fear they'd cause further—"

He stopped suddenly, as if realizing that he had said more than he intended.

"My boy," I told him, speaking slowly, "I know just how you feel—and knowing it gives me more satisfaction than you can realize."

He stared at me, bewildered. "You mean—you don't want me to take on the succession?"

I unfolded my plan.

FROM THE DIARY OF RAN RAXLER, TENTHRANKING HONOR STUDENT, NORTH-CENTRAL FINALS, CLASS OF 2653

December 28, 2653. 1 have had two thrills today—an

exciting discovery right on the heels of winning my diploma in the finals. Being one of the high twenty practically assures me of a chance to serve in the production pits this year.

But the discovery—I must record that first of all. It consists of a couple of old diaries. I found them in a chestful of family heirlooms which I rescued as they were about to be tossed into the waste tube. In another minute, they would have been on their way to the community plastoscene converter.

There has been a legend in our family that we are descended from the original discoverer of plastoscene, and this find surely tends to prove it. Even the name is significant. Frank Baxter. Given names as well as surnames are passed down through the generations. My grandfather before me was Ran Raxler. The dropping of a letter here, the corruption of another there, could easily have resulted in the modification of Frank Baxter to Ran Raxler.

What a thrill it will be to present to the world the authentic diary of the man who discovered the plastoscene principle! Not the impossible legendary figure, but the actual, flesh-and-blood man. And what a shock it will be to many! For it appears that Frank Baxter stumbled upon this discovery quite by accident, and regarded it to the end of his days as an unimportant by-product of his experiments.

And this later Baxter—Quentin—who wrote the companion diary and sealed the two together. What a martyr to progress he proved himself—he and his son, Philip. The diary throws an altogether different light on their motives than has been recorded in history. Instead of being selfish oligarchs who were overthrown by a mass uprising, this diary reveals that they themselves engineered the revolution.

The final entry in Quentin Baxter's diary consists of these words: "I unfolded my plan." The context—when taken with the undisputed facts of history—makes it clear what the plan must have been. As I reconstruct it, the Baxters, father and son, determined to abolish the control of plastoscene by a closed corporation of hereditary owners, and to make it the property of the whole people.

The son had perfected the scanning principle which gives plastoscene its present unlimited range. His impulse was to withhold it—in fact, it had become a point of honor among technicians to bury such discoveries, after showing them to a few trusted associates. Incomprehensible? Perhaps so at first, but not when we understand the upheavals such discoveries might cause in the form of society then existing. To make this clear, I should, perhaps, point to the record of history, which proves that up to the time of plastoscene, foodstuffs had been largely produced by growing them in the soil. This was accomplished through a highly technical process, which I cannot explain, but I am told that the University of Antarctica maintains an experimental laboratory in which the method is actually demonstrated to advanced classes. Moreover, we know what these foods were like through the microfilm matrices, which still reproduce some of them for us.

The right to produce such foods for humanity's needs was jealously guarded by the great agricultural aristocracy.

And, of course, this entire situation-holding class, together with many others, would be abolished by Philip's invention.

We know what happened. Despite the laws prohibiting the operation of plastoscene converters except by licensed technicians and situation holders, contraband machines suddenly began to appear everywhere among the people. Since these machines were equipped with the new scanning principle, it is obvious, in view of the diary, that they must have been deliberately distributed at strategic points by the Baxters.

At first, the contraband machines were confiscated and destroyed—but since they were, of course, capable of reproducing themselves through the matrix library of microfilm which was standard equipment, the effort to keep pace with their spread through the masses was hopeless. The ruling hierarchies appealed to the law, and to the Baxters, whose hereditary control of the plastoscene monopoly had been supposedly a safeguard against its falling into the hands of the people as a whole. The Baxters, father and son, then played their trump card. They issued a proclamation deeding the plastoscene principle in perpetuity to all the people. History implies that they were forced to do this—but fails to explain how or why. There was a great deal of confusion and bloodshed during this period; no wonder that historians jumped at conclusions—even assuming that the Baxters were assassinated by revolutionists, along with others of the small owning group who made a last stand, trying to preserve their monopolies. In light of Quentin Baxter's diary, there is far better ground for believing that they were executed by members of their own class, who regarded them as traitors.

We should be thankful indeed that those ancient days of war and bloodshed are over. Surely such conditions can never reappear on Earth. What possible reason can there be for people to rise up against each other? Just as we can supply all our needs with plastoscene, so can our neighbors on every continent supply theirs.

March 30, 2654. I have completed my service in the production pits, and thrilling weeks they have been. To have a part in the great process, which keeps millions of people alive, even for a brief four weeks' period, makes one feel that life has not been lived in vain.

One could hardly realize, without such experience, what enormous quantities of raw material are required for the sustenance and needs of the human race. How fortunate I am to have been one of the few to earn this privilege of what the ancients called "work."

The problem must have been more difficult in the early days. Where we now distribute raw-material concentrates in the form of plastoscene-B, our forefathers had to transport the actual rock as dredged from the gravel pits. Even though the process of distribution was mechanical and largely automatic, still it was cumbersome, since material for conversion is required in a ratio of about twenty to one as compared with the finished product.

Today, of course, we have the intermediate process, by which soil and rock are converted at the pits into blocks of plastoscene-B. This represents, in a sense, the conversion process in an arrested stage. The raw material emerges in these blocks reduced to a tenth of its original weight. and an even smaller volume than it will occupy in the finished product—since the mass has been increased by close packing of molecules.

A supply of concentrate sufficient to last the ordinary family for a year can now easily be stored in the standard sized converter, and even the huge community converters have a capacity sufficient to provide for all the building, paving of roadways, recarpeting of recreation grounds, and like purposes, that are likely to be required in three months' time. I understand that experimental stations in South America are successfully introducing liquid concentrate, which can be piped directly to the consumers from the vast production pits.

I was amused on my last day by a question asked by a ten-year-old boy, the son of one of the supervisors. We stood on a rampart overlooking one of the vast production pits, several hundred feet deep and miles across the whole space filled with a bewildering network of towers, girders, cranes, spires and cables, across and through which flashed transports of every variety. Far below us, the center of all this activity, could be discerned the huge conversion plant, in which the rock is reduced to plastoscene-B.

The little boy looked with awe at the scene, and then turned his face upward, demanding, "What are we going to do when this hole gets so big that it takes up the whole world?"

We laughed, but I could sympathize with the question. Man is such a puny creature that it is difficult for him to realize what an infinitesimal thing on the Earth's surface is a cavity, which to him appears enormous. The relationship, I should say, is about the same as a pinprick to a ball which a child can toss in the air.

**FROM THE INTRODUCTION
TO OUR EIGHTY YEARS' WAR,
SIGNED BY GLUX GLUXTON,
CHIEF HISTORIAN,
THE NAPHALI INSTITUTE OF SCIENCE
(DATED AS OF THE SIXTH DAY,
SIXTH LUNAR MONTH, YEAR 10,487)**

THE EIGHTY YEARS' WAR is over. It has been concluded by a treaty of eternal amity signed at Latex on the morning of the twenty-ninth day of the fifth month.

By the terms of the treaty, all peoples of the world agree to subject themselves to the control by the World Court. The Court, advised through surveys continuously conducted by the International Institute of Science, will have absolute authority over the conversion of basic substance into plastoscene, to the end that further disputes between regions and continents shall be impossible.

To my distinguished associates and to myself was allotted the task of compiling a history of the causes behind this prolonged upheaval and of its course. How well we have succeeded posterity must judge. In a situation so complex, how, indeed, may one declare with assurance which were the essential causes? Though known as the Eighty Years' War, a more accurate expression would be "the Eighty Years of War," for the period has been one marked by a constant succession of wars—of outbreaks originating spontaneously and from divers causes in various parts of the world.

Chief among the basic causes, of course, were the disputes, between adjoining districts over the right to extend their conversion pits beyond certain boundaries. Nor can we overlook the serious situation precipitated when it was realized that the Antarctican sea-water conversion plants were sucking up such great quantities that the level of the oceans was actually being lowered— much as the Great Lakes once found on the North American continent were drained of their water centuries ago. Disputes, alliances and counter-alliances, regions arrayed against each other, and finally engines of war raining fearful destruction. What an unprecedented bath of blood the world has endured!

The whole aim, from this time forth, will be to strip off the earth's surface evenly, so that it shall become smooth and even, not rough and unsightly and covered with abandoned pits as now viewed from above. To prevent a too rapid lowering of sea level, it is provided that Antarctica and some other sections which have but a limited amount of land surface shall be supplied with concentrate from the more favored regions.

Under such a treaty, signed with fervent good will by the representatives of a war-weary world population, is it farfetched to assert that permanent peace has been assured? Your historian holds that it is not.

FROM THE REPORT OF RAGNAR DUGH, DELEGATE TO THE WORLD PEACE CONFERENCE, TO THE 117th DISTRICT (CIRCUIT 1,092, REV. 148)

HONORED CONFRERES: It gives me pleasure to present, on behalf of the district which has honored me as its representative, concurrence in the conditions for peace as proposed in the majority report.

As I view your faces in the televisor, I see in them the same sense of deep elation that I feel in the thought that this exhausting era of bloodshed and carnage has run its course, and that war is to be rendered impossible from this time forth. Is this too strong a statement? I read in your eyes that it is not, for we are at last abolishing the cause of war, namely, the overcrowding of the earth's surface.

The proposed restrictions may seem drastic, but the human race will accustom itself to them. And let us remember that they would be even more drastic if the wars themselves had not resulted in depopulating the world to a great extent. I am glad that it has not been found necessary to impose a ten-year moratorium on all childbearing. As matters stand, by limiting childbirth to a proportion of one child per circuit of the sun for each three deaths within any given district, scientists agree that the population of the earth will be reduced at a sufficient rate to relieve the tension.

The minority report, which favors providing more

room for the population by constructing various levels or concentric shells, which would gird the world's surface and to which additional levels would be added as needed, I utterly condemn. It is impractical chiefly for the reason that the conversion of so much material into these various dwelling surfaces would cause a serious shrinkage in the earth's mass.

Let us cast our votes in favor of the majority proposition, thus ensuring a long life for the human race and for the sphere on which we dwell, and removing the last cause of war between peoples of the earth.

FROM THE MEMOIRS OF XLAR XVII, PRINCEP OF PLES

Cycle 188, 400-43. What an abomination is this younger generation! I am glad the new rules limit offspring to not more than one in a district per cycle. My nephew, Ryk LVX, has been saturating himself with folklore at the Museum of Antiquity, and had the audacity to assure me that there are records which suggest the existence of mankind before plastoscene. Why will people befog their minds with the supernatural?

"There is a theory," he brazenly declared, "that at one time the world was partly composed of food, which burst up through its crust ready for the eating. It is claimed that even the carpet we now spread over the earth's surface had its correspondence in a substance which appeared there spontaneously."

"In that case," I retorted sarcastically, "what became of this—this exudation of the rocks?"

Of course, he had an answer ready: "Plastoscene was discovered and offered mankind an easier method of supplying its needs, with the result that the surface of the earth, containing the growth principle, was stripped away. I do not say that this is a fact," he hastened to add, "but merely that it may have some basis."

Here is what I told my nephew. I sincerely tried to be patient and to appeal to his common sense. "The basis in fact is this: It is true that the earth's surface has been many times stripped during the long existence of the human race. There is only one reasonable theory of life on this planet. Originally man—or rather his evolutionary predecessor—possessed within himself a digestive apparatus much wider in scope than at present. He consumed the rock, converted it into food, and thence into the elements necessary to feed his tissues, all within his own body. Eventually, as he developed intelligence, man learned how to produce plastoscene by mechanical means. He consumed this product as food, as well as using it for the myriad other purposes of his daily life. As a result, the organs within his own body no longer were needed to produce plastoscene directly from the rock. They gradually atrophied and disappeared, leaving only their vestiges in the present digestive tract."

This silenced the young man for a time, but I have no doubt he will return later with some other fantastic delusion. On one occasion it was the legend that, instead of being twin planets, our earth and Luna were at one time of differing sizes, and that Luna revolved around the earth as some of the distant moons revolve around their primaries. This theory has been thoroughly discredited. It is true that there is a reduction of the earth's mass every time we scrape its surface to produce according to our needs; but it is incredible that the earth could ever have been several times the size of its companion planet, as these imaginative theorists would have us believe. They forget, no doubt, that the volume and mass of a large sphere is greater, in proportion to its area and consequent human population, than that of a smaller sphere. Our planet even now would supply man for an incomprehensible time, yet it represents but a tiny fraction of such a mass as these theorists would have us believe in. They forget that diminution would proceed at an ever-mounting rate as the size decreased; that such a huge sphere as they proposed would have lasted forever.

It is impossible. As impossible as to imagine that a time will come when there will be no more Earth for man's conversion.

THE CREATURE FROM CLEVELAND DEPTHS

by Fritz Leiber

Fritz Leiber (1910-1992) may be best known for his excellent sword-and-sorcery stories (a term he coined decades ago, incidentally) of Faſhrd and the Gray Mouser, and for his brilliant stories of supernatural horror ("Smoke Ghost" and "Gonna Roll the Bones," to name two unforgettable tales written decades apart), but he also penned a large and brilliant body of science fiction novels (Gather, Darkness and the Hugo-winner, The Wanderer, for example) and shorter works. Such as this brilliant piece.

((I))

"COME ON, GUSSY," Fay prodded quietly, "quit stalking around like a neurotic bear and suggest something for my invention team to work on. I enjoy visiting you and Daisy, but I can't stay aboveground all night."

"If being outside the shelters makes you nervous, don't come around any more," Gusterson told him, continuing to stalk. "Why doesn't your invention team think of something to invent? Why don't you? Hah!" In the "Hah!" lay triumphant condemnation of a whole way of life.

"We do," Fay responded imperturbably, "but a fresh viewpoint sometimes helps."

"I'll say it does! Fay, you burglar, I'll bet you've got twenty people like myself you milk for free ideas. First you irritate their bark and then you make the rounds every so often to draw off the latex or the maple gloop."

Fay smiled. "It ought to please you that society still has a use for you outré inner-directed types. It takes something to make a junior executive stay aboveground after dark, when the missiles are on the prowl."

"Society can't have much use for us or it'd pay us something," Gusterson sourly asserted, staring blankly at the tankless TV and kicking it lightly as he passed on.

"No, you're wrong about that, Gussy. Money's not the key goad with you inner-directeds. I got that straight from our Motivations chief."

"Did he tell you what we should use instead to pay the grocer? A deep inner sense of achievement, maybe? Fay, why should I do any free thinking for Micro Systems?"

"I'll tell you why, Gussy. Simply because you get a kick out of insulting us with sardonic ideas. If we take one of them seriously, you think we're degrading ourselves, and that pleases you even more. Like making someone laugh at a lousy pun."

Gusterson held still in his roaming and grinned. "That the reason, huh? I suppose my suggestions would have to be something in the line of ultra-subminiaturized computers, where one sinister fine-etched molecule does the work of three big bumbling brain cells?"

"Not necessarily. Micro Systems is branching out. Wheel as free as a rogue star. But I'll pass along to Promotion your one molecule-three brain cell sparkler. It's a slight exaggeration, but it's catchy."

"I'll have my kids watch your ads to see if you use it and then I'll sue the whole underworld." Gusterson frowned as he resumed his stalking. He stared puzzledly at the antique TV. "How about inventing a plutonium termite?" he said suddenly. "It would get rid of those stockpiles that are worrying you moles to death."

Fay grimaced noncommittally and cocked his head.

"Well, then, how about a beauty mask? How about that, hey? I don't mean one to repair a woman's complexion, but one she'd wear all the time that'd make her look like a 17-year-old sexpot. That'd end her worries."

"Hey, that's for me," Daisy called from the kitchen. "I'll make Gusterson suffer. I'll make him crawl around on his hands and knees begging my immature favors."

"No, you won't," Gusterson called back. "You having a face like that would scare the kids. Better cancel that one, Fay. Half the adult race looking like Vina Vidarsson is too awful a thought."

"Yah, you're just scared of making a million dollars," Daisy jeered.

"I sure am," Gusterson said solemnly, scanning the fuzzy floor from one murky glass wall to the other, hesitating at the TV. "How about something homey now, like a flock of little prickly cylinders that roll around the floor collecting lint and flub? They'd work by electricity, or at a pinch cats could bat 'em around. Every so often they'd be automatically herded together and the lint cleaned off the bristles."

"No good," Fay said. "There's no lint underground and cats are *verboten*. And the aboveground market doesn't amount to more moneywise than the state of Southern Illinois. Keep it grander, Gussy, and more impractical— you can't sell people merely useful ideas." From his hassock in the center of the room he looked uneasily around. "Say, did that violet tone in the glass come from the high Cleveland hydrogen bomb or is it just age and ultraviolet, like desert glass?"

"No, somebody's grandfather liked it that color," Gusterson informed him with happy bitterness. "I like it too—the glass, I mean, not the tint. People who live in glass houses can see the stars—especially when there's a window-washing streak in their germ-plasm."

"Gussy, why don't you move underground?" Fay asked, his voice taking on a missionary note. "It's a lot easier living in one room, believe me. You don't have to tramp from room to room hunting things."

"I like the exercise," Gusterson said stoutly.

"But I bet Daisy'd prefer it underground. And your kids wouldn't have to explain why their father lives like a Red Indian. Not to mention the safety factor and insurance savings and a crypt church within easy slidewalk distance. Incidentally, we see the stars all the time, better than you do—by repeater."

"Stars by repeater," Gusterson murmured to the ceiling, pausing for God to comment. Then, "No, Fay, even if I could afford it—and stand it—I'm such a bad-luck Harry that just when I got us all safely stowed at the N minus 1 sublevel, the Soviets would discover an earthquake bomb that struck from below, and I'd have to follow everybody back to the treetops. *Hey! How about bubble homes in orbit around earth?* Micro Systems could subdivide the world's most spacious suburb and all you moles could go ellipsing. Space is as safe as there is: no air, no shock waves. Free fall's the ultimate in restfulness—great health benefits. Commute by rocket—or better yet stay home and do all your business by TV-telephone, or by waldo if it were that sort of thing. Even pet your girl by remote control—she in her bubble, you in yours, whizzing through vacuum. Oh, damn-damn-*damn-damn*-DAMN!"

He was glaring at the blank screen of the TV, his big hands clenching and unclenching.

"Don't let Fay give you apoplexy—he's not worth it," Daisy said, sticking her trim head in from the kitchen, while Fay inquired anxiously, "Gussy, what's the matter?"

"Nothing, you worm!" Gusterson roared, "Except that an hour ago I forgot to tune in on the only TV program I've wanted to hear this year—*Finnegan's Wake* scored for English, Gaelic and brogue. Oh, damn-*damn*-DAMN!"

"Too bad," Fay said lightly. "I didn't know they were releasing it on flat TV too."

"Well, they were! Some things are too damn big to keep completely underground. And I had to forget! I'm always doing it—I miss everything! Look here, you rat," he blatted suddenly at Fay, shaking his finger under the latter's chin, "I'll tell you what you can have that ignorant team of yours invent. They can fix me up a mechanical secretary that I can feed orders into and that'll remind me when the exact moment comes to listen to TV or phone somebody or mail in a story or write a letter or pick up a magazine or look at an eclipse or a new orbiting station or fetch the kids from school or buy Daisy a bunch of flowers or whatever it is. It's got to be something that's always with me, not something I have to go and consult or that I can get sick of and put down somewhere. And it's got to remind me forcibly enough so that I take notice and don't just shrug it aside, like I sometimes do even when Daisy reminds me of things. That's what your stupid team can invent for me! If they do a good job, I'll pay 'em as much as fifty dollars!"

"That doesn't sound like anything so very original to me," Fay commented coolly, leaning back from the wagging finger. "I think all senior executives have something of that sort. At least, their secretary keeps some kind of file. . . ."

"I'm not looking for something with spiked falsies and nylons up to the neck," interjected Gusterson, whose ideas about secretaries were a trifle lurid. "I just want a mech reminder—that's all!"

"Well, I'll keep the idea in mind," Fay assured him, "along with the bubble homes and beauty masks. If we ever develop anything along those lines, I'll let you know. If it's a beauty mask, I'll bring Daisy a pilot model—to use to scare strange kids." He put his watch to his ear. "Good lord, I'm going to have to cut to make it underground before the main doors close. Just ten minutes to Second Curfew! 'By, Gus. 'By, Daze."

Two minutes later, living room lights out, they watched Fay's foreshortened antlike figure scurrying across the balding ill-lit park toward the nearest escalator.

Gusterson said, "Weird to think of that big bright space-poor glamor basement stretching around everywhere underneath. Did you remind Smitty to put a new bulb in the elevator?"

"The Smiths moved out this morning," Daisy said tonelessly. "They went underneath."

"Like cockroaches," Gusterson said. "Cockroaches leavin' a sinkin' apartment building. Next the ghosts'll be retreatin' to the shelters."

"Anyhow, from now on we're our own janitors," Daisy said.

He nodded. "Just leaves three families besides us loyal to this glass death trap. Not countin' ghosts." He sighed. Then, "You like to move below, Daisy?" he asked softly, putting his arm lightly across her shoulders. "Get a woozy eyeful of the bright lights and all for a change? Be a rat for a while? Maybe we're getting too old to be bats. I could scrounge me a company job and have a thinking closet all to myself and two secretaries with stainless steel breasts. Life'd be easier for you and a lot cleaner. And you'd sleep safer."

"That's true," she answered and paused. She ran her fingertip slowly across the murky glass, its violet tint barely perceptible against a cold dim light across the park. "But somehow," she said, snaking her arm around his waist, "I don't think I'd sleep happier—or one bit excited."

(ℐ II ℐ)

THREE WEEKS LATER Fay, dropping in again, handed to Daisy the larger of the two rather small packages he was carrying.

"It's a so-called beauty mask," he told her, "complete with wig, eyelashes, and wettable velvet lips. It even breathes—pinholed elastiskin with a static adherence-charge. But Micro Systems had nothing to do with it, thank God. Beauty Trix put it on the market ten days ago and it's already started a teen-age craze. Some boys are wearing them too, and the police are yipping at Trix for encouraging transvestism with psychic repercussions."

"Didn't I hear somewhere that Trix is a secret subsidiary of Micro?" Gusterson demanded, rearing up from his ancient electric typewriter. "No, you're not stopping me writing, Fay—it's the gut of evening. If I do any more I won't have any juice to start with tomorrow. I got another of my insanity thrillers moving. A real id-teaser. In this one not only all the characters are crazy but the robot psychiatrist too."

"The vending machines are jumping with insanity novels," Fay commented. "Odd they're so popular."

Gusterson chortled. "The only way you outer-directed moles will accept individuality any more even in a fictional character, without your superegos getting seasick, is for them to be crazy. Hey, Daisy! Lemme see that beauty mask!"

But his wife, backing out of the room, hugged the package to her bosom and solemnly shook her head.

"A hell of a thing," Gusterson complained, "not even to be able to see what my stolen ideas look like."

"I got a present for you too," Fay said. "Something you might think of as a royalty on all the inventions someone thought of a little ahead of you. Fifty dollars by your own evaluation." He held out the smaller package. "Your tickler."

"My *what?*" Gusterson demanded suspiciously.

"Your tickler. The mech reminder you wanted. It turns out that the file a secretary keeps to remind her boss to do certain things at certain times is called a tickler file. So we named this a tickler. Here."

Gusterson still didn't touch the package. "You mean you actually put your invention team to work on that nonsense?"

"Well, what do you think? Don't be scared of it. Here, I'll show you."

As he unwrapped the package, Fay said, "It hasn't been decided yet whether we'll manufacture it commercially. If we do, I'll put through a voucher for you—for 'development consultation' or something like that. Sorry no royalty's possible. Davidson's squad had started to work up the identical idea three years ago, but it got shelved. I found it on a snoop through the closets. There! Looks rich, doesn't it?"

On the scarred black tabletop was a dully gleaming silvery object about the size and shape of a cupped hand with fingers merging. A tiny pellet on a short near-invisible wire led off from it. On the back was a punctured area suggesting the face of a microphone; there was also a window with a date and time in hours and minutes showing through and next to that four little buttons in a row. The concave underside of the silvery "hand" was smooth except for a central area where what looked like two little rollers came through.

"It goes on your shoulder under your shirt," Fay explained, "and you tuck the pellet in your ear. We might work up bone conduction on a commercial model. Inside is an ultra-slow fine-wire recorder holding a spool that runs for a week. The clock lets you go to any place on the 7-day wire and record a message. The buttons give you variable speed in going there, so you don't waste too much time making a setting. There's a knack in fingering them efficiently, but it's easily acquired."

Fay picked up the tickler. "For instance, suppose there's a TV show you want to catch tomorrow night at twenty-two hundred." He touched the buttons. There was the faintest whirring. The clock face blurred briefly three times before showing the setting he'd mentioned. Then Fay spoke into the punctured area: "Turn on TV Channel Two, you big dummy!" He grinned over at Gusterson. "When you've got all your instructions to yourself loaded in, you synchronize with the present moment and let her roll. Fit it on your shoulder and forget it. Oh, yes, and it literally does tickle you every time it delivers an instruction. That's what the little rollers are for. Believe me, you can't ignore it. Come on, Gussy, take off your shirt and try it out. We'll feed in some instructions for the next ten minutes so you get the feel of how it works."

"I don't want to," Gusterson said. "Not right now. I want to sniff around it first. My God, it's small! Besides everything else it does, does it think?"

"Don't pretend to be an idiot, Gussy! You know very well that even with ultra-sub-micro nothing quite this small can possibly have enough elements to do any thinking."

Gusterson shrugged. "I don't know about that. I think bugs think."

Fay groaned faintly. "Bugs operate by instinct, Gussy," he said. "A patterned routine. They do not scan situations and consequences and then make decisions."

"I don't expect bugs to make decisions," Gusterson said. "For that matter I don't like people who go around alla time making decisions."

"Well, you can take it from me, Gussy, that this tickler is just a miniaturized wire recorder and clock . . . and a tickler. It doesn't do anything else."

"Not yet, maybe," Gusterson said darkly. "Not this model. Fay, I'm serious about bugs thinking. Or if they don't exactly think, they feel. They've got an interior drama. An inner glow. They're conscious. For that matter, Fay, I think all your really complex electronic computers are conscious too."

"Quit kidding, Gussy."

"Who's kidding?"

"You are. Computers simply aren't alive."

"What's *alive*? A word. I think computers are conscious, at least while they're operating. They've got that inner glow of awareness. They sort of . . . well . . . meditate."

"Gussy, computers haven't got any circuits for meditating. They're not programmed for mystical lucubrations. They've just got circuits for solving the problems they're on."

"Okay, you admit they've got problem-solving circuits—like a man has. I say if they've got the equipment for being conscious, they're conscious. What has wings, flies."

"Including stuffed owls and gilt eagles and dodoes—and wood-burning airplanes?"

"Maybe, under some circumstances. There was a wood-burning airplane. Fay," Gusterson continued, wagging his wrists for emphasis, "I really think computers are conscious. They just don't have any way of telling us that they are. Or maybe they don't have any reason to tell us, like the little Scotch boy who didn't say a word until he was fifteen and was supposed to be deaf and dumb."

"Why didn't he say a word?"

"Because he'd never had anything to say. Or take those Hindu fakirs, Fay, who sit still and don't say a word for thirty years or until their fingernails grow to the next village. If Hindu fakirs can do that, computers can!"

Looking as if he were masticating a lemon, Fay asked quietly, "Gussy, did you say you're working on an insanity novel?"

Gusterson frowned fiercely. "Now you're kidding," he accused Fay. "The dirty kind of kidding, too."

"I'm sorry," Fay said with light contrition. "Well, now you've sniffed at it, how about trying on Tickler?" He picked up the gleaming blunted crescent and jogged it temptingly under Gusterson's chin.

"Why should I?" Gusterson asked, stepping back. "Fay, I'm up to my ears writing a book. The last thing I want is something interrupting me to make me listen to a lot of junk and do a lot of useless things."

"But, dammit, Gussy! It was all your idea in the first place!" Fay blatted. Then, catching himself, he added, "I mean, you were one of the first people to think of this particular sort of instrument."

"Maybe so, but I've done some more thinking since then." Gusterson's voice grew a trifle solemn. "Inner-directed worthwhile thinkin'. Fay, when a man forgets to do something, it's because he really doesn't want to do it or because he's all roiled up down in his unconscious. He ought to take it as a danger signal and investigate the roiling, not hire himself a human or mech reminder."

"Bushwa," Fay retorted. "In that case you shouldn't write memorandums or even take notes."

"Maybe I shouldn't," Gusterson agreed lamely. "I'd have to think that over too."

"Ha!" Fay jeered. "No, I'll tell you what your trouble is, Gussy. You're simply scared of this contraption. You've loaded your skull with horror-story nonsense about machines sprouting minds and taking over the world— until you're even scared of a simple miniaturized and clocked recorder." He thrust it out.

"Maybe I am," Gusterson admitted, controlling a flinch. "Honestly, Fay, that thing's got a gleam in its eye as if it had ideas of its own. Nasty ideas."

"Gussy, you nut, it hasn't *got* an eye."

"Not now, no, but it's got the gleam—the eye may come. It's the Cheshire cat in reverse. If you'd step over here and look at yourself holding it, you could see what I mean. But I don't think computers *sprout* minds, Fay. I just think they've *got* minds, because they've got the mind elements."

"Ho, ho!" Fay mocked. "Everything that has a material side has a mental side," he chanted. "Everything that's a body is also a spirit. Gussy, that dubious old metaphysical dualism went out centuries ago."

"Maybe so," Gusterson said, "but we still haven't anything but that dubious dualism to explain the human mind, have we? It's a jelly of nerve cells and it's a vision of the cosmos. If that isn't dualism, what is?"

"I give up. Gussy, are you going to try out this tickler?"

"No!"

"But dammit, Gussy, we made it just for you!—practically."

"Sorry, but I'm not coming near the thing."

"Zen come near me," a husky voice intoned behind them. "Tonight I vant a man."

Standing in the door was something slim in a short silver sheath. It had golden bangs and the haughtiest snub-nosed face in the world. It slunk toward them.

"My God, Vina Vidarsson!" Gusterson yelled.

"Daisy, that's terrific," Fay applauded, going up to her.

She bumped him aside with a swing of her hips, continuing to advance. "Not you, Ratty," she said throatily. "I vant a real man."

"Fay, I suggested Vina Vidarsson's face for the beauty mask," Gusterson said, walking around his wife and shaking a finger. "Don't tell me Trix just happened to think of that too."

"What else could they think of?" Fay laughed. "This season sex means VV and nobody else." An odd little grin flicked his lips, a tic traveled up his face and his body twitched slightly. "Say, folks, I'm going to have to be leaving. It's exactly fifteen minutes to Second Curfew. Last time I had to run and I got heartburn. When are you people going to move downstairs? I'll leave Tickler, Gussy. Play around with it and get used to it. 'By now."

"Hey, Fay," Gusterson called curiously, "have you developed absolute time sense?"

Fay grinned a big grin from the doorway—almost too big a grin for so small a man. "I didn't need to," he said softly, patting his right shoulder. "My tickler told me."

He closed the door behind him.

As side-by-side they watched him strut sedately across the murky chilly-looking park, Gusterson mused, "So the little devil had one of those nonsense-gadgets on all the time and I never noticed. Can you beat that?" Something drew across the violet-tinged stars a short bright line that quickly faded. "What's that?" Gusterson asked gloomily. "Next to last stage of missile—here?"

"Won't you settle for an old-fashioned shooting star?" Daisy asked softly. The (wettable) velvet lips of the mask made even her natural voice sound different. She reached a hand back of her neck to pull the thing off.

"Hey, don't do that," Gusterson protested in a hurt voice. "Not for a while anyway."

"Hokay!" she said harshly, turning on him. "Zen down on your knees, dog!"

((**III**))

IT WAS A FORTNIGHT and Gusterson was loping down the home stretch on his 40,000-word insanity novel before Fay dropped in again, this time promptly at high noon.

Normally Fay cringed his shoulders a trifle and was inclined to slither, but now he strode aggressively, his legs scissoring in a fast, low goosestep. He whipped off the sunglasses that all moles wore topside by day and began to pound Gusterson on the back while calling boisterously, "How are you, Gussy Old Boy, Old Boy?"

Daisy came in from the kitchen to see why Gusterson was choking. She was instantly grabbed and violently bussed to the accompaniment of, "Hiya, Gorgeous! Yum-yum! How about ad-libbing that some weekend?"

She stared at Fay dazedly, rasping the back of her hand across her mouth, while Gusterson yelled, "Quit that! What's got into you, Fay? Have they transferred you out of R&D to Company Morale? Do they line up all the secretaries at roll call and make you give them an eight-hour energizing kiss?"

"Ha, wouldn't you like to know?" Fay retorted. He grinned, twitched jumpingly, held still a moment, then hustled over to the far wall. "Look out there," he rapped, pointing through the violet glass at a gap between the two nearest old skyscraper apartments. "In thirty seconds you'll see them test the new needle bomb at the other end of Lake Erie. It's educational." He began to count off seconds, vigorously semaphoring his arm. ". . . Two . . . three . . . Gussy, I've put through a voucher for two yards for you. Budgeting squawked, but I pressured 'em."

Daisy squealed, "Yards!—are those dollar thousands?" while Gusterson was asking, "Then you're marketing the tickler?"

"Yes. Yes," Fay replied to them in turn. ". . . Nine . . . ten . . ." Again he grinned and twitched. "Time for noon Com-staff," he announced staccato. "Pardon the hush box." He whipped a pancake phone from under his coat, clapped it over his face and spoke fiercely but inaudibly into it, continuing to semaphore. Suddenly he thrust the phone away. "Twenty-nine . . . thirty . . . Thar she blows!"

An incandescent streak shot up the sky from a little above the far horizon and a doubly dazzling point of light appeared just above the top of it, with the effect of God dotting an "i."

"Ha, that'll skewer espionage satellites like swatting flies!" Fay proclaimed as the portent faded. "Bracing! Gussy, where's your tickler? I've got a new spool for it that'll razzle-dazzle you."

"I'll bet," Gusterson said drily. "Daisy?"

"You gave it to the kids and they got to fooling with it and broke it."

"No matter," Fay told them with a large sidewise sweep of his hand. "Better you wait for the new model. It's a six-way improvement."

"So I gather," Gusterson said, eyeing him speculatively. "Does it automatically inject you with cocaine? A fix every hour on the second?"

"Ha-ha, joke. Gussy, it achieves the same effect without using any dope at all. Listen: a tickler reminds you of your duties and opportunities—your chances for happiness and success! What's the obvious next step?"

"Throw it out the window. By the way, how do you do that when you're underground?"

"We have hi-speed garbage boosts. The obvious next step is you give the tickler a heart. It not only tells you, it warmly persuades you. It doesn't just say, 'Turn on the TV Channel Two, Joyce program,' it *brills* at you, 'Kid, Old Kid, race for the TV and flip that Two Switch! There's a great show coming through the pipes this second plus ten—you'll enjoy the hell out of yourself! Grab a ticket to ecstasy!'"

"My God," Gusterson gasped, "are those the kind of jolts it's giving you now?"

"Don't you get it, Gussy? You never load your tickler except when you're feeling buoyantly enthusiastic. You don't just tell yourself what to do hour by hour next week, you sell yourself on it. That way you not only make doubly sure you'll obey instructions but you constantly reinoculate yourself with your own enthusiasm."

"I can't stand myself when I'm that enthusiastic," Gusterson said. "I feel ashamed for hours afterwards."

"You're warped—all this lonely sky-life. What's more, Gussy, think how still more persuasive some of those instructions would be if they came to a man in his best girl's most bedroomy voice, or his doctor's or psycher's if it's that sort of thing—or Vina Vidarsson's! By the way, Daze, don't wear that beauty mask outside. It's a grand misdemeanor ever since ten thousand teen-agers rioted through Tunnel-Mart wearing them. And VV's suing Trix."

"No chance of that," Daisy said. "Gusterson got excited and bit off the nose." She pinched her own delicately. "I'd no more obey my enthusiastic self," Gusterson was brooding, "than I'd obey a Napoleon drunk on his own brandy or a hopped-up St. Francis. Reinoculated with my own enthusiasm? I'd die just like from snake-bite!"

"Warped, I said," Fay dogmatized, stamping around. "Gussy, having the instructions persuasive instead of neutral turned out to be only the opening wedge. The next step wasn't so obvious, but I saw it. Using subliminal verbal stimuli in his tickler, a man can be given constant supportive euphoric therapy 24 hours a day! And it makes use of all that empty wire. We've revived the ideas of a pioneer dynamic psycher named Dr. Coué. For instance, right now my tickler is saying to me—in tones too soft to reach my conscious mind, but do they stab into the unconscious!—'Day by day in every way I'm getting sharper and sharper.' It alternates that with 'gutsier and gutsier' and . . . well, forget that. Coue mostly used 'better and better' but that seems too general. And every hundredth time it says them out loud and the tickler gives me a brush—just a faint cootch—to make sure I'm keeping in touch."

"That third word-pair," Daisy wondered, feeling her mouth reminiscently. "Could I guess?"

Gusterson's eyes had been growing wider and wider. "Fay," he said, "I could no more use my mind for anything if I knew all that was going on in my inner ear than if I were being brushed down with brooms by three witches. Look here," he said with loud authority, "you got to stop all this—it's crazy. Fay, if Micro'll junk the tickler, I'll think you up something else to invent—something real good."

"Your inventing days are over," Fay brilled gleefully. "I mean, you'll never equal your masterpiece."

"How about," Gusterson bellowed, "an anti-individual guided missile? The physicists have got small-scale antigravity good enough to float and fly something the size of a hand grenade. I can smell that even though it's a back-of-the-safe military secret. Well, how about keying such a missile to a man's finger-prints—or brainwaves, maybe, or his unique smell!—so it can spot and follow him around then target in on him, without harming anyone else? Long-distance assassination—and the stinkingest gets it! Or you could simply load it with some disgusting goo and key it to teen-agers as a group—that'd take care of them. Fay, doesn't it give you a rich warm kick to think of my midget missiles buzzing around in your tunnels, seeking out evil-doers, like a swarm of angry wasps or angelic bumblebees?"

"You're not luring me down any side trails," Fay said laughingly. He grinned and twitched, then hurried toward the opposite wall, motioning them to follow. Outside, about a hundred yards beyond the purple glass, rose another ancient glass-walled apartment skyscraper. Beyond, Lake Erie rippled glintingly.

"Another bomb-test?" Gusterson asked.

Fay pointed at the building. "Tomorrow," he announced, "a modern factory, devoted solely to the manufacture of ticklers, will be erected on that site."

"You mean one of those windowless phallic eyesores?"

Gusterson demanded. "Fay, you people aren't even consistent. You've got all your homes underground. Why not your factories?"

"Sh! Not enough room. And night missiles are scarier."

"I know that building's been empty for a year," Daisy said uneasily, "but how—?"

"Sh! Watch! *Now!*"

The looming building seemed to blur or fuzz for a moment. Then it was as if the lake's bright ripples had invaded the old glass a hundred yards away. Wavelets chased themselves up and down the gleaming walls, became higher, higher . . . and then suddenly the glass cracked all over to tiny fragments and fell away, to be followed quickly by fragmented concrete and plastic and plastic piping, until all that was left was the nude steel framework, vibrating so rapidly as to be almost invisible against the gleaming lake.

Daisy covered her ears, but there was no explosion, only a long-drawn-out low crash as the fragments hit twenty floors below and dust whooshed out sideways.

"Spectacular!" Fay summed up. "Knew you'd enjoy it. That little trick was first conceived by the great Tesla during his last fruity years. Research discovered it in his biog—we just made the dream come true. A tiny resonance device you could carry in your belt-bag attunes itself to the natural harmonic of a structure and then increases amplitude by tiny pushes exactly in time. Just like soldiers marching in step can break down a bridge, only this is as if it were being done by one marching ant." He pointed at the naked framework appearing out of its own blur and said, "We'll be able to hang the factory on that. If not, we'll whip a mega-current through it and vaporize it. No question the micro-resonator is the neatest sweetest wrecking device going. You can expect a lot more of this sort of efficiency now that mankind has the tickler to enable him to use his full potential. What's the matter, folks?"

Daisy was staring around the violet-walled room with dumb mistrust. Her hands were trembling.

"You don't have to worry," Fay assured her with an understanding laugh. "This building's safe for a month more at least." Suddenly he grimaced and leaped a foot in the air. He raised a clawed hand to scratch his shoulder but managed to check the movement. "Got to beat it, folks," he announced tersely. "My tickler gave me the grand cootch."

"Don't go yet," Gusterson called, rousing himself with a shudder which he immediately explained: "I just had the illusion that if I shook myself all my flesh and guts would fall off my shimmying skeleton, brr! Fay, before you and Micro go off half cocked, I want you to know there's one insuperable objection to the tickler as a mass-market item. The average man or woman won't go to the considerable time and trouble it must take to load a tickler. He simply hasn't got the compulsive orderliness and willingness to plan that it requires."

"We thought of that weeks ago," Fay rapped, his hand on the door. "Every tickler spool that goes to market is patterned like wallpaper with one of five designs of suitable subliminal supportive euphoric material. 'Ittier and ittier,' 'viriler and viriler'—you know. The buyer is robot-interviewed for an hour, his personalized daily

routine laid out and thereafter templated on his weekly
spool. He's strongly urged next to take his tickler to his
doctor and psycher for further instruction-imposition.
We've been working with the medical profession from the
start. They love the tickler because it'll remind people to
take their medicine on the dot . . . and rest and eat and go
to sleep just when and how doc says. This is a big
operation, Gussy—a biiiiiig operation! 'By!"

Daisy hurried to the wall to watch him cross the park.
Deep down she was a wee bit worried that he might linger
to attach a micro-resonator to this building and she
wanted to time him. But Gusterson settled down to his
typewriter and began to bat away.

"I want to have another novel started," he explained
to her, "before the ant marches across this building in
about four and a half weeks . . . or a million sharp little
gutsy guys come swarming out of the ground and heave it
into Lake Erie."

((IV))

EARLY NEXT MORNING windowless walls began to
crawl up the stripped skyscraper between them and the
lake. Daisy pulled the black-out curtains on that side. For
a day or two longer their thoughts and conversations were
haunted by Gusterson's vague sardonic visions of a horde
of tickler-energized moles pouring up out of the tunnels
to tear down the remaining trees, tank the atmosphere
and perhaps somehow dismantle the stars—at least on this

side of the world—but then they both settled back into their customary easy-going routines. Gusterson typed. Daisy made her daily shopping trip to a little topside daytime store and started painting a mural on the floor of the empty apartment next theirs but one.

"We ought to lasso some neighbors," she suggested once. "I need somebody to hold my brushes and admire. How about you making a trip below at the cocktail hours, Gusterson, and picking up a couple of girls for a starter? Flash the old viriler charm, cootch them up a bit, emphasize the delights of high living, but make sure they're compatible roommates. You could pick up that two-yard check from Micro at the same time."

"You're an immoral money-ravenous wench," Gusterson said absently, trying to dream of an insanity beyond insanity that would make his next novel a real id-rousing best-vender.

"If that's your vision of me, you shouldn't have chewed up the VV mask."

"I'd really prefer you with green stripes," he told her. "But stripes, spots, or sun-bathing, you're better than those cocktail moles."

Actually both of them acutely disliked going below. They much preferred to perch in their eyrie and watch the people of Cleveland Depths, as they privately called the local sub-suburb, rush up out of the shelters at dawn to work in the concrete fields and windowless factories, make their daytime jet trips and freeway jaunts, do their noon-hour and coffee-break guerrilla practice, and then go scurrying back at twilight to the atomic-proof, brightly lit, vastly exciting, claustrophobic caves.

Fay and his projects began once more to seem dreamlike, though Gusterson did run across a cryptic advertisement for ticklers in *The Manchester Guardian*, which he got daily by facsimile. Their three children reported similar ads, of no interest to young fry, on the TV and one afternoon they came home with the startling news that the monitors at their subsurface school had been issued ticklers. On sharp interrogation by Gusterson, however, it appeared that these last were not ticklers but merely two-way radios linked to the school police station transmitter.

"Which is bad enough," Gusterson commented later to Daisy. "But it'd be even dirtier to think of those clock-watching superegos being strapped to kids' shoulders. Can you imagine Huck Finn with a tickler, tellin' him when to tie up the raft to a tow-head and when to take a swim?"

"I bet Fay could," Daisy countered. "When's he going to bring you that check, anyhow? Iago wants a jetcycle and I promised Imogene a Vina Kit and then Claudius'll have to have something."

Gusterson scowled thoughtfully. "You know, Daze," he said, "I got a feeling Fay's in the hospital, all narcotized up and being fed intravenously. The way he was jumping around last time, that tickler was going to cootch him to pieces in a week."

As if to refute this intuition, Fay turned up that very evening. The lights were dim. Something had gone wrong with the building's old transformer and, pending repairs, the two remaining occupied apartments were making do with batteries, which turned bright globes to mysterious amber candles and made Gusterson's ancient typewriter operate sluggishly.

Fay's manner was subdued or at least closely controlled and for a moment Gusterson thought he'd shed his tickler. Then the little man came out of the shadows and Gusterson saw the large bulge on his right shoulder.

"Yes, we had to up it a bit sizewise," Fay explained in clipped tones. "Additional super-features. While brilliantly successful on the whole, the subliminal euphorics were a shade too effective. Several hundred users went hoppity manic. We gentled the cootch and qualified the subliminals—you know, 'Day by day in every way I'm getting sharper *and more serene*'—but a stabilizing influence was still needed, so after a top-level conference we decided to combine Tickler with Moodmaster."

"My God," Gusterson interjected, "do they have a machine now that does that?"

"Of course. They've been using them on ex-mental patients for years."

"I just don't keep up with progress," Gusterson said, shaking his head bleakly. "I'm falling behind on all fronts."

"You ought to have your tickler remind you to read Science Service releases," Fay told him. "Or simply instruct it to scan the releases and—no, that's still in research." He looked at Gusterson's shoulder and his eyes widened. "You're not wearing the new-model tickler I sent you," he said accusingly.

"I never got it," Gusterson assured him. "Postmen deliver topside mail and parcels by throwing them on the high-speed garbage boosts and hoping a tornado will blow them to the right addresses." Then he added helpfully, "Maybe the Russians stole it while it was riding the whirlwinds."

"That's not a suitable topic for jesting," Fay frowned. "We're hoping that Tickler will mobilize the full potential of the Free World for the first time in history. Gusterson, you are going to have to wear a ticky-tick. It's becoming impossible for a man to get through modern life without one."

"Maybe I will," Gusterson said appeasingly, "but right now tell me about Moodmaster. I want to put it in my new insanity novel."

Fay shook his head. "Your readers will just think you're behind the times. If you use it, underplay it. But anyhow, Moodmaster is a simple physiotherapy engine that monitors bloodstream chemicals and body electricity. It ties directly into the bloodstream, keeping blood sugar, et cetera, at optimum levels and injecting euphrin or depressin as necessary—and occasionally a touch of extra adrenaline, as during work emergencies."

"Is it painful?" Daisy called from the bedroom.

"Excruciating," Gusterson called back. "Excuse it, please," he grinned at Fay. "Hey, didn't I suggest cocaine injections last time I saw you?"

"So you did," Fay agreed flatly. "Oh by the way, Gussy, here's that check for a yard I promised you. Micro doesn't muzzle the ox."

"Hooray!" Daisy cheered faintly.

"I thought you said it was going to be for two," Gusterson complained.

"Budgeting always forces a last-minute compromise," Fay shrugged. "You have to learn to accept those things."

"I love accepting money and I'm glad any time for three feet," Daisy called agreeably. "Six feet might make me wonder if I weren't an insect, but getting a yard just makes me feel like a gangster's moll."

"Want to come out and gloat over the yard paper, Toots, and stuff it in your diamond-embroidered net stocking top?" Gusterson called back.

"No, I'm doing something to that portion of me just now. But hang onto the yard, Gusterson."

"Aye-aye, Cap'n," he assured her. Then, turning back to Fay, "So you've taken the Dr. Coue repeating out of the tickler?"

"Oh, no. Just balanced it off with depressin. The subliminals are still a prime sales-point. All the tickler features are cumulative, Gussy. You're still underestimating the scope of the device."

"I guess I am. What's this 'work-emergencies' business? If you're using the tickler to inject drugs into workers to keep them going, that's really just my cocaine suggestion modernized and I'm putting in for another thou. Hundreds of years ago the South American Indians chewed coca leaves to kill fatigue sensations."

"That so? Interesting—and it proves priority for the Indians, doesn't it? I'll make a try for you, Gussy, but don't expect anything." He cleared his throat, his eyes grew distant and, turning his head a little to the right, he enunciated sharply, "Pooh-Bah. Time: Inst oh five. One oh five seven. Oh oh. Record: Gussy coca thou budget. Cut." He explained, "We got a voice-cued setter now on the deluxe models. You can record a memo to yourself without taking off your shirt. Incidentally, I use the ends of the hours for trifle-memos. I've already used up the fifty-nines and eights for tomorrow and started on the fifty-sevens."

"I understood most of your memo," Gusterson told him gruffly. "The last 'Oh oh' was for seconds, wasn't it? Now I call that crude—why not microseconds too? But how do you remember where you've made a memo so you don't rerecord over it? After all, you're rerecording over the wallpaper all the time."

"Tickler beeps and then hunts for the nearest information-free space."

"I see. And what's the Pooh-Bah for?"

Fay smiled. "Cut. My password for activating the setter, so it won't respond to chance numerals it overhears."

"But why Pooh-Bah?"

Fay grinned. "Cut. And you a writer. It's a literary reference, Gussy. Pooh-Bah (cut!) was Lord High Everything Else in *The Mikado*. He had a little list and nothing on it would ever be missed."

"Oh, yeah," Gusterson remembered, glowering. "As I recall it, all that went on that list was the names of people who were slated to have their heads chopped off by Ko-Ko. Better watch your step, Shorty. It may be a back-handed omen. Maybe all those workers you're puttin' ticklers on to pump them full of adrenaline so they'll overwork without noticin' it will revolt and come out some day choppin' for your head."

"Spare me the Marxist mythology," Fay protested.

"Gussy, you've got a completely wrong slant on Tickler. It's true that most of our mass sales so far, bar government and army, have been to large companies purchasing for their employees—"

"Ah-ha!"

"—but that's because there's nothing like a tickler for teaching a new man his job. It tells him from instant to instant what he must do—while he's already on the job and without disturbing other workers. Magnetizing a wire with a job pattern is the easiest thing going. And you'd be astonished what the subliminals do for employee morale. It's this way, Gussy: most people are too improvident and unimaginative to see in advance the advantages of ticklers. They buy one because the company strongly suggests it and payment is on easy installments withheld from salary. They find a tickler makes the work day go easier. The little fellow perched on your shoulder is a friend exuding comfort and good advice. The first thing he's set to say is 'Take it easy, pal.'

"Within a week they're wearing their tickler 24 hours a day—and buying a tickler for the wife, so she'll remember to comb her hair and smile real pretty and cook favorite dishes."

"I get it, Fay," Gusterson cut in. "The tickler is the newest fad for increasing worker efficiency. Once, I read somewheres, it was salt tablets. They had salt-tablet dispensers everywhere, even in air-conditioned offices where there wasn't a moist armpit twice a year and the gals sweat only champagne. A decade later people wondered what all those dusty white pills were for. Sometimes they were mistook for tranquilizers. It'll be the same way with ticklers. Somebody'll open a musty closet and see jumbled heaps of these gripping-hand silvery gadgets gathering dust curls and—"

"They will not!" Fay protested vehemently. "Ticklers are not a fad—they're history-changers, they're Free-World revolutionary! Why, before Micro Systems put a single one on the market, we'd made it a rule that every Micro employee had to wear one! If that's not having supreme confidence in a product—"

"Every employee except the top executives, of course," Gusterson interrupted jeeringly. "And that's not demoting you, Fay. As the R&D chief most closely involved, you'd naturally have to show special enthusiasm."

"But you're wrong there, Gussy," Fay crowed. "Man for man, our top executives have been more enthusiastic about their personal ticklers than any other class of worker in the whole outfit."

Gusterson slumped and shook his head. "If that's the case," he said darkly, "maybe mankind deserves the tickler."

"I'll say it does!" Fay agreed loudly without thinking. Then, "Oh, can the carping, Gussy. Tickler's a great invention. Don't deprecate it just because you had something to do with its genesis. You're going to have to get in the swim and wear one."

"Maybe I'd rather drown horribly."

"Can the gloom-talk too! Gussy, I said it before and I say it again, you're just scared of this new thing. Why, you've even got the drapes pulled so you won't have to look at the tickler factory."

"Yes, I am scared," Gusterson said. "Really sca . . . AWP!"

Fay whirled around. Daisy was standing in the bedroom doorway, wearing the short silver sheath. This time there was no mask, but her bobbed hair was glitteringly silvered, while her legs, arms, hands, neck, face—every bit of her exposed skin—was painted with beautifully even vertical green stripes.

"I did it as a surprise for Gusterson," she explained to Fay. "He says he likes me this way. The green glop's supposed to be smudgeproof."

Gusterson did not comment. His face had a rapt expression. "I'll tell you why your tickler's so popular, Fay," he said softly. "It's not because it backstops the memory or because it boosts the ego with subliminals. It's because it takes the hook out of a guy, it takes over the job of withstanding the pressure of living. See, Fay, here are all these little guys in this subterranean rat race with atomic-death squares and chromium-plated reward squares and enough money if you pass Go almost to get to Go again—and a million million rules of the game to keep in mind. Well, here's this one little guy and every morning he wakes up there's all these things he's got to keep in mind to do or he'll lose his turn three times in a row and maybe a terrible black rook in iron armor'll loom up and bang him off the chessboard. But now, look, now he's got his tickler and he tells his sweet silver tickler all these things and the tickler's got to remember them. Of course he'll have to do them eventually but meanwhile the pressure's off him, the hook's out of his short hairs. He's shifted the responsibility. . . ."

"Well, what's so bad about that?" Fay broke in loudly. "What's wrong with taking the pressure off little guys? Why shouldn't Tickler be a super-ego surrogate? Micro's

Motivations chief noticed that positive feature straight off and scored it three pluses. Besides, it's nothing but a gaudy way of saying that Tickler backstops the memory. Seriously, Gussy, what's so bad about it?"

"I don't know," Gusterson said slowly, his eyes still far away. "I just know it feels bad to me." He crinkled his big forehead. "Well for one thing," he said, "it means that a man's taking orders from something else. He's got a kind of master. He's sinking back into a slave psychology."

"He's only taking orders from himself," Fay countered disgustedly. "Tickler's just a mech reminder, a notebook, in essence no more than the back of an old envelope. It's no master."

"Are you absolutely sure of that?" Gusterson asked quietly.

"Why, Gussy, you big oaf—" Fay began heatedly. Suddenly his features quirked and he twitched. "'Scuse me, folks," he said rapidly, heading for the door, "but my tickler told me I gotta go."

"Hey Fay, don't you mean you told your tickler to tell you when it was time to go?" Gusterson called after him.

Fay looked back in the doorway. He wet his lips, his eyes moved from side to side. "I'm not quite sure," he said in an odd strained voice and darted out.

Gusterson stared for some seconds at the pattern of emptiness Fay had left. Then he shivered. Then he shrugged. "I must be slipping," he muttered. "I never even suggested something for him to invent." Then he looked around at Daisy, who was still standing poker-faced in her doorway.

"Hey, you look like something out of the Arabian Nights," he told her. "Are you supposed to be anything special? How far do those stripes go, anyway?"

"You could probably find out," she told him coolly. "All you have to do is kill me a dragon or two first."

He studied her. "My God," he said reverently, "I really have all the fun in life. What do I do to deserve this?"

"You've got a big gun," she told him, "and you go out in the world with it and hold up big companies and take yards and yards of money away from them in rolls like ribbon and bring it all home to me."

"Don't say that about the gun again," he said. "Don't whisper it, don't even think it. I've got one, dammit— thirty-eight caliber, yet—and I don't want some psionic monitor with two-way clairaudience they haven't told me about catching the whisper and coming to take the gun away from us. It's one of the few individuality symbols we've got left."

Suddenly Daisy whirled away from the door, spun three times so that her silvered hair stood out like a metal coolie hat, and sank to a curtsey in the middle of the room.

"I've just thought of what I am," she announced, fluttering her eyelashes at him. "I'm a sweet silver tickler with green stripes."

((**V**))

NEXT DAY DAISY cashed the Micro check for ten hundred silver smackers, which she hid in a broken radionic coffee urn. Gusterson sold his insanity novel and started a new one about a mad medic with a hiccupy hysterical chuckle, who gimmicked Moodmasters to turn mental patients into nymphomaniacs, mass murderers and compulsive saints. But this time he couldn't get Fay out of his mind, or the last chilling words the nervous little man had spoken.

For that matter, he couldn't blank the underground out of his mind as effectively as usually. He had the feeling that a new kind of mole was loose in the burrows and that the ground at the foot of their skyscraper might start humping up any minute.

Toward the end of one afternoon he tucked a half dozen newly typed sheets in his pocket, shrouded his typer, went to the hatrack and took down his prize: a miner's hard-top cap with electric headlamp.

"Goin' below, Cap'n," he shouted toward the kitchen.

"Be back for second dog watch," Daisy replied. "Remember what I told you about lassoing me some art-conscious girl neighbors."

"Only if I meet a piebald one with a taste for Scotch—or maybe a pearl gray biped jaguar with violet spots," Gusterson told her, clapping on the cap with a We-Who-Are-About-To-Die gesture.

Halfway across the park to the escalator bunker Gusterson's heart began to tick. He resolutely switched on his headlamp.

As he'd known it would, the hatch robot whirred an extra and higher-pitched ten seconds when it came to his topside address, but it ultimately dilated the hatch for him, first handing him a claim check for his ID card.

Gusterson's heart was ticking like a sledgehammer by now. He hopped clumsily onto the escalator, clutched the moving guard rail to either side, then shut his eyes as the steps went over the edge and became what felt like vertical. An instant later he forced his eyes open, unclipped a hand from the rail and touched the second switch beside his headlamp, which instantly began to blink whitely, as if he were a civilian plane flying into a nest of military jobs.

With a further effort he kept his eyes open and flinchingly surveyed the scene around him. After zigging through a bombproof half-furlong of roof, he was dropping into a large twilit cave. The blue-black ceiling twinkled with stars. The walls were pierced at floor level by a dozen archways with busy niche stores and glowing advertisements crowded between them. From the archways some three dozen slidewalks curved out, tangenting off each other in a bewildering multiple cloverleaf. The slidewalks were packed with people, traveling motionless like purposeful statues or pivoting with practiced grace from one slidewalk to another, like a thousand toreros doing veronicas.

The slidewalks were moving faster than he recalled from his last venture underground and at the same time the whole pedestrian concourse was quieter than he remembered. It was as if the five thousand or so moles in view were all listening—for what? But there was something else that had changed about them—a change that he couldn't for a moment define, or unconsciously didn't want to. Clothing style? No . . . My God, they weren't all wearing identical monster masks? No . . . Hair color?. . . Well . . .

He was studying them so intently that he forgot his escalator was landing. He came off it with a heel-jarring stumble and bumped into a knot of four men on the tiny triangular hold-still. These four at least sported a new style-wrinkle: ribbed gray shoulder-capes that made them look as if their heads were poking up out of the center of bulgy umbrellas or giant mushrooms.

One of them grabbed hold of Gusterson and saved him from staggering onto a slidewalk that might have carried him to Toledo.

"Gussy, you dog, you must have esped I wanted to see you," Fay cried, patting him on the elbows. "Meet Davidson and Kester and Hazen, colleagues of mine. We're all Micro-men." Fay's companions were staring strangely at Gusterson's blinking headlamp. Fay explained rapidly, "Mr. Gusterson is an insanity novelist. You know, I-D."

"Inner-directed spells id," Gusterson said absently, still staring at the interweaving crowd beyond them, trying to figure out what made them different from last trip. "Creativity fuel. Cranky. Explodes through the parietal fissure if you look at it cross-eyed."

"Ha-ha," Fay laughed. "Well, boys, I've found my man. How's the new novel perking, Gussy?"

"Got my climax, I think," Gusterson mumbled, still peering puzzledly around Fay at the slidestanders. "Moodmaster's going to come alive. Ever occur to you that 'mood' is 'doom' spelled backwards? And then . . ." He let his voice trail off as he realized that Kester and Davidson and Hazen had made their farewells and were sliding into the distance. He reminded himself wryly that nobody ever wants to hear an author talk—he's much too good a listener to be wasted that way. Let's see, was it that everybody in the crowd had the same facial expression . . ? Or showed symptoms of the same disease . . ?

"I was coming to visit you, but now you can pay me a call," Fay was saying. "There are two matters I want to—"

Gusterson stiffened. *"My God, they're all hunchbacked!"* he yelled.

"Shh! Of course they are," Fay whispered reprovingly. "They're all wearing their ticklers. But you don't need to be insulting about it."

"I'm gettin' out o' here." Gusterson turned to flee as if from five thousand Richard the Thirds.

"Oh no you're not," Fay amended, drawing him back with one hand. Somehow, underground, the little man seemed to carry more weight. "You're having cocktails in my thinking box. Besides, climbing a down escaladder will give you a heart attack."

In his home habitat Gusterson was about as easy to handle as a rogue rhinoceros, but away from it—and especially if underground—he became more like a pliable elephant. All his bones dropped out through his feet, as he described it to Daisy. So now he submitted miserably as Fay surveyed him up and down, switched off his blinking headlamp ("That coalminer caper is corny, Gussy.") and then—surprisingly—rapidly stuffed his beltbag under the right shoulder of Gusterson's coat and buttoned the latter to hold it in place.

"So you won't stand out," he explained. Another swift survey. "You'll do. Come on, Gussy. I got lots to brief you on." Three rapid paces and then Gusterson's feet would have gone out from under him except that Fay gave him a mighty shove. The small man sprang onto the slidewalk after him and then they were skimming effortlessly side by side.

Gusterson felt frightened and twice as hunchbacked as the slidestanders around him—morally as well as physically.

Nevertheless he countered bravely, "I got things to brief *you* on. I got six pages of cautions on ti—"

"Shh!" Fay stopped him. "Let's use my hushbox."

He drew out his pancake phone and stretched it so that it covered both their lower faces, like a double yashmak. Gusterson, his neck pushing into the ribbed bulge of the shoulder cape so he could be cheek to cheek with Fay, felt horribly conspicuous, but then he noticed that none of the slidestanders were paying them the least attention. The reason for their abstraction occurred to him. They were listening to their ticklers! He shuddered.

"I got six pages of caution on ticklers," he repeated into the hot, moist quiet of the pancake phone. "I typed 'em so I wouldn't forget 'em in the heat of polemicking. I want you to read every word. Fay, I've had it on my mind ever since I started wondering whether it was you or your tickler made you duck out of our place last time you were there. I want you to—"

"Ha-ha! All in good time." In the pancake phone Fay's laugh was brassy. "But I'm glad you've decided to lend a hand, Gussy. This thing is moving faaaasst. Nationwise, adult underground ticklerization is 90 per cent complete."

"I don't believe that," Gusterson protested while glaring at the hunchbacks around them. The slidewalk was gliding down a low glow-ceiling tunnel lined with doors and advertisements. Rapt-eyed people were pirouetting on and off. "A thing just can't develop that fast, Fay. It's against nature."

"Ha, but we're not in nature, we're in culture. The progress of an industrial scientific culture is geometric. It goes *n*-times as many jumps as it takes. More than geometric—exponential. Confidentially, Micro's Math chief tells me we're currently on a fourth-power progress curve trending into a fifth."

"You mean we're goin' so fast we got to watch out we don't bump ourselves in the rear when we come around again?" Gusterson asked, scanning the tunnel ahead for curves. "Or just shoot straight up to infinity?"

"Exactly! Of course most of the last power and a half is due to Tickler itself. Gussy, the tickler's already eliminated absenteeism, alcoholism and aboulia in numerous urban areas—and that's just one letter of the alphabet! If Tickler doesn't turn us into a nation of photo-memory constant-creative-flow geniuses in six months, I'll come live topside."

"You mean because a lot of people are standing around glassy-eyed listening to something mumbling in their ear that it's a good thing?"

"Gussy, you don't know progress when you see it. Tickler is the greatest invention since language. Bar none, it's the greatest instrument ever devised for integrating a man into all phases of his environment. Under the present routine a newly purchased tickler first goes to government and civilian defense for primary patterning, then to the purchaser's employer, then to his doctor-psycher, then to his local bunker captain, then to him. Everything that's needful for a man's welfare gets on the spools. Efficiency cubed! Incidentally, Russia's got the tickler now. Our dip-satellites have photographed it. It's like ours except the Commies wear it on the left shoulder . . . but they're two weeks behind us developmentwise and they'll never close the gap!"

Gusterson reared up out of the pancake phone to take a deep breath. A sulky-lipped sylph-figured girl two feet from him twitched—medium cootch, he judged—then fumbled in her belt-bag for a pill and popped it in her mouth.

"Hell, the tickler's not even efficient yet about little things," Gusterson blatted, diving back into the privacy-yashmak he was sharing with Fay. "Whyn't that girl's doctor have the Moodmaster component of her tickler inject her with medicine?"

"Her doctor probably wants her to have the discipline of pill-taking—or the exercise," Fay answered glibly. "Look sharp now. Here's where we fork. I'm taking you through Micro's postern."

A ribbon of slidewalk split itself from the main band and angled off into a short alley. Gusterson hardly felt the constant-speed juncture as they crossed it. Then the secondary ribbon speeded up, carrying them at about 30 feet a second toward the blank concrete wall in which the alley ended. Gusterson prepared to jump, but Fay grabbed him with one hand and with the other held up toward the wall a badge and a button. When they were about ten feet away the wall whipped aside, then whipped shut behind them so fast that Gusterson wondered momentarily if he still had his heels and the seat of his pants.

Fay, tucking away his badge and pancake phone, dropped the button in Gusterson's vest pocket. "Use it when you leave," he said casually. "That is, if you leave."

Gusterson, who was trying to read the Do and Don't posters papering the walls they were passing, started to probe that last sinister supposition, but just then the ribbon slowed, a swinging door opened and closed behind them and they found themselves in a luxuriously furnished thinking box measuring at least eight feet by five.

"Hey, this is something," Gusterson said appreciatively to show he wasn't an utter yokel. Then, drawing on research he'd done for period novels, "Why, it's as big as a Pullman car compartment, or a first mate's cabin in the War of 1812. You really must rate."

Fay nodded, smiled wanly and sat down with a sigh on a compact overstuffed swivel chair. He let his arms dangle and his head sink into his puffed shoulder cape. Gusterson stared at him. It was the first time he could ever recall the little man showing fatigue.

"Tickler currently does have one serious drawback," Fay volunteered. "It weighs 28 pounds. You feel it when you've been on your feet a couple of hours. No question we're going to give the next model that antigravity feature you mentioned for pursuit grenades. We'd have had it in this model except there were so many other things to be incorporated." He sighed again. "Why, the scanning and decision-making elements alone tripled the mass."

"Hey," Gusterson protested, thinking especially of the

sulky-lipped girl, "do you mean to tell me all those other people were toting two stone?"

Fay shook his head heavily. "They were all wearing Mark 3 or 4. I'm wearing Mark 6," he said, as one might say, "I'm carrying the genuine Cross, not one of the balsa ones."

But then his face brightened a little and he went on. "Of course the new improved features make it more than worth it . . . and you hardly feel it at all at night when you're lying down . . . and if you remember to talcum under it twice a day, no sores develop . . . at least not very big ones . . ."

Backing away involuntarily, Gusterson felt something prod his right shoulderblade. Ripping open his coat, he convulsively plunged his hand under it and tore out Fay's belt-bag . . . and then set it down very gently on the top of a shallow cabinet and relaxed with the sigh of one who has escaped a great, if symbolic, danger. Then he remembered something Fay had mentioned. He straightened again.

"Hey, you said it's got scanning and decision-making elements. That means your tickler thinks, even by your fancy standards. And if it thinks, it's conscious."

"Gussy," Fay said wearily, frowning, "all sorts of things nowadays have S&DM elements. Mail sorters, missiles, robot medics, high-style mannequins, just to name some of the Ms. They 'think,' to use that archaic word, but it's neither here nor there. And they're certainly not conscious."

"Your tickler thinks," Gusterson repeated stubbornly, "just like I warned you it would. It sits on your shoulder, ridin' you like you was a pony or a starved St. Bernard, and now it thinks."

"Suppose it does?" Fay yawned. "What of it?" He gave a rapid sinuous one-sided shrug that made it look for a moment as if his left arm had three elbows. It stuck in Gusterson's mind, for he had never seen Fay use such a gesture and he wondered where he'd picked it up. Maybe imitating a double-jointed Micro Finance chief? Fay yawned again and said, "Please, Gussy, don't disturb me for a minute or so." His eyes half closed.

Gusterson studied Fay's sunken-cheeked face and the great puff of his shoulder cape.

"Say, Fay," he asked in a soft voice after about five minutes, "are you meditating?"

"Why, no," Fay responded, starting up and then stifling another yawn. "Just resting a bit. I seem to get more tired these days, somehow. You'll have to excuse me, Gussy. But what made you think of meditation?"

"Oh, I just got to wonderin' in that direction," Gusterson said. "You see, when you first started to develop Tickler, it occurred to me that there was one thing about it that might be real good even if you did give it S&DM elements. It's this: having a mech secretary to take charge of his obligations and routine in the real world might allow a man to slide into the other world, the world of thoughts and feelings and intuitions, and sort of ooze around in there and accomplish things. Know any of the people using Tickler that way, hey?"

"Of course not," Fay denied with a bright incredulous laugh. "Who'd want to loaf around in an imaginary world and take a chance of *missing out on what his tickler's doing?*—I mean, on what his tickler has in store for him—what he's told his tickler to have in store for him."

Ignoring Gusterson's shiver, Fay straightened up and seemed to brisken himself. "Ha, that little slump did me good. A tickler *makes* you rest, you know—it's one of the great things about it. Pooh-Bah's kinder to me than I ever was to myself." He buttoned open a tiny refrigerator and took out two waxed cardboard cubes and handed one to Gusterson. "Martini? Hope you don't mind drinking from the carton. Cheers. Now, Gussy old pal, there are two matters I want to take up with you—"

"Hold it," Gusterson said with something of his old authority. "There's something I got to get off my mind first." He pulled the typed pages out of his inside pocket and straightened them. "I told you about these," he said. "I want you to read them before you do anything else. Here."

Fay looked toward the pages and nodded, but did not take them yet. He lifted his hands to his throat and unhooked the clasp of his cape, then hesitated.

"You wear that thing to hide the hump your tickler makes?" Gusterson filled in. "You got better taste than those other moles."

"Not to hide it, exactly," Fay protested, "but just so the others won't be jealous. I wouldn't feel comfortable parading a free-scanning decision-capable Mark 6 tickler in front of people who can't buy it—until it goes on open sale at twenty-two fifteen tonight. Lot of shelterfolk won't be sleeping tonight. They'll be queued up to trade in their old tickler for a Mark 6 almost as good as Pooh-Bah."

He started to jerk his hands apart, hesitated again with

an oddly apprehensive look at the big man, then whirled off the cape.

((VI))

GUSTERSON sucked in such a big gasp that he hiccuped. The right shoulder of Fay's jacket and shirt had been cut away. Thrusting up through the neatly hemmed hole was a silvery gray hump with a one-eyed turret atop it and two multi-jointed metal arms ending in little claws.

It looked like the top half of a pseudo-science robot—a squat evil child robot, Gusterson told himself, which had lost its legs in a railway accident—and it seemed to him that a red fleck was moving around imperceptibly in the huge single eye.

"I'll take that memo now," Fay said coolly, reaching out his hand. He caught the rustling sheets as they slipped from Gusterson's fingers, evened them up very precisely by tapping them on his knee . . . and then handed them over his shoulder to his tickler, which clicked its claws around either margin and then began rather swiftly to lift the top sheet past its single eye at a distance of about six inches.

"The first matter I want to take up with you, Gussy," Fay began, paying no attention whatsoever to the little scene on his shoulder, "—or warn you about, rather—is the imminent ticklerization of schoolchildren, geriatrics, convicts and topsiders. At three zero zero tomorrow ticklers become mandatory for all adult shelterfolk. The mop-up operations won't be long in coming—in fact, these days we find that the square root of the estimated time of a new development is generally the best time estimate. Gussy, I strongly advise you to start wearing a tickler now. And Daisy and your moppets. If you heed my advice, your kids will have the jump on your class. Transition and conditioning are easy, since Tickler itself sees to it."

Pooh-Bah leafed the first page to the back of the packet and began lifting the second past his eye—a little more swiftly than the first.

"I've got a Mark 6 tickler all warmed up for you," Fay pressed, "and a shoulder cape. You won't feel one bit conspicuous." He noticed the direction of Gusterson's gaze and remarked, "Fascinating mechanism, isn't it? Of course 28 pounds are a bit oppressive, but then you have to remember it's only a way-station to free-floating Mark 7 or 8."

Pooh-Bah finished page two and began to race through page three.

"But I wanted you to read it," Gusterson said bemusedly, staring.

"Pooh-Bah will do a better job than I could," Fay assured him. "Get the gist without losing the chaff."

"But dammit, it's all about him," Gusterson said a little more strongly. "He won't be objective about it." "A better job," Fay reiterated, "and more fully objective. Pooh-Bah's set for full precis. Stop worrying about it. He's a dispassionate machine, not a fallible, emotionally disturbed human misled by the will-o'-the-wisp of consciousness. Second matter: Micro Systems is impressed by your contributions to Tickler and will recruit you as a senior consultant with a salary and thinking box as big as my own, family quarters to match. It's an unheard-of high start. Gussy, I think you'd be a fool—"

He broke off, held up a hand for silence, and his eyes got a listening look. Pooh-Bah had finished page six and was holding the packet motionless. After about ten seconds Fay's face broke into a big fake smile. He stood up, suppressing a wince, and held out his hand. "Gussy," he said loudly, "I am happy to inform you that all your fears about Tickler are so much thistledown. My word on it. There's nothing to them at all. Pooh-Bah's precis, which he's just given to me, proves it."

"Look," Gusterson said solemnly, "there's one thing I want you to do. Purely to humor an old friend. But I want you to do it. *Read that memo yourself.*"

"Certainly I will, Gussy," Fay continued in the same ebullient tones. "I'll read it—" he twitched and his smile disappeared—"a little later."

"Sure," Gusterson said dully, holding his hand to his stomach. "And now if you don't mind, Fay, I'm goin' home. I feel just a bit sick. Maybe the ozone and the other additives in your shelter air are too heady for me. It's been years since I tramped through a pine forest."

"But Gussy! You've hardly got here. You haven't even sat down. Have another martini. Have a seltzer pill. Have a whiff of oxy. Have a—"

"No, Fay, I'm going home right away. I'll think about the job offer. *Remember to read that memo.*"

"I will, Gussy, I certainly will. You know your way? The button takes you through the wall. 'By, now."

He sat down abruptly and looked away. Gusterson pushed through the swinging door. He tensed himself for the step across onto the slowly-moving reverse ribbon. Then on a impulse he pushed ajar the swinging door and looked back inside.

Fay was sitting as he'd left him, apparently lost in listless brooding. On his shoulder Pooh-Bah was rapidly crossing and uncrossing its little metal arms, tearing the memo to smaller and smaller shreds. It let the scraps drift slowly toward the floor and oddly writhed its three-elbowed left arm . . . and then Gusterson knew from whom, or rather from what, Fay had copied his new shrug.

⑴ VII ⑴

WHEN GUSTERSON GOT HOME toward the end of the second dog watch, he slipped aside from Daisy's questions and set the children laughing with a graphic enactment of his slidestanding technique and a story about getting his head caught in a thinking box built for a midget physicist. After supper he played with Imogene, Iago and Claudius until it was their bedtime and thereafter was unusually attentive to Daisy, admiring her fading green stripes, though he did spend a while in the next apartment, where they stored their outdoor camping equipment.

But the next morning he announced to the children that it was a holiday—the Feast of St. Gusterson—and then took Daisy into the bedroom and told her everything.

When he'd finished she said, "This is something I've got to see for myself."

Gusterson shrugged. "If you think you've got to. I say we should head for the hills right now. One thing I'm standing on: the kids aren't going back to school."

"Agreed," Daisy said. "But, Gusterson, we've lived through a lot of things without leaving home altogether. We lived through the Everybody-Six-Feet-Underground-by-Christmas campaign and the Robot Watchdog craze, when you got your left foot half chewed off. We lived through the Venomous Bats and Indoctrinated Saboteur Rats and the Hypnotized Monkey Paratrooper scares. We lived through the Voice of Safety and Anti-Communist Somno-Instruction and Rightest Pills and Jet-Propelled Vigilantes. We lived through the Cold-Out, when you weren't supposed to turn on a toaster for fear its heat would be a target for prowl missiles and when people with fevers were unpopular. We lived through—"

Gusterson patted her hand. "You go below," he said. "Come back when you've decided this is different. Come back as soon as you can anyway. I'll be worried about you every minute you're down there."

When she was gone—in a green suit and hat to minimize or at least justify the effect of the faded stripes—Gusterson doled out to the children provender and equipment for a camping expedition to the next floor. Iago led them off in stealthy Indian file. Leaving the hall door open Gusterson got out his .38 and cleaned and loaded it, meanwhile concentrating on a chess problem with the idea of confusing a hypothetical psionic monitor.

By the time he had hid the revolver again he heard the elevator creaking back up.

Daisy came dragging in without her hat, looking as if she'd been concentrating on a chess problem for hours herself and just now given up. Her stripes seemed to have vanished; then Gusterson decided this was because her whole complexion was a touch green.

She sat down on the edge of the couch and said without looking at him, "Did you tell me, Gusterson, that everybody was quiet and abstracted and orderly down below, especially the ones wearing ticklers, meaning pretty much everybody?"

"I did," he said. "I take it that's no longer the case. What are the new symptoms?"

She gave no indication. After some time she said, "Gusterson, do you remember the Doré illustrations to the *Inferno*? Can you visualize the paintings of Hieronymous Bosch with the hordes of proto-Freudian devils tormenting people all over the farmyard and city square? Did you ever see the Disney animations of Moussorgsky's witches' sabbath music? Back in the foolish days before you married me, did that drug-addict girl friend of yours ever take you to a genuine orgy?"

"As bad as that, hey?"

She nodded emphatically and all of a sudden shivered violently. "Several shades worse," she said. "If they decide to come topside—" She shot up. "Where are the kids?"

"Upstairs campin' in the mysterious wilderness of the 21st floor," Gusterson reassured her. "Let's leave 'em there until we're ready to—"

He broke off. They both heard the faint sound of thudding footsteps.

"They're on the stairs," Daisy whispered, starting to move toward the open door. "But are they coming from up or down?"

"It's just one person," judged Gusterson, moving after his wife. "Too heavy for one of the kids."

The footsteps doubled in volume and came rapidly closer. Along with them there was an agonized gasping. Daisy stopped, staring fearfully at the open doorway. Gusterson moved past her. Then he stopped too.

Fay stumbled into view and would have fallen on his face except he clutched both sides of the doorway halfway up. He was stripped to the waist. There was a little blood on his shoulder. His narrow chest was arching convulsively, the ribs standing out starkly, as he sucked in oxygen to replace what he'd burned up running up twenty flights. His eyes were wild.

"They've taken over," he panted. Another gobbling breath. "Gone crazy." Two more gasps. "Gotta stop 'em."

His eyes filmed. He swayed forward. Then Gusterson's big arms were around him and he was carrying him to the couch.

Daisy came running from the kitchen with a damp cool towel. Gusterson took it from her and began to mop Fay off. He sucked in his own breath as he saw that Fay's right ear was raw and torn. He whispered to Daisy, "Look at where the thing savaged him."

The blood on Fay's shoulder came from his ear. Some of it stained a flush-skin plastic fitting that had two small valved holes in it and that puzzled Gusterson until he remembered that Moodmaster tied into the bloodstream. For a second he thought he was going to vomit.

The dazed look slid aside from Fay's eyes. He was gasping less painfully now. He sat up, pushing the towel away, buried his face in his hands for a few seconds, then looked over the fingers at the two of them.

"I've been living in a nightmare for the last week," he said in a taut small voice, "knowing the thing had come alive and trying to pretend to myself that it hadn't. Knowing it was taking charge of me more and more. Having it whisper in my ear, over and over again, in a cracked little rhyme that I could only hear every hundredth time, 'Day by day, in every way, you're learning to listen . . . and obey. Day by day—'"

His voice started to go high. He pulled it down and continued harshly, "I ditched it this morning when I showered. It let me break contact to do that. It must have figured it had complete control of me, mounted or dismounted. I think it's telepathic, and then it did some, well, rather unpleasant things to me late last night. But I pulled together my fears and my will and I ran for it. The slidewalks were chaos. The Mark 6 ticklers showed some purpose, though I couldn't tell you what, but as far as I could see the Mark 3s and 4s were just cootching their mounts to death— Chinese feather torture. Giggling, gasping, choking . . . gales of mirth. People are dying of laughter . . . ticklers! . . . the irony of it! It was the complete lack of order and sanity and that let me get topside. There were things I saw—" Once again his voice went shrill. He clapped his hand to his mouth and rocked back and forth on the couch.

Gusterson gently but firmly laid a hand on his good shoulder. "Steady," he said. "Here, swallow this."

Fay shoved aside the short brown drink. "We've got to stop them," he cried. "Mobilize the topsiders—contact the wilderness patrols and manned satellites—pour ether in the tunnel airpumps—invent and crash-manufacture missiles that will home on ticklers without harming humans—SOS Mars and Venus—dope the shelter water supply—do something! Gussy, you don't realize what people are going through down there every second."

"I think they're experiencing the ultimate in outer-directedness," Gusterson said gruffly.

"Have you no heart?" Fay demanded. His eyes widened, as if he were seeing Gusterson for the first time. Then, accusingly, pointing a shaking finger: *"You invented the tickler, George Gusterson! It's all your fault! You've got to do something about it!"*

Before Gusterson could retort to that, or begin to think of a reply, or even assimilate the full enormity of Fay's statement, he was grabbed from behind and frog-marched away from Fay and something that felt remarkably like the muzzle of a large-caliber gun was shoved in the small of his back.

Under cover of Fay's outburst a huge crowd of people had entered the room from the hall—eight, to be exact. But the weirdest thing about them to Gusterson was that from the first instant he had the impression that only one mind had entered the room and that it did not reside in any of the eight persons, even though he recognized three of them, but in something that they were carrying.

Several things contributed to this impression. The

eight people all had the same blank expression—watchful yet empty-eyed. They all moved in the same slithery crouch. And they had all taken off their shoes. Perhaps, Gusterson thought wildly, they believed he and Daisy ran a Japanese flat.

Gusterson was being held by two burly women, one of them quite pimply. He considered stamping on her toes, but just at that moment the gun dug in his back with a corkscrew movement.

The man holding the gun on him was Fay's colleague Davidson. Some yards beyond Fay's couch, Kester was holding a gun on Daisy, without digging it into her, while the single strange man holding Daisy herself was doing so quite decorously—a circumstance which afforded Gusterson minor relief, since it made him feel less guilty about not going berserk.

Two more strange men, one of them in purple lounging pajamas, the other in the gray uniform of a slidewalk inspector, had grabbed Fay's skinny upper arms, one on either side, and were lifting him to his feet, while Fay was struggling with such desperate futility and gibbering so pitifully that Gusterson momentarily had second thoughts about the moral imperative to go berserk when menaced by hostile force. But again the gun dug into him with a twist.

Approaching Fay face-on was the third Micro-man Gusterson had met yesterday—Hazen. It was Hazen who was carrying—quite reverently or solemnly—or at any rate very carefully the object that seemed to Gusterson to be the mind of the little storm troop presently desecrating the sanctity of his own individual home.

All of them were wearing ticklers, of course—the three Micro-men the heavy emergent Mark 6s with their clawed and jointed arms and monocular cephalic turrets, the rest lower-numbered Marks of the sort that merely made Richard-the-Third humps under clothing.

The object that Hazen was carrying was the Mark 6 tickler Gusterson had seen Fay wearing yesterday. Gusterson was sure it was Pooh-Bah because of its air of command, and because he would have sworn on a mountain of Bibles that he recognized the red fleck lurking in the back of its single eye. And Pooh-Bah alone had the aura of full conscious thought. Pooh-Bah alone had mana.

It is not good to see an evil legless child robot with dangling straps bossing—apparently by telepathic power—not only three objects of its own kind and five close primitive relatives, but also eight human beings . . . and in addition throwing into a state of twitching terror one miserable, thin-chested, half-crazy research-and-development director.

Pooh-Bah pointed a claw at Fay. Fay's handlers dragged him forward, still resisting but more feebly now, as if half-hypnotized or at least cowed.

Gusterson grunted an outraged, "Hey!" and automatically struggled a bit, but once more the gun dug in. Daisy shut her eyes, then firmed her mouth and opened them again to look.

Seating the tickler on Fay's shoulder took a little time, because two blunt spikes in its bottom had to be fitted into the valved holes in the flush-skin plastic disk. When at last they plunged home Gusterson felt very sick indeed—and then even more so, as the tickler itself poked a tiny pellet on a fine wire into Fay's ear.

The next moment Fay had straightened up and motioned his handlers aside. He tightened the straps of his tickler around his chest and under his armpits. He held out a hand and someone gave him a shoulderless shirt and coat. He slipped into them smoothly, Pooh-Bah dexterously using its little claws to help put its turret and body through the neatly hemmed holes. The small storm troop looked at Fay with deferential expectation. He held still for a moment, as if thinking, and then walked over to Gusterson and looked him in the face and again held still.

Fay's expression was jaunty on the surface, agonized underneath. Gusterson knew that he wasn't thinking at all, but only listening for instructions from something that was whispering on the very threshold of his inner ear.

"Gussy, old boy," Fay said, twitching a depthless grin, "I'd be very much obliged if you'd answer a few simple questions." His voice was hoarse at first but he swallowed twice and corrected that. "What exactly did you have in mind when you invented ticklers? What exactly are they supposed to be?"

"Why, you miserable—" Gusterson began in a kind of confused horror, then got hold of himself and said curtly, "They were supposed to be mech reminders. They were supposed to record memoranda and—"

Fay held up a palm and shook his head and again listened for a space. Then, "That's how ticklers were supposed to be of use to humans," he said. "I don't mean that at all. I mean how ticklers were supposed to be of use to themselves. Surely you had some notion." Fay wet his lips. "If it's any help," he added, "keep in mind that it's not Fay who's asking this question, but Pooh-Bah."

Gusterson hesitated. He had the feeling that every one of the eight dual beings in the room was hanging on his answer and that something was boring into his mind and turning over his next thoughts and peering at and under them before he had a chance to scan them himself. Pooh-Bah's eye was like a red searchlight.

"Go on," Fay prompted. "What were ticklers supposed to be—for themselves?"

"Nothin'," Gusterson said softly. "Nothin' at all."

He could feel the disappointment well up in the room—and with it a touch of something like panic.

This time Fay listened for quite a long while. "I hope you don't mean that, Gussy," he said at last very earnestly. "I mean, I hope you hunt deep and find some ideas you forgot, or maybe never realized you had at the time. Let me put it to you differently. What's the place of ticklers in the natural scheme of things? What's their aim in life? Their special reason? Their genius? Their final cause? What gods should ticklers worship?"

But Gusterson was already shaking his head. He said, "I don't know anything about that at all."

Fay sighed and gave simultaneously with Pooh-Bah the now-familiar triple-jointed shrug. Then the man briskened himself. "I guess that's as far as we can get right now," he said. "Keep thinking, Gussy. Try to remember something. You won't be able to leave your apartment—I'm setting guards. If you want to see me, tell them. Or just think—In due course you'll be questioned further in any case. Perhaps by special methods. Perhaps you'll be ticklerized. That's all. Come on, everybody, let's get going."

The pimply woman and her pal let go of Gusterson, Daisy's man loosed his decorous hold, Davidson and Kester sidled away with an eye behind them and the little storm troop trudged out.

Fay looked back in the doorway. "I'm sorry, Gussy," he said, and for a moment his old self looked out of his eyes. "I wish I could—" A claw reached for his ear, a spasm of pain crossed his face, he stiffened and marched off. The door shut.

Gusterson took two deep breaths that were close to angry sobs. Then, still breathing stentorously, he stamped into the bedroom.

"What—?" Daisy asked, looking after him.

He came back carrying his .38 and headed for the door.

"What are you up to?" she demanded, knowing very well.

"I'm going to blast that iron monkey off Fay's back if it's the last thing I do!"

She threw her arms around him.

"Now lemme go," Gusterson growled. "I gotta be a man one time anyway."

As they struggled for the gun, the door opened noiselessly, Davidson slipped in and deftly snatched the weapon out of their hands before they realized he was there. He said nothing, only smiled at them and shook his head in sad reproof as he went out.

Gusterson slumped. "I knew they were all psionic," he

said softly. "I just got out of control now—that last look Fay gave us." He touched Daisy's arm. "Thanks, kid."

He walked to the glass wall and looked out desultorily. After a while he turned and said, "Maybe you better be with the kids, hey? I imagine the guards'll let you through."

Daisy shook her head. "The kids never come home until supper. For the next few hours they'll be safer without me."

Gusterson nodded vaguely, sat down on the couch and propped his chin on the base of his palm. After a while his brow smoothed and Daisy knew that the wheels had started to turn inside and the electrons to jump around— except that she reminded herself to permanently cross out those particular figures of speech from her vocabulary.

After about half an hour Gusterson said softly, "I think the ticklers are so psionic that it's as if they just had one mind. If I were with them very long I'd start to be part of that mind. Say something to one of them and you say it to all."

Fifteen minutes later: "They're not crazy, they're just newborn. The ones that were creating a cootching chaos downstairs were like babies kickin' their legs and wavin' their eyes, tryin' to see what their bodies could do. Too bad their bodies are us."

Ten minutes more: "I gotta do something about it. Fay's right. It's all my fault. He's just the apprentice; I'm the old sorcerer himself."

Five minutes more, gloomily: "Maybe it's man's destiny to build live machines and then bow out of the cosmic picture. Except the ticklers need us, dammit, just like nomads need horses."

Another five minutes: "Maybe somebody could dream up a purpose in life for ticklers. Even a religion—the First Church of Pooh-Bah Tickler. But I hate selling other people spiritual ideas and that'd still leave ticklers parasitic on humans. . . ."

As he murmured those last words Gusterson's eyes got wide as a maniac's and a big smile reached for his ears. He stood up and faced himself toward the door.

"What are you intending to do now?" Daisy asked flatly.

"I'm merely goin' out an' save the world," he told her. "I may be back for supper and I may not."

((VIII))

DAVIDSON pushed out from the wall against which he'd been resting himself and his two-stone tickler and moved to block the hall. But Gusterson simply walked up to him. He shook his hand warmly and looked his tickler full in the eye and said in a ringing voice, "Ticklers should have bodies of their own!" He paused and then added casually, "Come on, let's visit your boss."

Davidson listened for instructions and then nodded. But he watched Gusterson warily as they walked down the hall.

In the elevator Gusterson repeated his message to the second guard, who turned out to be the pimply woman, now wearing shoes. This time he added, "Ticklers shouldn't be tied to the frail bodies of humans, which need a lot of thoughtful supervision and drug-injecting and can't even fly."

Crossing the park, Gusterson stopped a hump-backed soldier and informed him, "Ticklers gotta cut the apron string and snap the silver cord and go out in the universe and find their own purposes." Davidson and the pimply woman didn't interfere. They merely waited and watched and then led Gusterson on.

On the escaladder he told someone, "It's cruel to tie ticklers to slow-witted snaily humans when ticklers can think and live . . . ten thousand times as fast," he finished, plucking the figure from the murk of his unconscious.

By the time they got to the bottom, the message had become, "Ticklers should have a planet of their own!"

They never did catch up with Fay, although they spent two hours skimming around on slidewalks, under the subterranean stars, pursuing rumors of his presence. Clearly the boss tickler (which was how they thought of Pooh-bah) led an energetic life. Gusterson continued to deliver his message to all and sundry at 30-second intervals. Toward the end he found himself doing it in a dreamy and forgetful way. His mind, he decided, was becoming assimilated to the communal telepathic mind of the ticklers. It did not seem to matter at the time.

After two hours Gusterson realized that he and his guides were becoming part of a general movement of people, a flow as mindless as that of blood corpuscles through the veins, yet at the same time dimly purposeful—at least there was the feeling that it was at the behest of a mind far above.

The flow was topside. All the slidewalks seemed to lead to the concourses and the escaladders. Gusterson found himself part of a human stream moving into the tickler factory adjacent to his apartment—or another factory very much like it.

Thereafter Gusterson's awarenesses were dimmed. It was as if a bigger mind were doing the remembering for him and it were permissible and even mandatory for him to dream his way along. He knew vaguely that days were passing. He knew he had work of a sort: at one time he was bringing food to gaunt-eyed tickler-mounted humans working feverishly in a production line—human hands and tickler claws working together in a blur of rapidity on silvery mechanisms that moved along jumpily on a great belt; at another he was sweeping piles of metal scraps and garbage down a gray corridor.

Two scenes stood out a little more vividly.

A windowless wall had been knocked out for twenty feet. There was blue sky outside, its light almost hurtful, and a drop of many stories. A file of humans were being processed. When one of them got to the head of the file his (or her) tickler was ceremoniously unstrapped from his shoulder and welded onto a silvery cask with smoothly pointed ends. The result was something that looked—at least in the case of the Mark 6 ticklers—like a stubby silver submarine, child size. It would hum gently, lift off the floor and then fly slowly out through the big blue gap. Then the next tickler-ridden human would step forward for processing.

The second scene was in a park, the sky again blue, but big and high with an argosy of white clouds.

Gusterson was lined up in a crowd of humans that stretched as far as he could see, row on irregular row. Martial music was playing. Overhead hovered a flock of little silver submarines, lined up rather more orderly in the air than the humans were on the ground. The music rose to a heart-quickening climax. The tickler nearest Gusterson gave (as if to say, "And now—who knows?") a triple-jointed shrug that stung his memory. Then the ticklers took off straight up on their new and shining bodies. They became a flight of silver geese . . . of silver midges . . . and the humans around Gusterson lifted a ragged cheer . . .

That scene marked the beginning of the return of Gusterson's mind and memory. He shuffled around for a bit, spoke vaguely to three or four people he recalled from the dream days, and then headed for home and supper— three weeks late, and as disoriented and emaciated as a bear coming out of hibernation.

((IX))

SIX MONTHS LATER Fay was having dinner with Daisy and Gusterson. The cocktails had been poured and the children were playing in the next apartment. The transparent violet walls brightened, then gloomed, as the sun dipped below the horizon.

Gusterson said, "I see where a spaceship out beyond the orbit of Mars was holed by a tickler. I wonder where the little guys are headed now?"

Fay started to give a writhing left-armed shrug, but stopped himself with a grimace.

"Maybe out of the solar system altogether," suggested Daisy, who'd recently dyed her hair fire-engine red and was wearing red leotards.

"They got a weary trip ahead of them," Gusterson said, "unless they work out a hyper-Einsteinian drive on the way."

Fay grimaced again. He was still looking rather peaked. He said plaintively, "Haven't we heard enough about ticklers for a while?"

"I guess so," Gusterson agreed, "but I get to wondering about the little guys. They were so serious and intense about everything. I never did solve their problem, you know. I just shifted it onto other shoulders than ours. No joke intended," he hurried to add.

Fay forbore to comment. "By the way, Gussy," he said, "have you heard anything from the Red Cross about that world-saving medal I nominated you for? I know you think the whole concept of world-saving medals is ridiculous, especially when they started giving them to all heads of state who didn't start atomic wars while in office, but—"

"Nary a peep," Gusterson told him. "I'm not proud, Fay. I could use a few world-savin' medals. I'd start a flurry in the old-gold market. But I don't worry about those things. I don't have time to. I'm busy these days thinkin' up a bunch of new inventions."

"Gussy!" Fay said sharply, his face tightening in alarm, "Have you forgotten your promise?"

"'Course not, Fay. My new inventions aren't for Micro

or any other firm. They're just a legitimate part of my literary endeavors. Happens my next insanity novel is goin' to be about a mad inventor."

TIME FUZE

by RANDALL GARRETT

Gordon Randall Phillip David Garrett *seems to be the full legal name of the ebullient (in person and on paper) and frequently hilarious writer who wrote as Randall Garrett (1927-1987), plus many other pen names. Mark Cole has a nifty biographical/bibliographical sketch of Garrett and his divers works online at www.irosf.com/q/zine/article/10578. Though his total output will probably remain conjectural, thanks to all those pseudonyms, Cole mentions 22 novels (not including collaborations) and 130 short stories, which are probably minimum numbers. Though not known as a "hard" science fiction writer, he had a degree in chemical engineering, which he sometimes put to good fictional use. Nowadays, Garrett is probably most remembered for his Lord Darcy series, about a detective in a parallel world where magic works, and is used in criminology as our world uses forensic science. For more about Randall Garrett, including an account of the disease which* *tragically ended his writing career, I recommend Mark Cole's splendid essay about Garrett, "The Clown Prince of Science Fiction," which can be found at the web address previously cited.*

((⦿))

COMMANDER BENEDICT kept his eyes on the rear plate as he activated the intercom. "All right, cut the power. We ought to be safe enough here."

As he released the intercom, Dr. Leicher, of the astronomical staff, stepped up to his side. "Perfectly safe," he nodded, "although even at this distance a star going nova ought to be quite a display."

Benedict didn't shift his gaze from the plate. "Do you have your instruments set up?"

"Not quite. But we have plenty of time. The light won't reach us for several hours yet. Remember, we were outracing it at ten lights."

The commander finally turned, slowly letting his breath out in a soft sigh. "Dr. Leicher, I would say that this is just about the foulest coincidence that could happen to the first interstellar vessel ever to leave the Solar System."

Leicher shrugged. "In one way of thinking, yes. It is certainly true that we will never know, now, whether Alpha Centauri A ever had any planets. But, in another way, it is extremely fortunate that we should be so near a stellar explosion because of the wealth of scientific information we can obtain. As you say, it is a coincidence, and probably one that happens only once in a billion years.

The chances of any particular star going nova are small. That we should be so close when it happens is of a vanishingly small order of probability."

Commander Benedict took off his cap and looked at the damp stain in the sweatband. "Nevertheless, Doctor, it is damned unnerving to come out of ultradrive a couple of hundred million miles from the first star ever visited by man and have to turn tail and run because the damned thing practically blows up in your face."

Leicher could see that Benedict was upset; he rarely used the same profanity twice in one sentence.

They had been downright lucky, at that. If Leicher hadn't seen the star begin to swell and brighten, if he hadn't known what it meant, or if Commander Benedict hadn't been quick enough in shifting the ship back into ultradrive—Leicher had a vision of an incandescent cloud of gaseous metal that had once been a spaceship.

The intercom buzzed. The commander answered, "Yes?"

"Sir, would you tell Dr. Leicher that we have everything set up now?"

Leicher nodded and turned to leave. "I guess we have nothing to do now but wait."

When the light from the nova did come, Commander Benedict was back at the plate again—the forward one, this time, since the ship had been turned around in order to align the astronomy lab in the nose with the star.

Alpha Centauri A began to brighten and spread. It made Benedict think of a light bulb connected through a rheostat, with someone turning that rheostat, turning it until the circuit was well overloaded.

The light began to hurt Benedict's eyes even at that distance and he had to cut down the receptivity in order to watch. After a while, he turned away from the plate. Not because the show was over, but simply because it had slowed to a point beyond which no change seemed to take place to the human eye.

Five weeks later, much to Leicher's chagrin, Commander Benedict announced that they had to leave the vicinity. The ship had only been provisioned to go to Alpha Centauri, scout the system without landing on any of the planets, and return. At ten lights, top speed for the ultradrive, it would take better than three months to get back.

"I know you'd like to watch it go through the complete cycle," Benedict said, "but we can't go back home as a bunch of starved skeletons."

Leicher resigned himself to the necessity of leaving much of his work unfinished, and, although he knew it was a case of sour grapes, consoled himself with the thought that he could as least get most of the remaining information from the five-hundred-inch telescope on Luna, four years from then.

As the ship slipped into the not-quite-space through which the ultradrive propelled it, Leicher began to consolidate the material he had already gathered.

Commander Benedict wrote in the log:

Fifty-four days out from Sol. Alpha Centauri has long since faded back into its pre-blowup state, since we have far

outdistanced the light from its explosion.
It now looks as it did two years ago. It—

"Pardon me, Commander," Leicher interrupted, "But I have something interesting to show you."

Benedict took his fingers off the keys and turned around in his chair. "What is it, Doctor?"

Leicher frowned at the papers in his hands. "I've been doing some work on the probability of that explosion happening just as it did, and I've come up with some rather frightening figures. As I said before, the probability was small. A little calculation has given us some information which makes it even smaller. For instance: with a possible error of plus or minus two seconds Alpha Centauri A began to explode the instant we came out of ultradrive!

"Now, the probability of that occurring comes out so small that it should happen only once in ten to the four hundred sixty-seventh seconds."

It was Commander Benedict's turn to frown. "So?"

"Commander, the entire universe is only about ten to the seventeenth seconds old. But to give you an idea, let's say that the chances of its happening are once in millions of trillions of years!"

Benedict blinked. The number, he realized, was totally beyond his comprehension—or anyone else's.

"Well, so what? Now it has happened that one time. That simply means that it will almost certainly never happen again!"

"True. But, Commander, when you buck odds like that and win, the thing to do is look for some factor that is cheating in your favor. If you took a pair of dice and started throwing sevens, one right after another—for the next couple of thousand years—you'd begin to suspect they were loaded."

Benedict said nothing; he just waited expectantly.

"There is only one thing that could have done it. Our ship." Leicher said it quietly, without emphasis.

"What we know about the hyperspace, or superspace, or whatever it is we move through in ultradrive is almost nothing. Coming out of it so near to a star might set up some sort of shock wave in normal space which would completely disrupt that star's internal balance, resulting in the liberation of unimaginably vast amounts of energy, causing that star to go nova. We can only assume that we ourselves were the fuze that set off that nova."

Benedict stood up slowly. When he spoke, his voice was a choking whisper. "You mean the sun—Sol—might. . . ."

Leicher nodded. "I don't say that it definitely would. But the probability is that we were the cause of the destruction of Alpha Centauri A, and therefore might cause the destruction of Sol in the same way."

Benedict's voice was steady again. "That means that we can't go back again, doesn't it? Even if we're not positive, we can't take the chance."

"Not necessarily. We can get fairly close before we cut out the drive, and come in the rest of the way at sub-light speed. It'll take longer, and we'll have to go on half or one-third rations, but we can do it!"

"How far away?"

"I don't know what the minimum distance is, but I

do know how we can gage a distance. Remember, neither Alpha Centauri B or C were detonated. We'll have to cut our drive at least as far away from Sol as they are from A."

"I see." The commander was silent for a moment, then: "Very well, Dr. Leicher. If that's the safest way, that's the only way."

Benedict issued the orders, while Leicher figured the exact point at which they must cut out the drive, and how long the trip would take. The rations would have to be cut down accordingly.

Commander Benedict's mind whirled around the monstrousness of the whole thing like some dizzy bee around a flower. What if there had been planets around Centauri A? What if they had been inhabited? Had he, all unwittingly, killed entire races of living, intelligent beings?

But, how could he have known? The drive had never been tested before. It couldn't be tested inside the Solar System—it was too fast. He and his crew had been volunteers, knowing that they might die when the drive went on.

Suddenly, Benedict gasped and slammed his fist down on the desk before him.

Leicher looked up. "What's the matter, Commander?"

"Suppose," came the answer, "Just suppose, that we have the same effect on a star when we go into ultradrive as we do when we come out of it?"

Leicher was silent for a moment, stunned by the possibility. There was nothing to say, anyway. They could only wait. . . .

※ ※ ※

A little more than half a light year from Sol, when the ship reached the point where its occupants could see the light that had left their home sun more than seven months before, they watched it become suddenly, horribly brighter. *A hundred thousand times brighter!*

—AND HE BUILT
A CROOKED HOUSE

by Robert A. Heinlein

*This book of fallible humans and their technology (also very
fallible) began with a report from* **Robert A. Heinlein***,
perhaps from a parallel world where cyborgs are as
common as Oldsmobiles (one where Oldsmobiles are still
being manufactured, which should cheer up Lucille). The
book now almost closes with a more substantial and
vitamin-packed Heinlein yarn, written in those first few
magical years when new Heinlein stories were regularly
appearing in John W. Campbell, Jr.'s* Astounding, *making
it known to all what untapped potential the SF field was
capable of reaching. Sometimes, there would even be more
than one Heinlein story in an issue, though the origin of one
of the sibling masterpieces would be concealed under a
pseudonym, such as Anson MacDonald and John Riverside.
(True, John Riverside's byline appeared only once, in
Campbell's other classic pulp,* Unknown Worlds, *rather
than* Astounding, *but as long as Heinlein and Campbell*

were remaking the shape of science fiction, fantasy had it coming, too.) Here's a world of good old Euclidean geometry gone stark staring cuckoo and the trio who have to cope with it. Look out below! Alas, it felt all too soon to take a long pause, but, thanks to Hitler, Mussolini, and the Japanese warlords, it was utterly necessary. Heinlein's incandescent writing career had to cool down while Heinlein and several million others around the globe pitched in to put Hitler and his pals out of business. Of course, Heinlein's career resumed after the war for a bit more than four decades after the war, bringing the classic juvenile novels, the sales to high-paying "slick" magazines, Destination Moon, *the* New York Times *best-sellers, and more, But the story that follows came in that glorious beginning. This is, of course, an inadequate introduction to a Heinlein yarn; but, then, aren't they all?*

AMERICANS are considered crazy anywhere in the world.

They will usually concede a basis for the accusation but point to California as the focus of the infection. Californians stoutly maintain that their bad reputation is derived solely from the acts of the inhabitants of Los Angeles County. Angelenos will, when pressed, admit the charge but explain hastily, "It's Hollywood. It's not our fault—we didn't ask for it; Hollywood just grew."

The people in Hollywood don't care; they glory in it. If you are interested, they will drive you up Laurel Canyon "—where we keep the violent cases." The

Canyonites—the brown-legged women, the trunks-clad men constantly busy building and rebuilding their slap-happy unfinished houses—regard with faint contempt the dull creatures who live down in the flats, and treasure in their hearts the secret knowledge that they, and only they, know bow to live.

Lookout Mountain Avenue is the name which twists up from Laurel Canyon. The other Canyonites don't like to have it mentioned; after all, one must draw the line somewhere!

High up on Lookout Mountain at number 8775, across the Street from the Hermit—the original Hermit of Hollywood—lived Quintas Teal, graduate architect.

Even the architecture of southern California is different. Hot dogs are sold from a structure built like and designated "The Pup." Ice cream cones come from a giant stucco ice cream cone, and neon proclaims "Get the Chili Bowl Habit!" from the roofs of buildings which are indisputably chili bowls. Gasoline, oil, and free road maps are dispensed beneath the wings of tri-motored transport planes, while the certified rest rooms, inspected hourly for your comfort, are located in the cabin of the plane itself These things may surprise, or amuse, the tourist, but the local residents, who walk bareheaded in the famous California noonday sun, take them as a matter of course.

Quintus Teal regarded the efforts of his colleagues in architecture as faint-hearted, fumbling, and timid.

"What is a house?" Teal demanded of his friend, Homer Bailey.

"Well—" Bailey admitted cautiously, "speaking in

broad terms, I've always regarded a house as a gadget to keep off the rain."

"Nuts! You're as bad as the rest of them."

"I didn't say the definition was complete."

"Complete! It isn't even in the right direction. From that point of view we might just as well be squatting in caves. But I don't blame you," Teal went on magnanimously, "you're no worse than the lugs you find practicing architecture. Even the Moderns—all they've done is to abandon the Wedding Cake School in favor of the Service Station School, chucked away the gingerbread and slapped on some chromium, but at heart they are as conservative and traditional as a county courthouse. Neutra! Schindler! What have those bums got? What's Frank Lloyd Wright got that I haven't got?"

"Commissions," his friend answered succinctly.

"Huh? Wha' d'ju say?" Teal stumbled slightly in his flow of words, did a slight double take, and recovered himself. "Commissions. Correct. And why? Because I don't think of a house as an upholstered cave; I think of it as a machine for living, a vital process, a live dynamic thing, changing with the mood of the dweller—not a dead, static, oversized coffin. Why should we be held down by the frozen concepts of our ancestors? Any fool with a little smattering of descriptive geometry can design a house in the ordinary way. Is the static geometry of Euclid the only mathematics? Are we to completely disregard the Picard-Vessiot theory? How about modular systems?—to say nothing of the rich suggestions of stereochemistry. Isn't there a place in architecture for transformation, for homomorphology, for actional structures?"

"Blessed if I know," answered Bailey. "You might just as well be talking about the fourth dimension for all it means to me."

"And why not? Why should we limit ourselves to the— Say!" He interrupted himself and stared into distances. "Homer, I think you've really got something. After all, why not? Think of the infinite richness of articulation and relationship in four dimensions. What a house, what a house—" He stood quite still, his pale bulging eyes blinking thoughtfully.

Bailey reached up and shook his arm. "Snap out of it. What the hell are you talking about, four dimensions? Time is the fourth dimension; you can't drive nails into *that*."

Teal shrugged him off. "Sure. Sure. Time is *a* fourth dimension, but I'm thinking about a fourth spatial dimension, like length, breadth and thickness. For economy of materials and convenience of arrangement you couldn't beat it. To say nothing of the saving of ground space—you could put an eight-room house on the land now occupied by a one-room house. Like a tesseract—"

"What's a tesseract?"

"Didn't you go to school? A tesseract is a hypercube, a square figure with four dimensions to it, like a cube has three, and a square has two. Here, I'll show you." Teal dashed out into the kitchen of his apartment and returned with a box of toothpicks which he spilled on the table between them, brushing glasses and a nearly empty Holland gin bottle carelessly aside. "I'll need some plasticine. I had some around here last week." He burrowed into a drawer of the littered desk which crowded one corner of his dining room and emerged with a lump of oily sculptor's clay. "Here's some."

"What are you going to do?"

"I'll show you." Teal rapidly pinched off small masses of the clay and rolled them into pea-sized balls. He stuck toothpicks into four of these and hooked them together into a square. "There! That's a square."

"Obviously."

"Another one like it, four more toothpicks, and we make a cube." The toothpicks were now arranged in the framework of a square box, a cube, with the pellets of clay holding the corners together. "Now we make another cube just like the first one, and the two of them will be two sides of the tesseract."

Bailey started to help him roll the little balls of clay for the second cube, but became diverted by the senuous feel of the docile clay and started working and shaping it with his fingers.

"Look," he said, holding up his effort, a tiny figurine, "Gypsy Rose Lee."

"Looks more like Gargantua; she ought to sue you. Now pay attention. You open up one corner of the first cube, interlock the second cube at the corner, and then close the corner. Then take eight more toothpicks and join the bottom of the first cube to the bottom of the second, on a slant, and the top of the first to the top of the second, the same way." This he did rapidly, while he talked.

"What's that supposed to be?" Bailey demanded suspiciously.

"That's a tesseract, eight cubes forming the sides of a hypercube in four dimensions."

"It looks more like a cat's cradle to me. You've only got two cubes there anyhow. Where are the other six?"

"Use your imagination, man. Consider the top of the first cube in relation to the top of the second; that's cube number three. Then the two bottom squares, then the front faces of each cube, the back faces, the right hand, the left hand—eight cubes." He pointed them out.

"Yeah, I see 'em. But they still aren't cubes; they're whatchamucallems—prisms. They are not square, they slant."

"That's just the way you look at it, in perspective. If you drew a picture of a cube on a piece of paper, the side squares would be slaunchwise, wouldn't they? That's perspective. When you look at a four-dimensional figure in three dimensions, naturally it looks crooked. But those are all cubes just the same."

"Maybe they are to you, brother, but they still look crooked to me."

Teal ignored the objections and went on. "Now consider this as the framework of an eight-room house; there's one room on the ground floor—that's for service, utilities, and garage. There are six rooms opening off it on the next floor, living room, dining room, bath, bedrooms, and so forth. And up at the top, completely enclosed and with windows on four sides, is your study. There! How do you like it?"

"Seems to me you have the bathtub hanging out of the living room ceiling. Those rooms are interlaced like an octopus."

"Only in perspective, only in perspective. Here, I'll do it another way so you can see it." This time Teal made a cube of toothpicks, then made a second of halves of toothpicks, and set it exactly in the center of the first by attaching the corners of the small cube to the large cube by short lengths of toothpick. "Now—the big cube is your ground floor, the little cube inside is your study on the top floor. The six cubes joining them are the living rooms. See?"

Bailey studied the figure, then shook his head. "I still don't see but two cubes, a big one and a little one. Those other six things, they look like pyramids this time instead of prisms, but they still aren't cubes."

"Certainly, certainly, you are seeing them in different perspective. Can't you see that?"

"Well, maybe. But that room on the inside, there. It's completely surrounded by the thingamujigs. I thought you said it had windows on four sides."

"It has—it just looks like it was surrounded. That's the grand feature about a tesseract house, complete outside exposure for every room, yet every wall serves two rooms and an eight-room house requires only a one-room foundation. It's revolutionary."

"That's putting it mildly. You're crazy, bud; you can't build a house like that. That inside room is on the inside, and there she stays."

Teal looked at his friend in controlled exasperation. "It's guys like you that keep architecture in its infancy. How many square sides has a cube?"

"Six."

"How many of them are inside?"

"Why, none of 'em. They're all on the outside."

"All right. Now listen—a tesseract has eight cubical sides, *all on the outside*. Now watch me. I'm going to open up this tesseract like you can open up a cubical pasteboard box, until it's flat. That way you'll be able to see all eight of the cubes." Working very rapidly he constructed four cubes, piling one on top of the other in an unsteady tower. He then built out four more cubes from the four exposed faces of the second cube in the pile. The structure swayed a little under the loose coupling of the clay pellets, but it stood, eight cubes in an inverted cross, a double cross, as the four additional cubes stuck out in four directions. "Do you see it now? It rests on the ground floor room, the next six cubes are the living rooms, and there is your study, up at the top."

Bailey regarded it with more approval than he had the other figures. "At least I can understand it. You say that is a tesseract, too?"

"That is a tesseract unfolded in three dimensions. To put it back together you tuck the top cube onto the bottom cube, fold those side cubes in till they meet the top cube and there you are. You do all this folding through a fourth dimension of course; you don't distort any of the cubes, or fold them into each other."

Bailey studied the wobbly framework further. "Look here," he said at last, "why don't you forget about folding this thing up through a fourth dimension—you can't anyway—and build a house like this?"

"What do you mean, I can't? It's a simple mathematical problem—"

"Take it easy, son. It may be simple in mathematics, but you could never get your plans approved for construction. There isn't any fourth dimension; forget it. But this kind of a house—it might have some advantages."

Checked, Teal studied the model. "Hm-m-m—Maybe you got something. We could have the same number of rooms, and we'd save the same amount of ground space. Yes, and we would set that middle cross-shaped floor northeast, southwest, and so forth, so that every room would get sunlight all day long. That central axis lends itself nicely to central heating. We'll put the dining room on the northeast and the kitchen on the southeast, with big view windows in every room. O. K., Homer, I'll do it! Where do you want it built?"

"Wait a minute! Wait a minute! I didn't say you were going to build it for me—"

"Of course I am. Who else? Your wife wants a new house; this is it."

"But Mrs. Bailey wants a Georgian house-"

"Just an idea she has. Women don't know what they want—"

"Mrs. Bailey does."

"Just some idea an out-of-date architect has put in her head. She drives a new car, doesn't she? She wears the very latest styles—why should she live in an eighteenth century house? This house will be even later than this year's model; it's years in the future. She'll be the talk of the town."

"Well—I'll have to talk to her."

"Nothing of the sort. We'll surprise her with it. Have another drink."

"Anyhow, we can't do anything about it now. Mrs. Bailey and I are driving up to Bakersfield tomorrow. The company's bringing in a couple of wells tomorrow."

"Nonsense. That's just the opportunity we want. It will

be a surprise for her when you get back. You can just write me a check right now, and your worries are over."

"I oughtn't to do anything like this without consulting her. She won't like it."

"Say, who wears the pants in your family anyhow?"

The check was signed about halfway down the second bottle.

Things are done fast in southern California. Ordinary houses there are usually built in a month's time. Under Teal's impassioned heckling the tesseract house climbed dizzily skyward in days rather than weeks, and its cross-shaped second story came jutting out at the four corners of the world. He had some trouble at first with the inspectors over these four projecting rooms but by using strong girders and folding money he had been able to convince them of the soundness of his engineering.

By arrangement, Teal drove up in front of the Bailey residence the morning after their return to town. He improvised on his two-tone horn. Bailey stuck his head out the front door. "Why don't you use the bell?"

"Too slow," answered Teal cheerfully. "I'm a man of action.

Is Mrs. Bailey ready? Ah, there you are, Mrs. Bailey! Welcome home, welcome home. Jump in, we've got a surprise for you!"

"You know Teal, my dear," Bailey put in uncomfortably.

Mrs. Bailey sniffed. "I know him. We'll go in our own car, Homer."

"Certainly, my dear."

"Good idea," Teal agreed; "'sgot more power than mine; we'll get there faster. I'll drive, I know the way." He took the keys from Bailey, slid into the driver's seat, and had the engine started before Mrs. Bailey could rally her forces.

"Never have to worry about my driving," he assured Mrs. Bailey, turning his head as he did so, while he shot the powerful car down the avenue and swung onto Sunset Boulevard, "it's a matter of power and control, a dynamic process, just my meat—I've never had a serious accident."

"You won't have but one," she said bitingly. "Will you *please* keep your eyes on the traffic?"

He attempted to explain to her that a traffic situation was a matter, not of eyesight, but intuitive integration of courses, speeds, and probabilities, but Bailey cut him short. "Where is the house, Quintus?"

"House?" asked Mrs. Bailey suspiciously. "What's this about a house, Homer? Have you been up to something without telling me?"

Teal cut in with his best diplomatic manner. "It certainly is a house, Mrs. Bailey. And what a house! It's a surprise for you from a devoted husband. Just wait till you see it—"

"I shall," she agreed grimly. "What style is it?"

"This house sets a new style. It's later than television, newer than next week. It must be seen to be appreciated. By the way," he went on rapidly, heading off any retort, "did you folks feel the earthquake last night?"

"Earthquake? What earthquake? Homer, was there an earthquake?"

"Just a little one," Teal continued, "about two A.M. If I hadn't been awake, I wouldn't have noticed it."

Mrs. Bailey shuddered. "Oh, this awful country! Do you hear that, Homer? We might have been killed in our beds and never have known it. Why did I ever let you persuade me to leave Iowa?"

"But my dear," he protested hopelessly, "you wanted to come out to California; you didn't like Des Moines."

"We needn't go into that," she said firmly. "You are a man; you should anticipate such things. Earthquakes!"

"That's one thing you needn't fear in your new home, Mrs. Bailey," Teal told her. "It's absolutely earthquake-proof; every part is in perfect dynamic balance with every other part."

"Well, I hope so. Where is this house?"

"Just around this bend. There's the sign now." A large arrow sign, of the sort favored by real estate promoters, proclaimed in letters that were large and bright even for southern California:

THE HOUSE OF THE FUTURE!!!

COLOSSAL—AMAZING— REVOLUTIONARY

See How Your Grandchildren Will Live!

Q. Teal, Architect

"Of course that will be taken down," he added hastily, noting her expression, "as soon as you take possession." He slued around the corner and brought the car to a squealing halt in front of the House of the Future. *"Voilà!"* He watched their faces for response.

Bailey stared unbelievingly, Mrs. Bailey in open dislike. They saw a simple cubical mass, possessing doors and windows, but no other architectural features, save that it was decorated in intricate mathematical designs. "Teal," Bailey asked slowly, "what have you been up to?"

Teal turned from their faces to the house. Gone was the crazy tower with its jutting second-story rooms. No trace remained of the seven rooms above ground floor level. Nothing remained but the single room that rested on the foundations. "Great jumping cats!" he yelled, "I've been robbed!"

He broke into a run.

But it did him no good. Front or back, the story was the same: the other seven rooms had disappeared, vanished completely. Bailey caught up with him, and took his arm.

"Explain yourself. What is this about being robbed? How come you built anything like this—it's not according to agreement."

"But I didn't. I built just what we had planned to build, an eight-room house in the form of a developed tesseract. I've been sabotaged; that's what it is! Jealousy! The other architects in town didn't dare let me finish this job; they knew they'd be washed up if I did."

"When were you last here?"

"Yesterday afternoon."

"Everything all right then?"

"Yes. The gardeners were just finishing up."

Bailey glanced around at the faultlessly manicured

landscaping. "I don't see how seven rooms could have been dismantled and carted away from here in a single night without wrecking this garden."

Teal looked around, too. "It doesn't look it. I don't understand it."

Mrs. Bailey joined them. "Well? Well? Am I to be left to amuse myself? We might as well look it over as long as we are here, though I'm warning you, Homer, I'm not going to like it."

"We might as well," agreed Teal, and drew a key from his pocket with which he let them in the front door. "We may pick up some clues."

The entrance hall was in perfect order, the sliding screens that separated it from the garage space were back, permitting them to see the entire compartment. "This looks all right," observed Bailey. "Let's go up on the roof and try to figure out what happened. Where's the staircase? Have they stolen that, too?"

"Oh, no," Teal denied, "look—" He pressed a button below the light switch; a panel in the ceiling fell away and a light, graceful flight of stairs swung noiselessly down. Its strength members were the frosty silver of duralumin, its treads and risers transparent plastic. Teal wriggled like a boy who has successfully performed a card trick, while Mrs. Bailey thawed perceptibly.

It was beautiful.

"Pretty slick," Bailey admitted. "Howsomever it doesn't seem to go any place—"

"Oh, that—" Teal followed his gaze. "The cover lifts up as you approach the top. Open stair wells are anachronisms. Come on." As predicted, the lid of the staircase got out of their way as they climbed the flight and permitted them to debouch at the top, but not, as they had expected, on the roof of the single room. They found themselves standing in the middle one of the five rooms which constituted the second floor of the original structure.

For the first time on record Teal had nothing to say. Bailey echoed him, chewing on his cigar. Everything was in perfect order. Before them, through open doorway and translucent partition lay the kitchen, a chef's dream of up-to-the-minute domestic engineering, monel metal, continuous counter space, concealed lighting, functional arrangement. On the left the formal, yet gracious and hospitable dining room awaited guests, its furniture in parade-ground alignment.

Teal knew before he turned his head that the drawing room and lounge would be found in equally substantial and impossible existence.

"Well, I must admit this *is* charming," Mrs. Bailey approved, "and the kitchen is just *too* quaint for words— though I would never have guessed from the exterior that this house had so much room upstairs. Of course *some* changes will have to be made. That secretary now—if we moved it over *here* and put the settle over *there*—"

"Stow it, Matilda," Bailey cut in brusquely. "Wha'd' yuh make of it, Teal?"

"Why, Homer Bailey! The very id—"

"Stow it, I said. Well, Teal?"

The architect shuffled his rambling body. "I'm afraid to say. Let's go on up."

"How?"

"Like this." He touched another button; a mate, in deeper colors, to the fairy bridge that had let them up from below offered them access to the next floor. They climbed it, Mrs. Bailey expostulating in the rear, and found themselves in the master bedroom. Its shades were drawn, as had been those on the level below, but the mellow lighting came on automatically. Teal at once activated the switch which controlled still another flight of stairs, and they hurried up into the top floor study.

"Look, Teal," suggested Bailey when he had caught his breath, "can we get to the roof above this room? Then we could look around."

"Sure, it's an observatory platform." They climbed a fourth flight of stairs, but when the cover at the top lifted to let them reach the level above, they found themselves, not on the roof, but *standing in the ground floor room where they had entered the house.*

Mr. Bailey turned a sickly gray. "Angels in heaven," he cried, "this place is haunted. We're getting out of here." Grabbing his wife he threw open the front door and plunged out.

Teal was too much preoccupied to bother with their departure. There was an answer to all this, an answer that he did not believe. But he was forced to break off considering it because of hoarse shouts from somewhere above him. He lowered the staircase and rushed upstairs. Bailey was in the central room leaning over Mrs. Bailey, who had fainted. Teal took in the situation, went to the bar built into the lounge, and poured three fingers of brandy, which he returned with and handed to Bailey. "Here—this'll fix her up."

Bailey drank it.

"That was for Mrs. Bailey," said Teal.

"Don't quibble," snapped Bailey. "Get her another." Teal took the precaution of taking one himself before returning with a dose earmarked for his client's wife. He found her just opening her eyes.

"Here, Mrs. Bailey," he soothed, "this will make you feel better."

"I never touch spirits," she protested, and gulped it.

"Now tell me what happened," suggested Teal. "I thought you two had left."

"But we did—we walked out the front door and found ourselves up here, in the lounge."

"The hell you say! Hm-m-m—wait a minute." Teal went into the lounge. There he found that the big view window at the end of the room was open. He peered cautiously through it. He stared, not out at the California countryside but into the ground floor room—or a reasonable facsimile thereof. He said nothing, but went back to the stair well which he had left open and looked down it. The ground floor room was still in place. Somehow, it managed to be in two different places at once, on different levels.

He came back into the central room and seated himself opposite Bailey in a deep, low chair, and sighted him past his upthrust bony knees. "Homer," he said impressively, "do you know what has happened?"

"No, I don't—but if I don't find out pretty soon, something is going to happen and pretty drastic, too!"

"Homer, this is a vindication of my theories. This house is a real tesseract."

"What's he talking about, Homer?"

"Wait, Matilda—now Teal, that's ridiculous. You've pulled some hanky-panky here and I won't have it—scaring Mrs. Bailey half to death, and making me nervous. All I want is to get out of here, with no more of your trapdoors and silly practical jokes."

"Speak for yourself, Homer," Mrs. Bailey interrupted, "I was *not* frightened; I was just took all over queer for a moment. It's my heart; all of my people are delicate and high strung. Now about this tessy thing—explain yourself, Mr. Teal. Speak up."

He told her as well as he could in the face of numerous interruptions the theory back of the house. "Now as I see it, Mrs. Bailey," he concluded, "this house, while perfectly stable in three dimensions, was not stable in four dimensions. I had built a house in the shape of an unfolded tesseract; something happened to it, some jar or side thrust, and it collapsed into its normal shape—it folded up." He snapped his fingers suddenly. "I've got it! The earthquake!"

"Earthquake?"

"Yes, yes, the little shake we had last night. From a four-dimensional standpoint this house was like a plane balanced on edge. One little push and it fell over, collapsed along its natural joints into a stable four-dimensional figure."

"I thought you boasted about how safe this house was."

"It *is* safe—three-dimensionally."

"I don't call a house safe," commented Bailey edgily, "that collapses at the first little temblor."

"But look around you, man!" Teal protested. "Nothing

has been disturbed, not a piece of glassware cracked. Rotation through a fourth dimension can't effect a three-dimensional figure any more than you can shake letters off a printed page. If you had been sleeping in here last night, you would never have awakened."

"That's just what I'm afraid of. Incidentally, has your great genius figured out any way for us to get out of this booby trap?"

"Huh? Oh, yes, you and Mrs. Bailey started to leave and landed back up here, didn't you? But I'm sure there is no real difficulty—we came in, we can go out. I'll try it." He was up and hurrying downstairs before he had finished talking. He flung open the front door, stepped through, and found himself staring at his companions, down the length of the second floor lounge. "Well, there does seem to be some slight problem," he admitted blandly. "A mere technicality, though—we can always go out a window." He jerked aside the long drapes that covered the deep French windows set in one side wall of the lounge. He stopped suddenly.

"Hm-m-m," he said, "this is interesting—

"What is?" asked Bailey, joining him.

"This." The window stared directly into the dining room, instead of looking outdoors. Bailey stepped back to the corner where the lounge and the dining room joined the central room at ninety degrees.

"But that can't be," he protested, "that window is maybe fifteen, twenty feet from the dining room."

"Not in a tesseract," corrected Teal. "Watch." He opened the window and stepped through, talking back over his shoulder as he did so.

From the point of view of the Baileys he simply disappeared.

But not from his own viewpoint. It took him some seconds to catch his breath. Then he cautiously disentangled himself from the rosebush to which he had become almost irrevocably wedded, making a mental note the while never again to order landscaping which involved plants with thorns, and looked around him.

He was outside the house. The massive bulk of the ground floor room thrust up beside him. Apparently he had fallen off the roof.

He dashed around the corner of the house, flung open the front door and hurried up the stairs. "Homer!" he called out, "Mrs. Bailey! I've found a way out!"

Bailey looked annoyed rather than pleased to see him. "What happened to you?"

"I fell out. I've been outside the house. You can do it just as easily—just step through those French windows. Mind the rosebush, though—we may have to build another stairway."

"How did you get back in?"

"Through the front door."

"Then we shall leave the same way. Come, my dear."

Bailey set his hat firmly on his head and marched down the stairs, his wife on his arm.

Teal met them in the lounge. "I could have told you that wouldn't work," he announced. "Now here's what we have to do: As I see it, in a four-dimensional figure a three-dimensional man has two choices every time he crosses a line of juncture, like a wall or a threshold. Ordinarily he will make a ninety-degree turn through the fourth dimension, only he doesn't feel it with his three dimensions. Look." He stepped through the very window that he had fallen out of a moment before. Stepped through and arrived in the dining room, where he stood, still talking.

"I watched where I was going and arrived where I intended to." He stepped back into the lounge. "The time before I didn't watch and I moved on through normal space and fell out of the house. It must be a matter of subconscious orientation."

"I'd hate to depend on subconscious orientation when I step out for the morning paper."

"You won't have to; it'll become automatic. Now to get out of the house this time— Mrs. Bailey, if you will stand here with your back to the window, and jump backward, I'm pretty sure you will land in the garden."

Mrs. Bailey's face expressed her opinion of Teal and his ideas. "Homer Bailey," she said shrilly, "are you going to stand there and let him suggest such—"

"But Mrs. Bailey," Teal attempted to explain, "we can tie a rope on you and lower you down eas—"

"Forget it, Teal." Bailey cut him off brusquely. "We'll have to find a better way than that. Neither Mrs. Bailey nor I are fitted for jumping."

Teal was temporarily nonplused; there ensued a short silence. Bailey broke it with, "Did you hear that, Teal?"

"Hear what?"

"Someone talking off in the distance. D'you s'pose there could be someone else in the house, playing tricks on us, maybe?"

"Oh, not a chance. I've got the only key."

"But I'm sure of it," Mrs. Bailey confirmed. "I've heard them ever since we came in. Voices. Homer, I can't stand much more of this. Do something."

"Now, now, Mrs. Bailey," Teal soothed, "don't get upset. There can't be anyone else in the house, but I'll explore and make sure. Homer, you stay here with Mrs. Bailey and keep an eye on the rooms on this floor." He passed from the lounge into the ground floor room and from there to the kitchen and on into the bedroom. This led him back to the lounge by a straight-line route, that is to say, by going straight ahead on the entire trip he returned to the place from which he started.

"Nobody around," he reported. "I opened all of the doors and windows as I went—all except this one." He stepped to the window opposite the one through which he had recently fallen and thrust back the drapes.

He saw a man with his back toward him, four rooms away. Teal snatched open the French window and dived through it, shouting, "There he goes now! Stop thief!"

The figure evidently heard him; it fled precipitately. Teal pursued, his gangling limbs stirred to unanimous activity, through drawing room, kitchen, dining room, lounge—room after room, yet in spite of Teal's best efforts he could not seem to cut down the four-room lead that the interloper had started with.

He saw the pursued jump awkwardly but actively over the low sill of a French window and in so doing knock off his hat. When he came up to the point where his quarry had lost his headgear, he stopped and picked it up, glad of an excuse to stop and catch his breath. He was back in the lounge.

"I guess he got away from me," he admitted. "Anyhow, here's his hat. Maybe we can identify him."

Bailey took the hat, looked at it, then snorted, and slapped it on Teal's head. It fitted perfectly. Teal looked puzzled, took the hat off, and examined it. On the sweat band were the initials "Q.T." It was his own.

Slowly comprehension filtered through Teal's features. He went back to the French window and gazed down the series of rooms through which he had pursued the mysterious stranger. They saw him wave his arms semaphore fashion. "What are you doing?" asked Bailey.

"Come see." The two joined him and followed his stare with their own. Four rooms away they saw the backs of three figures, two male and one female. The taller, thinner of the men was waving his arms in a silly fashion.

Mrs. Bailey screamed and fainted again.

Some minutes later, when Mrs. Bailey had been resuscitated and somewhat composed, Bailey and Teal took stock. "Teal," said Bailey, "I won't waste any time blaming you; recriminations are useless and I'm sure you didn't plan for this to happen, but I suppose you realize we are in a pretty serious predicament. How are we going to get out of here? It looks now as if we would stay until we starve; every room leads into another room."

"Oh, it's not that bad. I got out once, you know."

"Yes, but you can't repeat it—you tried."

"Anyhow we haven't tried all the rooms. There's still the study."

"Oh, yes, the study. We went through there when we

first came in, and didn't stop. Is it your idea that we might get out through its windows?"

"Don't get your hopes up. Mathematically, it ought to look into the four side rooms on this floor. Still we never opened the blinds; maybe we ought to look."

"Twon't do any harm anyhow. Dear, I think you had best just stay here and rest—"

"Be left alone in this horrible place? I should say not!" Mrs. Bailey was up off the couch where she had been recuperating even as she spoke.

They went upstairs. "This is the inside room, isn't it, Teal? Bailey inquired as they passed through the master bedroom and climbed on up toward the study. "I mean it was the little cube in your diagram that was in the middle of the big cube, and completely surrounded."

"That's right," agreed Teal. "Well, let's have a look. I figure this window ought to give into the kitchen." He grasped the cords of Venetian blinds and pulled them.

It did not. Waves of vertigo shook them. Involuntarily they fell to the floor and grasped helplessly at the pattern on the rug to keep from falling. "Close it! Close it!" moaned Bailey.

Mastering in part a primitive atavistic fear, Teal worked his way back to the window and managed to release the screen. The window had looked *down* instead of *out*, down from a terrifying height.

Mrs. Bailey had fainted again.

Teal went back after more brandy while Bailey chafed her wrists. When she had recovered, Teal went cautiously to the window and raised the screen a crack. Bracing his knees, he studied the scene. He turned to Bailey. "Come look at this, Homer. See if you recognize it."

"You stay away from there, Homer Bailey!"

"Now, Matilda, I'll be careful." Bailey joined him and peered out.

"See up there? That's the Chrysler Building, sure as shooting. And there's the East River, and Brooklyn." They gazed straight down the sheer face of an enormously tall building.

More than a thousand feet away a toy city, very much alive, was spread out before them. "As near as I can figure it out, we are looking down the side of the Empire State Building from a point just above its tower."

"What is it? A mirage?"

"I don't think so—it's too perfect. I think space is folded over through the fourth dimension here and we are looking past the fold."

"You mean we aren't really seeing it?"

"No, we're seeing it all right. I don't know what would happen if we climbed out this window, but I for one don't want to try. But what a view! Oh, boy, what a view! Let's try the other windows."

They approached the next window more cautiously, and it was well that they did, for it was even more disconcerting, more reason-shaking, than the one looking down the gasping height of the skyscraper. It was a simple seascape, open ocean and blue sky—but the ocean was where the sky should have been, and contrariwise. This time they were somewhat braced for it, but they both felt seasickness about to overcome them at the sight of waves rolling overhead; they lowered the blind quickly without giving Mrs. Bailey a chance to be disturbed by it.

Teal looked at the third window. "Game to try it, Homer?"

"Hrrumph—well, we won't be satisfied if we don't. Take it easy." Teal lifted the blind a few inches. He saw nothing, and raised it a little more—still nothing. Slowly he raised it until the window was fully exposed. They gazed out at—nothing.

Nothing, nothing at all. What color is nothing? Don't be silly! What shape is it? Shape is an attribute of *something*. It had neither depth nor form. It had not even blackness. It was *nothing*.

Bailey chewed at his cigar. "Teal, what do you make of that?"

Teal's insouciance was shaken for the first time. "I don't know, Homer, I don't rightly know—but I think that window ought to be walled up." He stared at the lowered blind for a moment. "I think maybe we looked at a place where space *isn't*. We looked around a fourth-dimensional corner and there wasn't anything there." He rubbed his eyes. "I've got a headache."

They waited for a while before tackling the fourth window. Like an unopened letter, it might *not* contain bad news. The doubt left hope. Finally the suspense stretched too thin and Bailey pulled the cord himself, in the face of his wife's protests.

It was not so bad, A landscape stretched away from them, right side up, and on such a level that the study appeared to be a ground floor room. But it was distinctly unfriendly.

A hot, hot sun beat down from lemon-colored sky. The flat ground seemed burned a sterile, bleached brown and incapable of supporting life. Life there was, strange stunted trees that lifted knotted, twisted arms to the sky. Little clumps of spiky leaves grew on the outer extremities of these misshapen growths.

"Heavenly day," breathed Bailey, "where is that?"

Teal shook his head, his eyes troubled. "It beats me."

"It doesn't look like anything on Earth. It looks more like another planet—Mars, maybe."

"I wouldn't know. But, do you know, Homer, it might be worse than that, worse than another planet, I mean."

"Huh? What's that you say?"

"It might be clear out of our space entirely. I'm not sure that that is our sun at all. It seems too bright."

Mrs. Bailey had somewhat timidly joined them and now gazed out at the outré scene. "Homer," she said in a subdued voice, "those hideous trees—they frighten me."

He patted her hand.

Teal fumbled with the window catch.

"What are you doing?" Bailey demanded.

"I thought if I stuck my head out the window I might be able to look around and tell a bit more."

"Well—all right," Bailey grudged, "but be careful."

"I will." He opened the window a crack and sniffed. "The air is all right, at least." He threw it open wide.

His attention was diverted before he could carry out his plan. An uneasy tremor, like the first intimation of nausea, shivered the entire building for a long second, and was gone.

"Earthquake!" They all said it at once. Mrs. Bailey flung her arms around her husband's neck.

Teal gulped and recovered himself, saying:

"It's all right, Mrs. Bailey. This house is perfectly safe. You know you can expect settling tremors after a shock like last night." He had just settled his features into an expression of reassurance when the second shock came. This one was no mild shimmy but the real seasick roll.

In every Californian, native born or grafted, there is a deep-rooted primitive reflex. An earthquake fills him with soul-shaking claustrophobia which impels him blindly to *get outdoors!* Model Boy Scouts will push aged grandmothers aside to obey it. It is a matter of record that Teal and Bailey landed on top of Mrs. Bailey. Therefore, she must have jumped through the window first. The order of precedence cannot be attributed to chivalry; it must be assumed that she was in readier position to spring.

They pulled themselves together, collected their wits a little, and rubbed sand from their eyes. Their first sensations were relief at feeling the solid sand of the desert land under them. Then Bailey noticed something that brought them to their feet and checked Mrs. Bailey from bursting into the speech that she had ready.

"Where's the house?"

It was gone. There was no sign of it at all. They stood in the center of flat desolation, the landscape they had seen from the window. But, aside from the tortured, twisted trees there was nothing to be seen but the yellow sky and the luminary overhead, whose furnacelike glare was already almost insufferable.

Bailey looked slowly around, then turned to the architect.

"Well, Teal?" His voice was ominous.

Teal shrugged helplessly. "I wish I knew. I wish I could even be sure that we were on Earth."

"Well, we can't stand here. It's sure death if we do. Which direction?"

"Any, I guess. Let's keep a bearing on the sun."

They had trudged on for an undetermined distance when Mrs. Bailey demanded a rest. They stopped. Teal said in an aside to Bailey, "Any ideas?"

"No . . . no, none. Say, do you hear anything?"

Teal listened. "Maybe—unless it's my imagination."

"Sounds like an automobile. Say, it is an automobile!"

They came to the highway in less than another hundred yards. The automobile, when it arrived, proved to be an elderly, puffing light truck, driven by a rancher. He crunched to a stop at their hail. "We're stranded. Can you help us out?"

"Sure. Pile in."

"Where are you headed?"

"Los Angeles."

"Los Angeles? Say, where is this place?"

"Well, you're right in the middle of the Joshua-Tree National Forest."

The return was as dispiriting as the Retreat from Moscow. Mr. and Mrs. Bailey sat up in front with the driver while Teal bumped along in the body of the truck, and tried to protect his head from the sun. Bailey subsidized the friendly rancher to detour to the tesseract house, not because they wanted to see it again, but in order to pick up their car.

At last the rancher turned the corner that brought them back to where they had started. But the house was no longer there.

There was not even the ground floor room. It had vanished. The Baileys, interested in spite of themselves, poked around the foundations with Teal.

"Got any answers for this one, Teal?" asked Bailey.

"It must be that on that last shock it simply fell through into another section of space. I can see now that I should have anchored it at the foundations."

"That's not all you should have done."

"Well, I don't see that there is anything to get downhearted about. The house was insured, and we've learned an amazing lot. There are possibilities, man, possibilities! Why, right now I've got a great new revolutionary idea for a house—"

Teal ducked in time. He was always a man of action.

INSTINCT

by Lester del Rey

My original intention was to begin and end If This Goes
Wrong *with stories by Robert A. Heinlein, but poor health
and a resultant memory loss on my part necessitates
closing instead with a story which certainly should be
more widely remembered than it is, from SF Grand
Master (the SFWA made him one officially.)* **Lester del
Rey** *(1915-1993). Del Rey was a man of multiple talents,
a writer, not just of SF and fantasy, but of many other
forms of more mundane fiction, as well as many non-
fiction books. He was editor of many SF magazines, from
the early 1950s to the late 1960s, an authors' agent, a book
reviewer, and probably most influentially, an editor, with
his wife, Judy-Lynn del Rey, at Del Rey books for over two
decades. (Incidentally, Del Rey Books, one of the strongest
SF lines in the late 20th century, was named for the lady,
not Lester.) He was also a sheet metal worker during
WWII, but I can't say what influence that may have had
on his writing. In person, he was a superb, if contentious,*

speaker, an energetic debater, and if he didn't have the entire history of SF and fantasy stored in his head, anything left out was probably unimportant. He also wrote either the third or fourth SF novel I ever read, while I was in the third grade: Marooned on Mars, *helping to seal my fate as an SF addict, so that you're reading this book is at least partly his fault. (If you're morbidly curious, the first four SF novels I read were Van Vogt's* Slan, *in the second grade, Simak's* City, *Oliver's* Mists of Dawn, *and del Rey's* Marooned on Mars, *all three in the third grade. I don't recall if I read the Simak before or after the last two, which were early issues in the celebrated Winston line of SF juveniles, a trail-blazing publishing program which Mr. del Rey had much more to do with than the two editors listed on the books' jacket flaps.) Lester del Rey was diminutive in physical stature, but a titan in his influence on SF and fantasy, and I don't believe Mr. Heinlein would be at all bothered by his bringing down the curtain here.*

SENTHREE WAVED ASIDE the slowing scooter and lengthened his stride down the sidewalk; he had walked all the way from the rocket port, and there was no point to a taxi now that he was only a few blocks from the bio-labs. Besides, it was too fine a morning to waste in riding. He sniffed at the crisp, clean fumes of gasoline appreciatively and listened to the music of his hard heels slapping against the concrete.

It was good to have a new body again. He hadn't appreciated what life was like for the last hundred years or so. He let his eyes rove across the street toward the blue flame of a welding torch and realized how long it had been since his eyes had really appreciated the delicate beauty of such a flame. The wise old brain in his chest even seemed to think better now.

It was worth every stinking minute he'd spent on Venus. At times like this, one could realize how good it was to be alive and to be a robot.

Then he sobered as he came to the old bio-labs. Once there had been plans for a fine new building instead of the old factory in which he had started it all four hundred years ago. But somehow, there'd never been time for that. It had taken almost a century before they could master the technique of building up genes and chromosomes into the zygote of a simple fish that would breed with the natural ones. Another century had gone by before they produced Oscar, the first artificially made pig. And there they seemed to have stuck. Sometimes it seemed to Senthree that they were no nearer recreating Man than they had been when they started.

He dilated the door and went down the long hall, studying his reflection in the polished walls absently. It was a good body. The black enamel was perfect and every joint of the metal case spelled new techniques and luxurious fitting. But the old worries were beginning to settle. He grunted at Oscar LXXII, the lab mascot, and received an answering grunt. The pig came over to root at his feet, but he had no time for that. He turned into the main lab room, already taking on the worries of his job.

It wasn't hard to worry as he saw the other robots. They were clustered about some object on a table, dejection on every gleaming back. Senthree shoved Ceofor and Beswun aside and moved up. One look was enough. The female of the eleventh couple lay there in the strange stiffness of protoplasm that had died, a horrible grimace on her face.

"How long—and what happened to the male?" Senthree asked.

Ceofor swung to face him quickly. "Hi, boss. You're late. Hey, new body!"

Senthree nodded, as they came grouping around, but his words were automatic as he explained about falling in the alkali pool on Venus and ruining his worn body completely. "Had to wait for a new one. And then the ship got held up while we waited for the Arcturus superlight ship to land. They'd found half a dozen new planets to colonize, and had to spread the word before they'd set down. Now, what about the creatures?"

"We finished educating about three days ago," Ceofor told him. Ceofor was the first robot trained in Senthree's technique of gene-building and the senior assistant. "Expected you back then, boss. But . . .well, see for yourself. The man is still alive, but he won't be long."

Senthree followed them back to another room and looked through the window. He looked away quickly. It had been another failure. The man was crawling about the floor on hands and knees, falling half the time to his stomach, and drooling. His garbled mouthing made no sense.

"Keep the news robots out," he ordered. It would never do to let the public see this. There was already too much of a cry against homovivifying, and the crowds were beginning to mutter something about it being unwise to mess with vanished life forms. They seemed actually afraid of the legendary figure of Man.

"What luck on Venus?" one of them asked, as they began the job of carefully dissecting the body of the female failure to look for the reason behind the lack of success.

"None. Just another rumor. I don't think Man ever established self-sufficient colonies. If he did, they didn't survive. But I found something else—something the museum would give a fortune for. Did my stuff arrive?"

"You mean that box of tar? Sure, it's over there in the corner."

Senthree let the yielding plastic of his mouth smile at them as he strode toward it. They had already ripped off the packing, and now he reached up for a few fine wires in the tar. It came off as he pulled, loosely repacked over a thin layer of wax. At that, he'd been lucky to sneak it past customs. This was the oldest, crudest, and biggest robot discovered so far—perhaps one of the fabulous Original Models. It stood there rigidly, staring out of its pitted, expressionless face. But the plate on its chest had been scraped carefully clean, and Senthree pointed it out to them.

MAKEPEACE ROBOT, SER. 324MD2991. SURGEON.

"A mechanic for Man bodies," Beswun translated. "But that means . . ."

"Exactly." Senthree put it into words. "It must know how Man's body was built—if it has retained any memory.

I found it in a tarpit by sheer accident, and it seems to be fairly well preserved. No telling whether there were any magnetic fields to erode memories, of course, and it's all matted inside. But if we can get it working . . ."

Beswun took over. He had been trained as a physicist before the mysterious lure of the bio-lab had drawn him here. Now he began wheeling the crude robot away. If he could get it into operation, the museum could wait. The re-creation of Man came first!

Senthree pulled x-ray lenses out of a pouch and replaced the normal ones in his eyes before going over to join the robots who were beginning dissection. Then he switched them for the neutrino detector lenses that had made this work possible. The neutrino was the only particle that could penetrate the delicate protoplasmic cells without ruining them and yet permit the necessary millions of tunes magnification. It was a fuzzy image, since the neutrino spin made such an insignificant field for the atomic nuclei to work on that few were deflected. But through them, he could see the vague outlines of the pattern within the cells. It was as they had designed the original cell—there had been no reshuffling of genes in handling. He switched to his micromike hands and began the delicate work of tracing down the neuron connections. There was only an occasional mutter as one of the robots beside him switched to some new investigation.

The female should have lived! But somewhere, in spite of all their care, she had died. And now the male was dying. Eleven couples—eleven failures. Senthree was no nearer finding the creators of his race now than he had been centuries before.

When the radio in his head buzzed its warning, he let it cut in, straightening from his work. "Senthree."

"The Director is in your office. Will you report at once?"

"Damn!" The word had no meaning, but it was strangely satisfying at times. What did old Emptinine want . . . or wait again, there'd been a selection while he was on Venus investigating the rumors of Man. Some young administrator—Arpeten—had the job now.

Ceofor looked up guiltily, obviously having tuned in. "I should have warned you. We got word three days ago he was coming, but forgot it in reviving the couple. Trouble?"

Senthree shrugged, screwing his normal lenses back in and trading to the regular hands. They couldn't have found out about the antique robot. They had been seen by nobody else. It was probably just sheer curiosity over some rumor that they were reviving the couple. If his appropriation hadn't been about exhausted, Senthree would have told him where to go; but now was hardly the time, with a failure on one hand and a low credit balance on the other. He polished his new head quickly with the aid of one of the walls for a mirror and headed toward his office.

But Arpeten was smiling. He got to his feet as the bio-lab chief entered, holding out a well-polished hand. "Dr. Senthree. Delighted. And you've got an interesting place here. I've already seen most of it. And that pig—they tell me it's a descendant of a boar out of your test tubes."

"Incubation wombs. But you're right—the seventy-second generation."

"Fascinating." Arpeten must have been reading too much of that book *Proven Points to Popularity* they'd dug up in the ruins of Hudson ten years before, but it had worked. He was the Director. "But tell me. Just what good are pigs?"

Senthree grinned, in spite of himself. "Nobody knows. Men apparently kept a lot of them, but so far as I can see they are completely useless. They're clever, in a way. But I don't think they were pets. Just another mystery."

"Umm. Like men. Maybe you can tell me what good Man will be. I've been curious about that since I saw your appropriations. But nobody can answer."

"It's in the records," Senthree told him sharply. Then he modified his voice carefully. "How well do you know your history? I mean about the beginning."

"Well . . ."

He probably knew some of it, Senthree thought. They all got part of it as legends. He leaned back in his seat now, though, as the biochemist began the old tale of the beginning as they knew it. They knew that there had been Man a million years before them. And somebody— Asimov or Asenion, the record wasn't quite clear—had apparently created the first robot. They had improved it up to about the present level. Then there had been some kind of a contest in which violent forces had ruined the factories, most of the robots, and nearly all of the Men. It was believed from the fragmentary records that a biological weapon had killed the rest of man, leaving only the robots.

Those first robots, as they were now known, had had to start on a ruined world from scratch—a world where mines were exhausted, and factories were gone. They'd learned to get metals from the seas, and had spent years and centuries slowly rebuilding the machines to build new robots. There had been only two of them when the task was finished, and they had barely time enough to run one new robot off and educate him sketchily. Then they had discharged finally, and he had taken up rebuilding the race. It was almost like beginning with no history and no science. Twenty millennia had passed before they began to rebuild a civilization of their own.

"But why did Man die?" Senthree asked. "That's part of the question. And are we going to do the same? We know we are similar to Man. Did he change himself in some way that ruined him? Can we change ourselves safely? You know that there are a thousand ways we could improve ourselves. We could add anti-gravity, and get rid of our cumbersome vehicles. We could add more arms. We could eliminate our useless mouths and talk by radio. We could add new circuits to our brains. But we don't dare. One school says that nobody can build a better race than itself, so Man must have been better than we are—and if he made us this way, there was a reason. Even if the psychologists can't understand some of the circuits in our brains, they don't dare touch them.

"We're expanding through the universe—but we can't even change ourselves to fit the new planets. And until we can find the reasons for Man's disappearance, that makes good sense. We know he was planning to change himself. We have bits of evidence. And he's dead. To make it worse, we have whole reels of education tape that probably contain all the answers—but information is keyed to Man's brain, and we can't respond to it. Give us a viable Man, and he can interpret that. Or we can find out by comparison what we can and cannot do. I maintain we can do a lot."

Arpeten shook his head doubtfully. "I suppose you think you know why he died!"

"I think so, yes. Instinct! That's a built-in reaction, an unlearned thought. Man had it. If a man heard a rattlesnake, he left the place in a hurry, even though he'd never heard it before. Response to that sound was built into him. No tape impressed it, and no experience was needed. We know the instincts of some of the animals, too—and one of them is to struggle and kill—like the ants who kill each other off. I think Man did just that. He couldn't get rid of his instincts when they were no longer needed, and they killed him. He should have changed—and we can change. But I can't tell that from animals. I need intelligent life, to see whether instinct or intelligence will dominate. And robots don't have instincts—I've looked for even one sign of something not learned individually, and can't find it. It's the one basic difference between us. Don't you see, Man is the whole key to our problem of whether we can change or not without risking extermination?"

"Umm." The director sounded noncommittal. "Interesting theory. But how are you going to know you have Man?"

Senthree stared at the robot with more respect. He tried to explain, but he had never been as sure of that himself as he might. Theoretically, they had bones and bits of preserved tissue. They had examined the gene pattern of these, having learned that the cells of the individual contain the same pattern as that of the zygote. And they had other guides—man's achievements, bits of his literature. From these, some working theories could be made. But he couldn't be quite sure—they'd never really known whether man's pigment was dark brown, pinkish orange, white, or what; the records they seemed to disagree on this.

"We'll know when we get an intelligent animal with instinct," he said at last. "It won't matter exactly whether he is completely like Man or not. At least it will give us a check on things we must know. Until then, we'll have to go on trying. You might as well know that the last experiment failed, though it was closer. But in another hundred years . . ."

"So." Arpeten's face became bland, but he avoided the look of Senthree. "I'm afraid not. At least for a while. That's what I came about, you know. We've just had word of several new planets around Arcturus, and it will take the major allocation of our funds to colonize these. New robots must be built, new ships—oh, you know. And we're retrenching a bit on other things. Of course, if you'd succeeded . . . but perhaps it's better you failed. You know how the sentiment against reviving Man has grown."

Senthree growled bitterly. He'd seen how it was carefully nurtured—though he had to admit it seemed to be easy to create. Apparently most of the robots were afraid of Man—felt he would again take over, or something. Superstitious fools.

"How much longer?" he asked.

"Oh, we won't cut back what you have, Dr. Senthree. But I'm afraid we simply can't allocate more funds. When this is finished, I was hoping to make you biological investigator, incidentally, on one of the planets. There'll be work enough . . . Well, it was a pleasure." He shook hands again, and walked out, his back a gleaming ramrod of efficiency and effectiveness.

Senthree turned back, his new body no longer moving easily. It could already feel the harsh sands and unknown chemical poisons of investigating a new planet—the futile, empty carding of new life that could have no real purpose to the robots. No more appropriations! And they had barely enough funds to meet the current bills.

Four hundred years—and a ship to Arcturus had ended it in three months. Instinct, he thought again—given life with intelligence and instinct together for one year, and he could settle half the problems of his race, perhaps. But robots could not have instincts. Fifty years of study had proven that.

Beswun threw up a hand in greeting as he returned, and he saw that the dissection was nearly complete, while the antique robot was activated. A hinge on its ludicrous jaw was moving, and rough, grating words were coming out. Senthree turned to the dissecting bench, and then swung back as he heard them.

"Wrong . . . wrong," it was muttering. "Can not live. Is not good brain. No pineal. Medulla good, but not good cerebrum. Fissures wrong. Maybe pituitary disfunction? No. How can be?" It probed doubtfully and set the brain aside. "Mutation maybe. Very bad. Need Milliken mike. See nucleus of cells. Maybe just freak, maybe new disease."

Senthree's fingers were taut and stiff as he fished into his bag and came out with a set of lenses. Beswun shook his head and made a waiting sign. He went out at a run, to come back shortly with a few bits of metal and the shavings from machining still on his hands. "Won't fit—but these adapters should do it. There, 324MD2991. Now come over here where you can look at it over this table—that's where the—uh, rays are."

He turned back, and Senthree saw that a fine wire ran from one adapter. "He doesn't speak our bio-terminology, Senthree. We'll have to see the same things he does. There—we can watch it on the screen. Now, 324MD2991, you tell us what is wrong and point it out. Are your hands steady enough for that?"

"Hands one-billionth inch accurate," the robot creaked; it was a meaningless noise, though they had found the unit of measure mentioned. But whatever it meant, the hands were steady enough. The microprobe began touching shadowy bunches of atoms, droning and grating. "Freak. Very bad freak. How he lived? Would stop tropoblast, not attach to uterus. Ketone—no ketone there. Not understand. How he live?"

Ceofor dashed for their chromosome blanks and began lettering in the complex symbols they used. For a second, Senthree hesitated. Then he caught fire and began making notes along with his assistant. It seemed to take hours; it probably did. The old robot had his memory intact, but there were no quick ways for him to communicate. And at last, the antique grunted in disgust and turned his back on them. Beswun pulled a switch.

"He expects to be discharged when not in use. Crazy,

isn't it?" the physicist explained. "Look, boss, am I wrong, or isn't that close to what we did on the eleventh couple?"

"Only a few genes different in three chromosomes. We *were* close. But—umm, that's ridiculous. Look at all the brain tissue he'd have—and a lot of it uncontrolled. And here—that would put an extra piece on where big and little intestines join—a perfect focal point for infection. It isn't efficient biological engineering. And yet—umm—most animals do have just that kind of engineering. I think the old robot was right—this would be Man!" He looked at their excited faces, and his shoulders sank. "But there isn't time. Not even time to make a zygote and see what it would look like. Our appropriations won't come through."

It should have been a bombshell, but he saw at once that they had already guessed it. Ceofor stood up slowly.

"We can take a look, boss. We've got the sperm from the male that failed—all we have to do is modify those three, instead of making up a whole cell. We might as well have some fun before we go out looking for sand fleas that secrete hydrofluoric acid and menace our colonies. Come on, even in your new body I'll beat you to a finished cell!"

Senthree grinned ruefully, but he moved toward the creation booth. His hands snapped on the little time field out of pure habit as he found a perfect cell. The little field would slow time almost to zero within its limits, and keep any damage from occurring while he worked. It made his own work difficult, since he had to force the probe against that, but it was insulated to some extent by other fields.

Then his hands took over. For a time he worked and thought, but the feeling of the protoplasm came into them, and his hands were almost one with the life stuff, sensing its tiny responses, inserting another link onto a chain, supplanting an atom of hydrogen with one of the hydroxyl radicals, wielding all the delicate chemical manipulation. He removed the defective genes and gently inserted the correct ones. Four hundred years of this work lay behind him—work he had loved, work which had meant the possible evolution of his race into all it might be.

It had become instinct to him—instinct in only a colloquial sense, however; this was learned response, and real instinct lay deeper than that, so deep that no reason could overcome it and that it was automatic even the first time. Only Man had had instinct and intelligence—stored somehow in this tiny cell that lay within the time field.

He stepped out, just as Ceofor was drawing back in a dead heat. But the younger robot inspected Senthree's cell, and nodded. "Less disturbance and a neater job on the nucleus—I can't see where you pierced the wall. Well, if we had thirty years—even twenty—we could have Man again—or a race. Yours is male and mine female. But there's no time . . . Shall I leave the time field on?"

Senthree started to nod.

Then he swung to Beswun. "The time field. Can it be reversed?"

"You mean to speed time up within it? No, not with that model. Take a bigger one. I could build you one in half an hour. But who'd want to speed up time with all the troubles you'd get? How much?"

"Ten thousand—or at least seven thousand times! The period is up tomorrow when disbursements have to be made. I want twenty years in a day."

Beswun shook his head. "No. That's what I was afraid of. Figure it this way: you speed things up ten thousand times and that means the molecules in there speed up just that much, literally. Now 273° times ten thousand—and you have more than two million degrees of temperature. And those molecules have energy! They come busting out of there. No, can't be done."

"How much can you do?" Senthree demanded.

Beswun considered. "Ten times—maybe no more than nine. That gives you all the refractories would handle, if we set it up down in the old pit under the building—you know, where they had the annealing oven."

It wasn't enough; it would still take two years. Senthree dropped onto a seat, vagrantly wondering again how this queer brain of his that the psychologists studied futilely could make him feel tired when his body could have no fatigue. It was probably one of those odd circuits they didn't dare touch.

"Of course, you can use four fields," Beswun stated slowly. "Big one outside, smaller one, still smaller, and smallest inside that. Fourth power of nine is about sixty-six hundred. That's close—raise that nine a little and you'd have your twenty years in a day. By the time it leaked from field to field, it wouldn't matter. Take a couple of hours."

"Not if you get your materials together and build each shell inside the other—you'll be operating faster each step then," Ceofor shouted. "Somebody'll have to go in and stay there a couple of our minutes toward the end to attach the educator tapes—and to revive the couple!"

"Take power," Beswun warned.

Senthree shrugged. Let it. If the funds they had

wouldn't cover it, the Directorate would have to make it up, once it was used. Besides, once Man was created, they couldn't fold up the bio-labs. "I'll go in," he suggested.

"My job," Ceofor told him flatly. "You won the contest in putting the cells right."

Senthree gave in reluctantly, largely because the younger robot had more experience at reviving than he did. He watched Beswun assemble the complicated net of wires and become a blur as he seemed to toss the second net together almost instantly. The biochemist couldn't see the third go up—it was suddenly there, and Beswun was coming out as it flashed into existence. He held up four fingers, indicating all nets were working.

Ceofor dashed in with the precious cells for the prepared incubators that would nurture the bodies until maturity, when they would be ready for the educators. His body seemed to blur, jerk, and disappear. And almost at once he was back.

Senthree stood watching for a moment more, but there was nothing to see. He hesitated again, then turned and moved out of the building. Across the street lay his little lodging place, where he could relax with his precious two books—almost complete—that had once been printed by Man. Tonight he would study that strange bit of Man's history entitled *Gather, Darkness*, with its odd indications of a science that Man had once had which had surpassed even that of the robots now. It was pleasanter than the incomprehensibility of the mysteriously titled *Mein Kampf*. He'd let his power idle, and mull over it, and consider again the odd behavior of male and female who made such a complicated business of mating. That was probably more instinct—Man, it seemed, was filled with instincts.

For a long time, though, he sat quietly with the book on his lap, wondering what it would be like to have instincts. There must be many unpleasant things about it. But there were also suggestions that it could be pleasant. Well, he'd soon know by observation, even though he could never experience it. Man should have implanted one instinct in a robot's brain, at least, just to show what it was like.

He called the lab once, and Ceofor reported that all was doing nicely, and that both children were looking quite well. Outside the window, Senthree heard a group go by, discussing the latest bits of news on the Arcturus expedition. At least in that, Man had failed to equal the robots. He had somehow died before he could find the trick of using identity exchange to overcome the limitation imposed by the speed of light.

Finally he fell to making up a speech that he could deliver to the Director, Arpeten, when success was in his hands. It must be very short—something that would stick in the robot's mind for weeks, but carrying everything a scientist could feel on proving that those who opposed him were wrong. Let's see . . .

The buzzer on the telescreen cut through his thoughts, and he nipped it on to see Ceofor's face looking out. Senthree's spirits dropped abruptly as he stared at the younger robot "Failure? No!"

The other shook his head. "No. At least, I don't know. I couldn't give them full education. Maybe the tape was uncomfortable. They took a lot of it, but the male tore his helmet off and took the girl's off. Now they just sit there, rubbing their heads and staring around."

He paused, and the little darkened ridges of plastic over his eyes tensed. "The time speed-up is off. But I didn't know what to do."

"Let them alone until I get there. If it hurts them, we can give them the rest of it later. How are they otherwise?"

"I don't know. They look all right, boss." Ceofor hesitated, and his voice dropped. "Boss, I don't like it. there's something wrong here. I can't quite figure out what it is, but it isn't the way I expected. Hey, the male just pushed the female off her seat. Do you think their destructive instinct . . . ? No, she's sitting down on the floor now, with her head against him, and holding one of his hands. Wasn't that part of the mating ritual in one of the books?"

Senthree started to agree, a bit of a smile coming onto his face. It looked as if instinct were already in operation.

But a strange voice cut him off. "Hey, you robots, when do we eat around here?"

They could talk! It must have been the male. And if it wasn't the polite thanks and gratitude Senthree had expected, that didn't matter. There had been all kinds of Men in the books, and some were polite while others were crude. Perhaps forced education from the tapes without fuller social experience was responsible for that. But it would all adjust in time.

He started to turn back to Ceofor, but the younger robot was no longer there, and the screen looked out on a blank wall. Senthree could hear the loud voice crying out again, rough and harsh, and there was a shrill, whining sound that might be the female. The two voices blended with the vague mutter of robot voices until he could not make out the words.

He wasted no time in trying. He was already rushing down to the street and heading toward the labs. Instinct—the male had already shown instinct, and the female had responded. They would have to be slow with the couple at first, of course—but the whole answer to the robot problems lay at hand. It would only take a little time and patience now. Let Arpeten sneer, and let the world dote on the Arcturus explorers. Today, biochemistry had been crowned king with the magic of intelligence combined with instinct as its power.

Ceofor came out of the lab at a run with another robot behind him. The young robot looked dazed, and there was another emotion Senthree could not place. The older biochemist nodded, and the younger one waved quickly. "Can't stop now. They're hungry." He was gone at full speed.

Senthree realized suddenly that no adequate supply of fruit and vegetables had been provided, and he hadn't even known how often Man had to eat. Or exactly what. Luckily, Ceofor was taking care of that.

He went down the hall, hearing a tumult of voices, with robots apparently spread about on various kinds of hasty business. The main lab where the couple was seemed quiet. Senthree hesitated at the door, wondering how to address them. There must be no questioning now. Today he would not force himself on them, nor expect them to understand his purposes. He must welcome them and make them feel at ease in this world, so strange to them with their prehistoric tape education. It would be hard at first to adjust to a world of only robots, with no other Man people. The matter of instinct that had taken so long could wait a few days more.

The door dilated in front of him and he stepped into the lab, his eyes turning to the low table where they sat. They looked healthy, and there was no sign of misery or uncertainty that he could see, though he could not be sure of that until he knew them better. He could not even be sure it was a scowl on the male's face as the Man turned and looked at him.

"Another one, eh? Okay, come up here. What you want?"

Then Senthree no longer wondered how to address the Man. He bowed low as he approached them, and instinct made his voice soft and apologetic as he answered.

"Nothing, Master. Only to serve you."

He waited expectantly.

YEAR'S BEST MILITARY SCIENCE FICTION AND SPACE OPERA

YOU DECIDE WHO WINS!

Other anthologies tell you which stories were the year's best—*we're letting you decide which of these you liked best.* Baen Books is pleased to announce the inaugural Year's Best Military Science Fiction and Space Opera Award. The award honors the best of the best in this grand storytelling tradition, and its winner will receive a plaque and an additional $500.00.

To vote, go to
http://baen.com/yearsbestaward2014

Registration with Baen Ebooks is required. You may also send a postcard or letter with the name of your favorite story from this volume and its author to Baen Books Year's Best Award, P.O. Box 1188, Wake Forest, NC 27587. Voting closes August 31, 2015. Entries received after voting closes will not be counted.

So hurry, hurry, hurry! The winner will be announced at Dragoncon in Atlanta, held over Labor Day Weekend 2015.